I0600718

Praise for

THE MIRROR LIES

You've heard that "the mirror never lies" but in this case, that's a lie. With a single look at this mirror, I was helplessly pulled into a riveting story of intrigue and suspense that would not let me look away until the last page. Sandy Brownlee's *The Mirror Lies* is a masterful novel that will keep you gazing, guessing and groping for the truth.

Jenny L. Cote
Award winning Author of
he Epic Order of the Seven series.

Hidden rooms, secret diaries, old graveyards, and dusty attics—*The Mirror Lies* is layered in mystery, history, and a deep, dark well of secrets which must be revealed before the truth is brought to light. Historical fiction with just the right dash of mystery, intrigue and romance.

River Jordan
Acclaimed author of
Praying for Strangers: An Adventure of the Human Spirit

Sandy Brownlee's debut novel is a gem of a book for anyone who enjoys suspense! There's romance too, and a dash of history, and a dollop of humor—all the ingredients of a truly engaging read.

Ann Tatlock
Christy Award winning author of
Once Beyond a Time

Secrecy, scary graveyards, old diaries, and keepsakes hidden in dusty, musty attics are the backdrop for *The Mirror Lies*. Sandy Brownlee has mastered the art of weaving mystery, history, and romance. Better make room on your Keepers Shelf for this one, because you'll want to read it again… and again!

Loree Lough
Bestselling author of
50 Hours

THE MIRROR LIES

Published by WordCrafts Press
Cody, Wyoming 82414
www.wordcrafts.net

THE MIRROR LIES

SANDY BROWNLEE

WordCrafts

The Last Will & Testament
of
Sir Thaddeus Thomas Graymoor

I, Thaddeus Thomas Graymoor, being of sound and clear mind, do set my hand to write this, my last will and testament. I, as my father before me, and every Graymoor from the time of Henry VIII, bestow all my worldly goods and every form of wealth on my eldest male child. If two are born, as is the common lot of the Graymoors, then the inheritance is to be split equally between them. For my wife, Anna, she has in trust her own income bestowed on her at the time of our marriage, as well as rights to live as she has always lived at the family estate, Graywyck, the rest of her natural life.

Should I die without producing a male heir, or should my heir, God forbid, predecease me, all the earthly goods and fortune of the Graymoors shall pass in full to my brother Samuel so that the Graymoor name might never perish. This legacy to the eldest male is to be carried on in perpetuity or be forfeited and dispersed to the poor.

Sir Thaddeus Thomas Graymoor
15 February 1882
Cambridgeshire, England

1

CHAPTER 1

*"You must suffer me to go my own dark way. I
have brought on myself a punishment and a danger
that I cannot name."*
—*The Strange Case of Dr. Jekyll & Mr. Hyde*

White Rock River Road, Outskirts of Graystone Estate
—October 1907

"Fool!" The hooves of the dun mare dug into the mire as
man and horse cut through the wind and rain. Why? Why on
a night like this? "And if he's as full of rum as I think he is…"

Peter Graymoor spoke aloud, the sound of his voice lost in
the storm around him. His wet, fair hair hung like a veil over
his eyes. He pushed it aside and peered into the blackness.
Ahead of him, the road was a river of mud, and a fog formed
a thick curtain across his path. Somewhere ahead was an old
and narrow bridge, and a misstep there could send him…

"Best not tempt God or Fate," he muttered, slowing his horse
to a trot. The mare suddenly balked, spooked by a bolt of
lightning that seemed to strike just ahead. For a moment, he
regretted not taking the motorcar, though it would have most
likely got stuck in the muck and ruts. No matter.

Peter leaned forward, whispering calming words to the shivering beast, then spurred her into the gloom ahead, hoping

the road was still beneath them. On a night like this, a horse might easily stumble and fall—even his horse. But his horse was gone, his clothing taken, and God alone knew what was being done in his name. Pity? Anger? Which should he feel? Disgust? Shame? No, not shame, not even if his reputation was ripped to shreds. A frown marred the strong lines of his face as he looked around him. Nothing. He saw nothing. Had he failed yet again? Should he still fight this losing battle?

Pounding hoof beats broke through the thunder and into his thoughts. Peter pulled up. "Ho! Who goes there?" The galloping drew closer. "I say, stop! Name yourself!" The sound slowed to a trot, and a familiar laugh echoed in the mist.

"Can't you tell by my attire? I'm Peter Graymoor, Esquire, at your service…"

"Simon." Laughter came from the shadows again. With clenched jaw and clenched fist, Peter advanced, speaking to the unseen figure in front of him. "First you take my horse and my clothes; must you steal my name and reputation, too?" Simon emerged from the mist, bloodied, muddied, and dressed in Peter's finest.

"Don't worry, Peter, no one would mistake me for you! Hah— no one would ever mistake the prodigal for his most perfect brother. Do you think our father would kill the fatted calf for me? I think not."

Peter could see him clearly now, a twisted picture of himself with a bottle in his hand. Simon laughed. "No, even if they mistook the face, they would never, never mistake the heart. Mine is black and full of drink, while your pure heart is…"

"Stop it. I know your heart, and it isn't black. But you are full of that—that devilish drink. Come, Simon, I'm taking you home." Peter moved his horse slowly toward his brother's.

"Take me home? So I can revel in the servants' pitying whispers of poor Peter's cross to bear? Or better yet, listen to that black-souled clergyman you've made a pet of condemn me to Hell?"

Simon Graymoor's slouched figure slowly straightened, as the two brothers locked eyes. There was silence—a silence thicker than the mantle of murkiness surrounding them. Only the rain and the roar of the river filled the empty space between them.

Suddenly, Simon spurred his horse forward, and grabbed his brother's reins.

"No, you shall not take me home. I shall take *you*. Come, and I will show you the bliss of the bottle. We shall drink and let Hell's fire burn away all memory!" Simon pulled Peter's horse toward him—and toward the swollen stream.

"Simon, let go; you'll kill us both!" The two horses clashed, rearing up in fright as each man reached for the other's reins. As the brothers battled toward the bridge, the voice of rushing waters grew louder until it rumbled right beneath them.

It was a graceless, dangerous dance of hooves and hands along the narrow strip of wood and stone, pushing the railings until they began to creak and snap, like breaking bones. Suddenly, the ancient timbers gave way, tumbling them, horses and all, into the roiling waters of the White Rock River.

For an awful moment, both brothers went under, until one man and horse struggled to the bank, battered by the torrent, but alive. Behind him came a desperate cry.

"Help—help me!"

A riderless horse emerged from the waters, and one man, shaken but safe, turned to see his brother clinging to a twisted root.

"For the love of God, do something!"

One brother clung for life in the relentless torrent. One brother stood on the riverbank, frozen by fear—or by design. One last word came up from the waters as they swallowed the man: "Save me!"

Chapter 2

"I put my hand to write this, the hand of the Lord,
His mighty fist coming down to bring His judgment.
Yes, so shall I bring it; so shall I bring the Al-
mighty's mastery over my domain. God help me in
this righteous cause."
—*Diary of Absalom Bane*

"I'm sorry, I am so sorry..." Clifford Graymoor stooped to pick up the scattered folders of the very pretty, very irritated woman he had just knocked down. He was on the polished marble steps outside the foundation, which made him feel even more unpolished and awkward. "Really, I'm sorry. I was just... Uh, you see, I'm late, and I was looking at my watch and didn't see—"

The icy stare of the woman stopped him cold. "Then I suggest you try being on time, instead of making *other* people late." The woman took her papers from Cliff, and without a word, he stepped back to let her pass.

Working with university politics had taught him when to speak and when to keep his mouth shut, and it looked like he was entering a world where the mouth-shut strategy might be his best chance of not getting eaten alive. He was just a professor, not an executive. What the heck was he doing here, anyway? Sure, he had the "name," but not the bloodline—not really.

7

Cliff gathered his own scattered papers and made his way up the stairs and through the glass doors. Funny how a building could look historic and modern at the same time. He shook off the random thought and approached the reception desk. The young woman behind it looked like she was freshly minted from a corporate brochure. No gum-chewing here, like at the college. She swiftly appraised Cliff, categorized him as a supplicant, and put on her chilliest smile. "Yes? Do you have an appointment, sir?"

Cliff gave his characteristic crooked smile. "Appointment? Yeah, I guess you could say that. My name is Clifford Graymoor, and I'm supposed to be in a—"

The receptionist's demeanor instantly changed. "Dr. Graymoor! We've been expecting you! What a pleasure to meet you, sir! If you'll just come this way..." She rose and placed her thumb on a print reader. As she did, two massive oak doors parted as if by incantation. The receptionist smiled and led him through those doors and into a world he'd always dreamed about, but had never had the magic to enter: the world of the Graymoor Foundation.

"Mr. Chairman, he's here." The receptionist spoke to a tall, distinguished man—diplomat-style distinguished—who stood at the head of a massive board room table. The hard, gray eyes softened when they saw Cliff.

"Ladies and Gentlemen of the board, we will come to order. I would like to introduce the only living man who still carries our foundation's name, Dr. Clifford Graymoor."

Cliff looked around at twelve faces who held the power—well, most of the power—over the vast wealth of the Graymoor Foundation. He had seen their names in newspapers, magazines, and had even seen a few on TV, but he'd never imagined that he'd be sitting across from them at a conference table that looked ten times more expensive than all his furniture combined. Sure, he'd corresponded with some of them; worked with a few of them on some archival projects, but to be here... Cliff's mind wandered into a fantasy, almost like a memory: dark halls, lined by portraits of men who looked like—but *not* like him. Faces from the past, watching him as he...

"Dr. Graymoor... Dr. Graymoor!"

Cliff was shaken from his reverie. "Huh? Oh, yes, sorry, I was just carbon-dating some of my thoughts." Cliff looked around. *Tough room. That line usually killed in History 101.*

Dexter Heathstone hid a slight smile. He was the only one of the board who actually knew Clifford Graymoor well. Dexter knew that, despite his slightly rumpled, distracted look, Cliff knew his stuff. There was no one on Earth as knowledgeable on the history of the Graymoors as Cliff.

"Since our Director seems to be delayed, shall we begin our discussion of—?"

The heavy doors swung open. "Sorry I'm late. Some idiot knocked me down and—" The pretty woman stopped and stared at Cliff.

"Madame Director, so glad you could join us. I'd like to introduce Dr. Clifford Graymoor—only living bearer of the Graymoor name—and the nation's foremost expert on the Graymoor family."

She cast a cold eye toward the Chairman of the Board.

"With the exception of yourself, of course." Dexter deftly side-stepped the awkward moment and took his seat. "Now that Director Bainbridge is here, I suggest we get down to business."

"And I suggest that this is highly inappropriate!" Lyndsie Bainbridge was not used to being side-stepped, and she was definitely not used to her authority being challenged. "We don't need to bring in an outsider who doesn't…" Lyndsie checked herself. "I suggest we discuss this further, without the presence of—"

"Madame Director, there's nothing more to discuss." The tone of Dexter's voice was firm. "Sorry, Lyndsie—the board's overruling you on this one."

"But I'm perfectly qualified to…"

Dexter rose from his seat. "So is he—maybe more so. And he's a Graymoor. We need that name attached to this project; that is, if Professor Graymoor agrees."

Cliff's adrenaline began to spike. The mighty Graymoor Foundation—the foundation that built children's hospitals and orphanages; the foundation that had been featured on the cover of Time magazine and in The Washington Post. The foundation that had become a global force in the past ten years was calling on him? "Agree to what?"

The cool voice of Lyndsie cut through. "Professor Graymoor, I hope you realize what a challenging, time-consuming mountain of work the board is about to ask you to undertake. You know you are under no obligation to—"

Dexter countered, "Let the man decide for himself, Lyndsie."

Cliff couldn't stand it any longer, "Decide what? Could someone please tell me what this is all about?"

Dexter winked at Cliff. "Madame Director, on behalf of the *governing* board of the Graymoor Foundation, please present to Dr. Graymoor 'Project Graystone.'"

Lyndsie gave an icy smile toward Dexter. "As you wish." The lights dimmed as Lyndsie began her PowerPoint. "As you know, Dr. Graymoor, we're entering into the centennial celebration of the official establishment of the Graymoor Foundation. Since the early 1900s when it began its work under the name of Atonement Missions, it's grown into a philanthropic organization of international importance."

Clifford frowned. *Good grief—she lifted that right from my book!*

"I know. I wrote my doctoral thesis on the foundation, and my published work says exactly..."

"Of course. Then I'll get to the point." Lyndsie advanced the slides forward. "As part of the centennial celebration, the board has decided to restore Graystone."

The vision of marble staircases and stained glass, of rose gardens and high, white walls gleaming in the sun flooded Cliff's imagination. "Restore Graystone?"

"It's the ancient ancestral estate of the Graymoor family, built in..."

"In 1902, I know... I know. I played there as a kid. Restore Graystone—wow! Who's going to handle the project?"

Dexter couldn't hold back a grin. "You are, Professor Graymoor. That is, if you're willing—and able."

Lyndsie shot a dark look at the Chairman. "As I mentioned, there is going to be a massive mountain of work involved, and with your duties at the University, I don't see how—"

"That's enough, Lyndsie." The edge to Dexter's voice silenced her. "We've talked to the Chancellor at the University and already arranged for a paid sabbatical for Professor Graymoor—as well as additional compensation for handling the restoration." Dexter turned to Cliff. "But she is right about one thing—the decision is yours. Are you ready to tackle this 'mountain of work,' Cliff?"

"Ready? Are you kidding?" Cliff caught himself. "I mean, I would be honored to tackle, uh, undertake the restoration of Graystone."

A stately, gray-suited woman rose from her seat. "I move that Professor Clifford Graymoor be placed in charge of Project Graystone."

Dexter scanned the faces around him. "All in favor, say, 'Aye.'"

Around the table the motion went: "Aye… Aye… Aye…" until every voice was heard.

"By unanimous decision of the board—"

"But I—" Lyndsie cut in, and just as quickly, Dexter cut her off.

"By unanimous decision of the board, motion carried. Congratulations, Cliff—you are now head of Project Graystone." Dexter turned to face the glare of the Director of the Graymoor Foundation. "I know you wanted this, Lyndsie, but you have to trust us. Cliff is the man for the job. You're not going to be left out of the loop. I expect you to work closely with him. You've got a lot of resources he could use. What do you say, Madame Director?"

Lyndsie's face softened into a smile. "Of course, Dex. But, you can't blame a girl for trying."

Dexter nodded to those around him. "This meeting is adjourned." The board of the most powerful foundation in the world rose, one by one congratulating and thanking Cliff.

"Professor Graymoor, you don't know how much this means…"

"Dr. Graymoor, the foundation thanks you…"

"We know the project couldn't be in better hands…"

As the board dispersed, exiting the inner sanctum, Lyndsie turned, flashing her brightest smile on Cliff. "Look, I think we got off on the wrong foot." Lyndsie extended her hand. "Hi, I'm Lyndsie Bainbridge."

Cliff cautiously took her hand. "Uh, hi. I'm Dr. Gray—I mean, I'm—"

Lyndsie dimpled. "I know. I've done my due diligence."

"I guess so. You quoted my book in your presentation." The dimples disappeared. Mentally, Cliff kicked himself. "Sorry. I have a tendency to blurt."

Lyndsie gave him a studied look. "Most men would consider it an homage if a woman publicly quoted his book." Cliff felt himself losing the battle. He wasn't used to handling words like weapons. "It's just that, it's my book…" He paused helplessly. "And I didn't mean to, you know, take something from—I mean Graystone's—"

Lyndsie coolly cut him off. "Don't worry about it. It's just organizational politics. This is going to be a very high-profile project. I had to give it a shot."

Cliff blurted again. "It's not a project; it's Graystone. You've got to understand, this has been a dream of mine since I was a kid. I used to peer in the windows and imagine what it looked like." He grasped for words. "I mean, it's why I wrote my book, and—"

Lyndsie gave her dazzling smile. "Enough, enough! You win. I wanted this project—you don't know how badly I wanted it. But, I know when I've been beaten. I'm sure we can find a way to work together. Truce, Professor Graymoor?"

Cliff took her extended hand. It was soft and warm, but her grasp was strong. "It's Cliff—and, uh, sure. Truce."

"Good. Let's set a lunch meeting today to discuss—"

"I can't—I still have classes and—"

Lyndsie pulled out her phone, checking her calendar. "Fine. Cocktails at six and then—"

"I don't drink. Ever. Fogs the brain." *I definitely have to stop blurting.*

Lyndsie gave a curious smile. "Alright, then just dinner. 7:30

p.m. at Le Chateau. Their nouvelle cuisine is exquisite. By the way, don't forget a coat and tie. Oh, and Cliff…" There was that smile again. "Don't be late."

Cliff called after, "Huh? Nouvelle… What?"

Coat and tie? What kind of place…? It twigged in. *Le Chateau!* The place was ultra-posh and out-the-roof expensive. He called after Lyndsie, "Hey, Le Chateau's a little pricey, don't you…?" But Lyndsie was already gone. Cliff sighed. Maybe he could get by with just ordering a salad. He hoped his good jacket wasn't at the cleaners.

Cliff's thoughts drifted back to the project at hand. He slowly gathered his papers in a daze. "Graystone—I can't believe it." He turned to Dexter, who had remained behind, watching the Lyndsie–Cliff battle of wits.

"Dex, I don't know how to thank—"

The chairman waved his words aside. "Nonsense. You're the man for the job." Then, in an uncharacteristically fatherly gesture, he placed a hand on Cliff's shoulder. "Just a word to the wise, Cliff: don't be charmed into letting your guard down. Lyndsie Bainbridge is as ambitious as she is beautiful—and if you think she's in this for anyone but herself, think again."

CHAPTER 3

Cliff wandered the canopied walkway that laced the campus of Graywood State, the small university more or less named after his ancestors. His classes were finally over, and the afternoon was postcard picture perfect: a blend of ivied halls and autumn leaves, with sunlight playfully peeking through. Not that he noticed.

His mind was bouncing back and forth between two opposing emotions: anger at the thought of high-level politics and manipulation, and rapture at the thought of restoring Graystone. A vision of Graystone in its grandeur loomed up before him; a vision he was now going to bring to life. This idyllic picture was shattered as the face of Lyndsie Bainbridge filled the frame. To no one in particular, he grumbled, "To just stand there and quote me like she… I mean, *I'm* the one who wrote the book—the real book! I don't care if she is 'Madame Director;' where does she get off—?"

His reverie was cut short by a voice from behind him, "Well if you told me who 'she' is, maybe I could tell you."

Cliff jumped and turned. In front of him was a tall woman, frosted with gray—and grinning.

"Aunt Kate! You nearly scared me out of my skin."

"Good thing I didn't. I'm not cleaning up a mess like that."

Cliff laughed and relaxed. Good old Aunt Kate; although he'd never say the word "old" to her face.

"Come on, boy. You need a cup of my herb tea." Kate was famous for her herb teas. She grew the herbs herself and was always concocting new brews.

Cliff turned toward her cottage. "As long as you don't give me that licorice stuff again. That was pretty nasty." Cliff held open the door as she entered.

"Yep, I know. That's what Amy said, too."

Cliff furrowed his brows. "Amy?"

A familiar petite figure emerged from the kitchen. Dark hair, big green doe-eyes, and dimples that put Lyndsie's to shame. "Cliff!" Amy flung herself toward Cliff, catching him in a bear hug. Or more like a baby bear hug.

As he disengaged himself, he pushed her at arm's length. "Amy?"

Amy placed her hands on her hips in mock protest. "Why Clifford Graymoor, don't tell me you don't remember me! After all the apples you chucked at me in the schoolyard, and the bugs you put in my hair, and the time you played pirate and tied me to a tree, and—"

Cliff laughed. "Enough already! Of course I remember you. There's no way anybody could forget the likes of you!" Amy Newgate. It was Newgate, now. Used to be "Daley," but that changed a few years back. She hadn't changed a bit since high school, except that—yeah, she *had* changed.

Boy, had she changed. His memory drifted back. First, she was that pig-tailed tag-a-long he knew from childhood, then that flirty cheerleader that he just missed asking to the senior prom. But Amy was a woman now—she most certainly was—but what was she doing back in Granville?

The whistle on the tea kettle started singing as Kate brought the cups out. "Yep. Amy's my new roomie. She's settin' up her salon right next to my pottery barn."

Before he could stop himself, he looked at Amy and blurted. "Roomie? I thought you were married." Only the whistling of the tea kettle could be heard. Cliff hung his head. "I did it again, didn't I?"

Amy put her hand on his arm. "No, no, it's okay. Jake died about a year ago. Cancer. Kate found out about it and was… Well, you know how Aunt Kate is." Amy looked at her and smiled. "She was right there for me. So, when she offered her extra bedroom, and half her shop for my salon…"

Kate blew her nose, waved the words away. "No point in both of us being alone. Just made sense for her to move in." Kate moved off to the kitchen.

Cliff smiled. Aunt Kate: crusty on the outside, soft as cotton candy on the inside. Just about as sweet, too. He turned to Amy. "So, how long have you been in town?"

"Two months. You know, you really ought to visit your Aunt Kate more often."

"Wait a sec. We have lunch once a month, out at the University."

"Only once a month? Hmm…"

"Oh, here we go again…"

"Settle down, you two. Still arguing like you were a couple of kids." Kate had re-entered with a tray laden with cookies, milk and honey, and a cozy-covered teapot. "Peppermint-pomegranate."

Amy and Cliff exchanged a look.

Kate caught it. "You never know till you try."

They bravely filled their cups and got comfortable. Amy curled up like a kitten on the couch next to Kate. All Cliff could think was, *I don't remember her being this cute…*

"Cliff. Cliff!" Aunt Kate's voice jarred him out of his thoughts. "Are you gonna tell us or not?" Cliff looked at her blankly. "The 'she' of, 'where does *she* get off?'"

It twigged in. "Oh, that. It's this, this woman, Lyndsie Bainbridge—"

Amy popped in sympathetically, "Oh, girlfriend problems?"

"Girlfriend? Huh? No, no! It's that—I have to work with this high-powered, female shark who just happens to run the Graymoor Foundation. And who also just happened to steal most of *Dark and Light—A History of the Graymoors* for her best seller. *Her* book shot to number one in the Times, leaving my book in the dust, when everybody knows that I spent *years* studying the Graymoor family and—"

"You're losing me, boy." Aunt Kate never minced words.

Cliff got to the point. "Here's the thing. I get to restore Graystone, but I have to work with the woman who stole my book."

Kate nodded. "So, you thought you'd wander back and eyeball the old estate." She smiled. "You never could keep away from that place as a kid."

Cliff's mind went back. How vast and mysterious the old place had seemed. Broken windows that the wind swirled through. How the house would moan on an autumn day—almost like it was crying. Cliff shook himself out of his reverie. "Could you blame me, Aunt Kate? I mean, an empty old mansion everybody said was haunted? It was a boy's dream." He leaned forward. "And you'll love this, Kate—I get to restore Granville Church, too."

Silence filled the room. Kate finally broke it. "You're going to restore the church?"

"Top to bottom. It's about time someone gave you a hand in it. Now you'll have all the help you need. You ought to be ecstatic, Aunt Kate!"

Silence.

Kate's husband had been the last vicar at the old Granville

Church—and the last man to carry the Bane name. Absalom Bane had founded the church, and the position of vicar had been passed down, father to son, since the time of Peter Graymoor. Since her husband's death, Kate had made it her job to, inch by inch, restore the legacy of the Bane name and bring the old place to its original charm.

Amy filled the silence with a squeal of delight. "You get to fix up Graystone? I could just pop all over the place! You must be so excited. Remember how we'd sneak around the outside of that big old house, trying to peek in the windows? You used to try to scare me all the time. Ooh, you were so mean."

"Well if you weren't such a little pest, I wouldn't have tried—"

"Oh, never mind—I forgive you!"

"Forgive me?"

"I am so excited we're doing this!"

"Huh? Wait, *we're* not doing—"

"Hold on, Clifford Graymoor! You're not leaving me out of this—no way."

Cliff turned to his Aunt Kate. "A little help here, Aunt Kate…?"

"You're on your own, boy."

Amy and Kate exchanged fist bumps. Clifford groaned. "What is it with you women? I just came here for a—a little tea and sympathy, and…" A thought hit him. "And maybe—"

Kate interrupted. "Uh-oh. What is it now?"

"Aunt Kate, I need to see the diaries of Absalom and Rebecca Bane."

Once again, silence.

Cliff got a strange, uncomfortable feeling, and he didn't know why. Kate began to clear the tea cups, though Cliff had barely taken a sip of his. He repeated his request. "C'mon, Aunt Kate, please?"

"I don't know what Absalom's diaries have to do with fixing up Graystone." Kate's voice sounded small, swallowed by the dark, narrow stairway. Her flashlight flickered, making a strange dance of shadows on the walls. Cobwebs hung like a tattered curtain across the doorway to the attic.

A nervous twitch began in Cliff's left eye. *Don't be stupid—it's just an attic.* Just an attic. His Uncle Nate had always teased him, telling him that's where he kept his pet monsters. Cliff brushed a cobweb out of his twitching eye, and gave his sound, reasonable reply. "There are some holes in the family history, and I remember reading some pages from Absalom's diary—"

"You read Absalom's diaries? His *private* diaries? Without my permission?"

"*Diaries?* As in, more than one?"

"Not the point, boy."

A voice from behind them piped up. "Ohh—I told you we'd get in trouble!"

Cliff jumped and turned to see a petite form behind him. "Amy, I told you to stay downstairs!"

"Yeah, right."

Cliff turned back to a stony-faced Kate. He had an uncomfortable *caught with a hand in the cookie jar* feeling.

"Don't look at me like that. I just found a few pages of it; random bits and pieces. Most of it's a blur—I mean, I was just a kid—but I know there was something that…" The memory that started to form evaporated. "Ah, I can't remember."

"That still doesn't answer my question, boy. Why do you need the diaries?"

"Because Peter Graymoor didn't keep anything from his

mentor. There were things, just some really curious things that
made me think…" Something in Cliff told him to hold back.
"I just need all the information I can get if I'm going to make
the restoration really authentic."

"You know plenty. Why do you—"

Cliff stepped closer and took her hand. "Come on, Aunt
Kate. This is important. Really important. Please?"

Reluctantly, Kate pushed open the attic door. The hinge
squeaked like a kitten crying.

"Ooh, spooky. Like monsters."

Cliff shot Amy a dagger look. She simply giggled. They carefully felt their way across the room, the main illumination
filtering from a set of small, dust-laden windows. Cliff shined
his flashlight around until it fell on an old steamer trunk. Kate
pointed. "Well, there it is."

All three carefully negotiated a path through boxes and
broken furniture. And all three leaned in expectantly as Cliff
pulled it open. He shined the flashlight and saw…

Busted toys.

An old duvet.

A lady's morning gown, fragile like a dandelion, ready to
fall apart. And underneath it all, a hatbox bound with string.
Before Cliff could speak, Amy blurted out, "That's it! I think.
At least it looks like it."

Some things never change, Cliff thought. *Amy never could
hold back.*

"I know, Amy—I was there." Cliff pulled at the knot. Too
tight. "Now, if we just had—"

Before he could finish, she placed a small pair of scissors in
his hand. "I'm a hairdresser. I've always got scissors."

Cliff snipped the string and opened the box.

"Letters? Old novels? Papers? Where are the diary pages? I don't get it!"

Kate sat down and shook her head. "That's all I got, boy. Your memory must be playing tricks on you."

Amy jumped in again. "Wait, wasn't there a suitcase or something? No, no—it was a trunk! Another trunk; kind of a small one. And it was green!"

"You know, you may actually be right this time. Aunt Kate…" Cliff turned to look at her. "Uh, Aunt Kate, what's that you're sitting on?"

It was Amy's turn to blurt. "It's a trunk! Look Cliff, it's a—" One look from Kate stopped her, but it didn't stop Cliff.

"Uh, what's in the trunk, Kate?"

"Personal things. Family things. *My* things. There's nothing in here for you."

"Are you sure, because I—"

"Take your time with the papers. I'm going to make some more tea." Kate left, shutting the attic door behind her.

"Boy, that was weird." Amy sat on the floor, staring at the green trunk.

"Huh? What's weird?"

Amy shook her head, "Kate, you dummy! She never acts that way."

"What way is that?"

"Ya know—secretive. I don't think she wants us to look in that trunk."

Clifford reached over and rattled the lock. "Looks like she's gonna get her way, too." He picked up the hatbox of papers and carried them toward the silvery light falling from the windows. "C'mon—let's see what we've got."

Amy followed him to the window where they both sat on an

antique couch with dirty cushions. Cliff pulled out the papers, one by one. "Letters, sermon notes… Hmm, no lack of fire and brimstone here."

"Yuk. Wait a sec—now that's weird."

"No, it's not. Lots of country parsons preached hell-fire and—"

"Not that—*this*." Amy pointed to a letter on heavy parchment.

"'*To Sir Thaddeus Thomas Graymoor*
Cambridgeshire…'"

CHAPTER 4

Parlor, Graystone Manor

—1907

The bedraggled figure of the only remaining son of Sir Thaddeus Graymoor paced restlessly across the rich carpet of the parlor, staining it with mud. His left hand pushed the wet hair away from his face. *How long? For God's sake, how long can it take to...?* He could take it no longer. "Where's that fool doctor? Why does he send no word about my—?"

"He is at rest."

The words came from behind him. He froze, then slowly turned. Before him stood, not the doctor, but the visage of the man he always dreaded to see. "You! What are you...?" He swallowed his dread. "So, Reverend Bane, you bring word that my brother's—"

"Dead."

"Dead? What? I thought you said—"

"Yes, he is at rest. His labors are no more."

Absalom Bane placed a boney hand on his shoulder, causing him to flinch. A Graymoor should fear no man, but this cold-eyed cleric made him feel as if his soul was being drained out of him.

Absalom continued. "Death is but the soul's passing to its final reward—or judgment. I pray that, for your brother, it is not judgment but—" A tray clattered behind them. A shivering servant girl stood motionless in the doorway.

"Master Simon's dead? God help us!" Nelly crossed herself as she began to cry into her apron. "God's hand; it was God's hand. Forgive me for speaking my mind, sir, but you can't live as Master Simon lived and not expect to—"

Absalom swiftly turned to her. "Impertinent girl! How dare you—a serving girl—claim the right of judgment that is only in the hands of God and His chosen servants. If God punishes anyone, it will be you, for your insolence." Absalom seemed to grow like a shadow in front of her, and Nelly cowered before it. "Go—gather your cups and leave us. Your master and I have much to discuss."

Nelly cast a fearful eye to her master, who gave her a slight nod.

As Nelly left, the grieving brother turned from the cold stare of Absalom Bane. "Leave me. Whatever it is that you want to say can wait. Can't you see I am grieving my—my brother, Simon?"

Absalom stepped within a whisper's breath of him. "So, you grieve for your brother, *Simon*?"

Wariness and apprehension mixed with grief as he lifted his eyes to the preacher's face.

Absalom leaned in closer. "Yes, I know. In this last hour, I became your brother's most intimate confessor. I heard his final breath. I know what happened."

He turned away from the preacher, fear filling his mind like a fog.

Absalom pressed in. "I know what happened at the bridge. I know about the drunken struggle that sent you both into the river. I know how you watched your brother cling for his life to a broken branch and—"

He cried out, "No! I went to him—"

"Too late!"

The last Graymoor sunk down on the high-backed chair that was his brother's.

Absalom leaned down. "I know how you watched him, waiting for him to be swept away to his death."

The broken man looked up, tears carving furrows down his face. "Then go—tell my father, tell the servants—tell them all how he died. Tell them, then tell the hangman too, if you like. I no longer care. The only one who ever truly loved me is dead. My brother is dead."

An ancient shuffle was heard at the door, and the creaking voice of Henry, the family's butler, gently coughed. "Excuse me sir, but the servants want to know where you would like to set Master Simon's body, once it is prepared? The neighbors will wish to come and comfort you in your vigil. They have already arranged for food and are asking when the service for dear Master Simon will—?"

The servant was interrupted by the survivor's laughter. "Master Simon? You wish to know about your dear Master Simon?"

Absalom Bane's voice broke in. "Leave us. You will be answered soon." Henry shuffled out of the door.

The grief-stricken brother began to chuckle, then laugh hysterically. A sharp rap from Absalom's cane silenced him. "Pull yourself together, man!" The cold gray eyes met the tear-filled blue ones.

"You're right. I will answer him now." He rose to his feet. "The hand of doom is upon me."

Once more, Absalom placed his hand on the broken man's shoulder. "No. It is the hand of mercy."

The young man didn't flinch at his touch this time. Instead, he looked at him, hope flickering in his face.

"Listen to me; listen carefully, for God has placed before you a chance to redeem your sins."

"How? How can a man who has—?"

"Heed my counsel, and I will help you purify your soul."

"Then help me, Absalom, help me! I will do anything you say…"

CHAPTER 5

Adust-covered Cliff and Amy once again made their way into Kate's parlor with arms full of papers. They settled comfortably on the couch and spread the papers out in front of them. Amy pointed to the death notice they had discovered.

"So, you're telling me he had a brother?"

"Yes. Peter and Simon Graymoor were—"

"So, did you find anything?" Kate entered the parlor with a tray laden with cookies and peppermint tea.

Amy spoke excitedly. "Did you know that this Peter Graymoor had a brother?"

"Of course I know. I married a Bane. So, I'll ask again—did you find anything?"

Cliff sighed. "Nothing much. The only thing of real interest is this letter informing Sir Thaddeus that his son, Simon, had died. That letter may prove what I've always suspected. Simon came with his brother, Peter, to America."

"Anything else?"

"Not really. But it at least has some good information on the appearance of the Gardens and the Church back in the day." Cliff hesitated. "Aunt Kate? Do you mind if I take this box with me?"

"Well, I supposed you can. Just be sure to bring it back. My Nathanial was mighty proud of his Bane family heritage." She continued softly, almost sadly, "Five generations. Five generations of serving the Lord."

Cliff smiled. "I'll guard it with my life, Aunt Kate."

Kate stood, and planted her hands on her hips. "You better. I don't want anything to happen to that box. Now I gotta check on that chicken." With that, she exited to the kitchen.

Amy squirmed impatiently on the couch. "So, tell me."

Cliff turned to her, confused. "Huh?"

"Tell me about Simon Peter—I mean, Peter and Simon!"

"Well, they were brothers. In fact, they were more than just brothers. They were…"

Kate's voice called from the kitchen. "Dinner's ready."

Suddenly Cliff remembered. "Dinner! Oh, crap. I gotta get out of here!"

Cliff reached the door of Le Chateau out of breath and slightly disheveled. He took a moment to straighten his tie, then with a sigh, opened the door. He looked straight into the face of a man in a black tuxedo. Tuxedo Man met him with a polite smile—after giving Cliff the subtly critical once-over. He felt like a twelve-year-old in the principal's office. Were his palms sweating? *Buck up. He's just the maître d.'* "Excuse me. I'm meeting a woman—I mean a lady who's expecting—I mean, she's expecting *me*, not that she's expecting or anything like—uh, anyway, her name's Lyndsie Bain—"

"Ah, yes, Ms. Bainbridge. Right this way, sir." Cliff followed the Tuxedo through a large room, that looked more suited for a ballroom than a restaurant, into a smaller, but no less plush, banquet room. He finally stopped at an intimate corner table.

Cliff rushed in with his apologies. "Sorry I'm late. I got caught up in some research and—wow!" Cliff looked up and saw a different Lyndsie in front of him. Her copper-colored hair fell in loose waves across her bare shoulders. The blue of her dress made her eyes appear bluer than he could ever imagine eyes could look. *Cornflowers. Freshly picked cornflowers,* was all Cliff could think. Gone were all the hard edges. Before him sat a beautiful, alluring woman.

"If 'wow' is an apology, apology accepted." Lyndsie flashed a smile that wasn't so much dazzling as it was warm and inviting.

"I, I didn't mean—well, I did mean, it's just… I have a blurting problem."

Lyndsie gave a genuine laugh. "I've kind of picked up on that. Here." She handed him a menu. "Shall we order?"

Cliff grabbed his glass of water. *If I just keep my mouth busy, maybe I won't stick my foot in it.* He opened the menu and almost did a spit take. "What? Whoa. Uh, these prices are—"

"Taken care of." Lyndsie smiled.

"No. No way. I can't let you pay for—"

"Relax. I'm not. The foundation is. Ever heard of expense accounts?"

Cliff hesitated and looked at the menu again. "I mean if you're sure."

"Scouts honor." She laughed again. A cozy laugh, like they were sharing a private joke.

"Okay, well, here goes." Cliff studied the menu. Unfortunately, all his college French had just flown out of his brain. "Uh, my French is kind of rusty. Could you help me out with—?"

Lyndsie leaned in. "Would you like me to order for you?" Cliff nodded in relief.

Magically, a waiter appeared. Lyndsie gave their order in fluent French, and as the waiter nodded and left, another appeared carrying a bottle of wine. Before Cliff could protest, he had filled both of their glasses.

Lyndsie took a sip. "I'm glad you're here. I was afraid you weren't coming."

Cliff shook his head. "No, I just, well, I was in the middle of research and I just forgot. Absent-minded professor, I guess."

"I find the idea of an absent-minded professor rather… charming. I find you charming."

Cliff blurted, "You do? Why?"

Lyndsie threw up her hands with a laugh. "I give up! You are obviously one man who is immune to my feminine wiles!"

Cliff stammered, "Immune? Well, I wouldn't say—I mean, I'm not really, I just—"

"Close enough. I was going to try to persuade you to let me handle the restoration, and I would give you some of the credit—" She dimpled. "Okay, most of the credit."

Cliff put his napkin down. "Look, Ms. Bainbridge—"

"Lyndsie, please—"

"Lyndsie. I'm not in this for the *credit*; it's not about that. It's about Graystone. Ever since I was a kid, I felt, I don't know, drawn to it. I felt a connection with it and with all the history and mystery buried in those walls. I know I come from the wrong side of the family, but I've always felt like I didn't. I felt like Graystone was mine."

Lyndsie placed her hand on his. "But it's not yours. It belongs to the Graymoor Foundation. You have a beautiful, beautiful dream, Cliff, but I should be the one handling this restoration."

Cliff felt his spine stiffen. "Look, I know Graystone's not mine. I know I have no part of the foundation. But I do have the Graymoor name, and there's nobody, *nobody* who knows more about the Graymoors—and Graystone—than me. I'm doing the restoration." Cliff saw a familiar flash of anger in her eyes.

Lyndsie took a deep breath and a sip of wine. She sighed. "Well, that's that, I guess. I just ask one thing."

"What's that?" Cliff feared another volley from those beautiful red lips.

"Let me help." She added softly, "Please?"

With relief, Cliff smiled. "Let you? Of course, I'll let you. Man, that would be great!"

"Wonderful! I've got some great ideas about—"

Cliff interrupted, "Lyndsie. I just need you to remember—"

"I know, I know—you're in charge. Don't worry, I'll be good. Promise."

A plate was set down in front of Cliff. "Huh, what's this? It looks…wiggly."

"Calamari—you're going to love it."

CHAPTER 6

Cliff walked up to his door with a spring in his step. He grabbed the handle; found it unlocked. He must have forgotten. No problem. In a small town like Granville, you didn't have to worry. Talking to himself, he opened the door, "Not a bad night, Clifford, not a bad night at all. Pretty girl, fancy dinner and—"

"Well, it's about time you got home!" A familiar voice popped his happy balloon.

"Amy? What are you doing here?"

"Waiting for you."

"Huh? Waiting? Why?"

"I found something—after you left."

Cliff turned on the lights. "Found something? What do you mean you found something?"

Amy pointed to the window.

"Close the blinds."

"Close the blinds? Why should I—"

"Good grief. Just do it, Cliff!"

Cliff obediently closed the blinds, then sat down across from Amy. She looked like some cuddly bear cub curled up on the couch—warm, cute, lovable. Not like Lyndsie, who...

"Stop it, Cliff! Focus." Amy looked at him quizzically.

"Huh? Stop what?" Did he just say those things out loud? He hoped not. "Never mind. Now, what do you mean you 'found something?'"

Amy uncurled herself on the couch, patting the soft leather. "Nice couch; it's cushy."

"Amy…"

"Okay, okay. I went back up to the attic. I'd forgotten something, as usual. I don't know why, but I'm always forgetting—"

"Amy, the attic?"

"Okay, I'm getting there! So, I went back up to the attic and just kind of happened to see a piece of paper sticking out of that green trunk. So, I jimmied up the lid a little, and I managed to pull it right—"

"Those are Aunt Kate's personal papers!"

"Personal, huh? Boy, you got that right. Read this." Amy held out a piece of paper.

"I'm not gonna read Kate's—"

"It's not Kate's. Just read it."

Reluctantly, Cliff took the piece of paper and began to read it out loud.

> *I know I've done all you've desired, but despite it all, I know I'm not the man you hoped I would be, Absalom. The thought of what I've done torments me day and night. My mind is never at rest. You tell me I must serve the greater good, but I don't know how much longer I can bear the weight of this. To save my family, must I ruin my soul? God help me! Must I carry this secret to my grave?*

The handwriting trailed off. Cliff stared at the paper in his hand.

"Secret? What secret?"

Bournemouth, England
                                        —Early November 1897

A twelve-year-old boy sat on a dune, a book in hand, staring out to sea. Either mist or tears lightly sprinkled his attractive features. The skies were gray, unsettled, and the seagull's cries seemed panicky rather than plaintive. Below the dunes, the ocean crashed against the craggy shoreline, matching the chaos of emotions on the youth's face. A voice called out to him, coming closer. "Simon! Simon!" A second boy plopped down beside the first. "There you are. Nanny Ives has been looking all over for you." The two brothers looked at one another, each with a face that exactly mirrored the other's, but for the trouble that marred Simon's.

Peter's Graymoor's eyes went from Simon to the book in his hand. "What are you doing out here? Nanny says you'll catch your death—"

"I hope I do."

Peter's brow furrowed in worry, a look he often had when in the company of his brother. "Don't say that, Simon—please! It's wicked!"

Simon snapped. "I say it because I *am* wicked!" The book fell from his hand. "Don't you see? I say wicked things because that's what I am. It's what I was born to be—wicked."

Peter sighed. How often he'd sighed for the sake of his brother, he couldn't begin to count. Though he wouldn't say it, it seemed as if sorrow and sighing for his brother were built into his own soul even before he was born. "What have you done now, Simon?"

"I haven't done anything wrong; not this time. It's me—don't you see it? It's me what's wrong." Simon dashed a tear from his eye—or was it just the mist from the sea?

"What are you talking about?"

Simon brushed the sand from the book he had dropped and handed it to Peter. "This. You'll see, good brother. It's this."

Peter took the book from Simon. "A book? You're wicked because of a book?"

"I found it in Mumsie's secret drawer."

"Simon." Peter drew in a breath and sighed. He looked at the cover. "'The Strange Case of Dr. Jekyll and Mr. Hyde.' Have you read it? What is it about?"

"It's about a man—a doctor, Dr. Jekyll—who has evil inside him, only he doesn't know it. At least not till he mixes up some chemicals and drinks them. Then he—he—"

"He what?"

"He turns into another person; one who's wicked and strong and does terrible, terrible things in the night. It's not Dr. Jekyll, but it is. It's Mr. Hyde; the bad that looks just like the good!"

Alarmed, Peter laid his hand on his brother's arm. "It's just a bogey story, Simon. You shouldn't read such things."

Simon shook his brother's hand away. "Don't you see? Don't you see it's you and me? We are Dr. Jekyll and Mr. Hyde!"

Real concern began to fill Peter's face. "That's silly. It's just a story, Simon! It's not you and—"

"Mumsie thinks it is. That's why she hid the book from us." Simon took the book from his brother, opening it to the cover page.

"Here. Read."

Peter took the book from Simon's hand. Firmly scrawled in an artistic hand were the words:

To Anna Graymoor, for your kindness in my distress. May fate prove kinder to you—and to your sons—than this tale forebodes. God help you!

CHAPTER 7

"Okay, guys, back it up... More... More... Stop! I said stop!" The small moving truck came to a halt. Cliff shivered. He didn't know if it was from excitement, the chill in the air, or from a lack of coffee this morning. He stepped toward the truck, but quickly hopped back up on the curb, narrowly being missed by a BMW racing into the driveway in front of Graystone Manor. Adrenaline pumping, Cliff strode up to the car. "What, are you crazy? You could have killed—" He halted when a slim figure, impeccably dressed, emerged from the car.

"Cliff! There you are! I swung by your apartment to take you out to breakfast, but they said you've moved?"

Cliff grinned. "Moving." He pointed to the truck. "The Graystone Gardener's Cottage is perfect for me! It's clean; it's been remodeled. Even has indoor plumbing now."

"Wait a sec. You're moving *onto* the estate?" Lyndsie frowned. "Are you sure you want to do that—I mean, isn't that a bit extreme?"

"Not if I'm going to be here every day."

"Look, Cliff, I appreciate your enthusiasm, but I wouldn't want you to do anything to interfere with the restoration of—"

"Interfere? Not a chance. I'm furnishing it with all original stuff. It's going to be absolutely picture perfect." Seeing the beginnings of protest, he added, "I already cleared it with

Dexter Heathstone, and the board has given it the 'thumbs up.' Dex even said I could live here rent-free."

"Oh, he did, did he? Well, it looks like 'Dex' and I need to have a little chat about things. There is such a thing as going through the proper channels. He may be Chairman of the Board, but *I'm* the Director of—" Lyndsie caught herself. She turned back to Cliff with a sweetly concerned look. "Please, Cliff, this really isn't a good idea. I don't want the grounds compromised by any—"

Cliff cut her off. "They won't be. I know what I'm doing, Lyndsie, and I'm in charge, remember?" Now he knew why he was sweating, in spite of the chilly morning. He'd never backed down a woman as pretty and powerful as Lyndsie Bainbridge—except for one. Andrea. Beautiful, treacherous Andrea. Lyndsie's voice dissolved the memory.

"Yes," she answered in a voice like shaved ice. "I remember."

Cliff continued. "Anyway, I'm glad you're here. I said I'd keep you in the loop, so here's the loop. I wanted to tell you—" Cliff heard a soft thud behind him. He turned. "No, no, no!" He walked past Lyndsie and up to the men unloading the truck. "Stop right now! Guys, put on some kid gloves and be careful how you handle that. It's an antique! They're all antiques, so don't do anything that will—"

"Tell me what?" The voice cut through, insistent.

"Just a minute, Lyndsie. I'm—"

"Tell me what, Cliff?" Something else was in the voice. *Man, she sounds ticked.* He motioned the movers to continue, then turned back to Lyndsie. "Okay. I wanted to tell you that—"

"I brought goodies!" The bright sound of Amy's voice sang out through the morning air. "Hi! I figured you could use a good sugar high this morning. I got a box of coffee in the car, too."

Cliff grabbed a fritter. "Mmm, thanks."

Amy stuffed a napkin into his hand. "By the way, I think I left my sweater at your place last night."

Lyndsie looked from Amy to Cliff. "Last night?"

"Yeah, last night," Amy repeated, a glint of mischief in her eye.

Cliff caught Lyndsie's look, his eyes widening. "No—no! Nothing like that. I mean, we're not... We didn't..."

"My, my, you *are* full of surprises, Clifford Graymoor." The voice had gone from insistent to cold.

"Huh?" Another soft thud caught Cliff's attention. "No! Don't set it on the ground like that. That's a mirror—there's a mirror inside! And turn it sideways to get it through the door." Cliff turned back to Lyndsie. "I'm sorry; can we talk later, Lyndsie? I really need to—"

Lyndsie's brilliant smile returned. "Of course! Just let me know when you're ready for the keys to the main house and I'll—"

"Already got 'em. Dex had them hand-delivered this morning."

"Well, Mr. Heathstone is certainly on top of things. I'll remember that next time I talk to the board. Yes, I'll definitely remember it." The razor-sharp chill returned to Lyndsie's voice. "Just make sure you call me before you go into the—"

"To the left! To the left!"

"...into the manor. Goodbye, Professor Graymoor."

Too absorbed to notice the ice in Lyndsie's tone, Cliff absently responded, "Huh? Oh, goodbye, Lyndsie."

After giving a hard, almost warning look toward Amy, Lyndsie walked back to her BMW and squealed out of the parking lot.

Amy came up next to Cliff and began in a mocking voice, "Goodbye, Lyndsie. Talk to you soon, Lyndsie..."

Cliff turned to Amy, annoyed. "What?"

"That's Lyndsie Bainbridge, right?"

"Yeah, so?"

"Your Aunt Kate calls her 'the barracuda.' You know, the kind that eats men alive!"

"Huh? What's Aunt Kate got against Lyndsie?" Cliff reached for another donut; Amy smacked his hand away.

"Your Lyndsie tried to take over the church yard—and kick Kate out of the old Gatekeeper's Cottage. She claimed it was foundation property."

Cliff reached again, and got a hand smack again. "Ow! Cut it out! I'm sure she just—"

"She just tried to *steal* something that had been in the Bane family for generations, that's all. And I think she's still planning to take it over as part of all this Graystone renovation stuff."

Cliff bristled. "Wait a sec, how do you know all this? She didn't say anything about it over dinner last night."

"Dinner? *That's* who you had dinner with last night?"

"Well, yeah." He grabbed another fritter before Amy could smack again. "Look, I didn't like her at first either. I mean, she does come on kind of strong. But we patched things up last night—and I made it clear that I'm in charge of this. Aunt Kate doesn't have anything to worry about."

Amy grabbed the fritter from his hand, frowned and said, "Just be careful, Cliff; I don't trust her. And you shouldn't either."

A grin slowly spread across Cliff's face. "Amy, are you actually…jealous?"

A flush crept up Amy's face. "No—I mean—no. It's just that—oh, it's hard to explain. It's like I can sometimes 'see' into people. Kate calls it a kind of radar about, well, about dark and light." Her big, green eyes looked right into Cliff's. "And let me tell you, buddy, my radar's pingin' all over the place with her—and not on the light side!"

"Oh, c'mon Amy."

"Your Aunt Kate knows what I mean. She says it's a kind of a gift. Like I said, I don't trust her, and you shouldn't either!" Amy looked down at her donuts.

Cliff placed his finger under her chin, lifting her face. She flushed again.

"Don't worry, I don't trust her. At least not completely. I know she really, really wanted the job of restoring Graystone, so I have to watch my back."

"That's not all she wants, Cliff. I think—no, I *know* she's after—"

A familiar voice behind them interrupted. "Don't you two ever stop arguing?"

Cliff jumped. "Aunt Kate? Don't sneak up on me like that."

"I can't help it if you're jumpier than a jackrabbit. Just thought you could use some expert help unpacking, Son."

Cliff walked over and kissed Kate on the cheek. "Thanks! You're the best!" He turned and saw the empty truck. "Everything in, guys? Great! Oh, and here's some donuts."

The driver grunted a thank you, and the movers descended on Amy's box like vultures. With full mouths, they re-entered the truck, taking the box with them. Amy frowned as she watched the truck pull away. "Did you ever think, Cliff, that *I* might have wanted one of those donuts? And that maybe I brought those goodies just for us?"

"Huh? Oh, you did?"

Amy crossed her arms and frowned. "I swear, Clifford Graymoor, sometimes I think that you have the—the intuition of a turnip!"

"Well, why didn't you say something?"

"Well, why didn't you ask?"

"How was I supposed to even know to ask? You think I'm some sort of mind reader who—"

Aunt Kate's voice cut through. "Good grief, here you are, burning daylight pickin' at one another, when you could be eating the *cookies* I brought for you."

Cliff kissed Kate again. "I love you, Aunt Kate!"

Amy smacked his arm. "Oh sure. You *love* Aunt Kate when she brings cookies, but when I bring donuts…"

A mischievous twinkle lit up Kate's eyes. "You saying you want Cliff to say 'I love you?'"

A simultaneous flush crept up both Cliff and Amy's faces. Amy turned on her heels and practically ran back to her car. As she was driving off, Cliff called out, "Hey, what about my coffee?"

The afternoon sun streamed through the small, stained-glass window of the Gardener's Cottage.

"I'm glad you came back." Cliff turned and faced Amy, who was emptying the last box of knickknacks.

Amy smiled. "Me too."

They both turned to survey their handiwork. It took all day, but the cottage finally looked like a home. In fact, it looked like a home from another place and time. Everything, from the wing-backed chairs to the Sheraton sideboard, spoke of a less complicated way of life. Visions from a century past danced through Cliff's imagination. He could almost see an afternoon tea being set, and a rosy-cheeked boy and girl eating sweet cakes as they clung to their mother's apron. His daydream drifted to a vision of himself in Edwardian garb, being welcomed home by his laughing children and loving wife. He looked in the face of the wife, which looked a lot like Amy, but it suddenly morphed into Lyndsie's face, laughing… And the laughing face became a laughing skull…

"Cliff. Cliff! Quit your daydreaming, boy! I said that just about does it." Kate's common-sense voice drove away the nightmare image.

Cliff was himself again, in a cozy room, with a cup of tea in front of him. It was just a daydream, that's all. "Uh, yeah. Wait, not quite." Cliff grabbed a hammer and nail. "We almost forgot the most important thing!" He pulled the step ladder over to the fireplace, selected a spot on the wall above it, and pounded the nail in.

Amy exchanged looks with Kate. "So that's why you wanted Kate's hammer? What's that for?"

Cliff jumped down from the step ladder. "For this!" He carefully tore brown wrapping paper from what was obviously a frame.

"A picture? Why's a picture the most important thing?"

"Because," Cliff struggled up the ladder with the heavy frame, "it's not just any picture. It's an *exact* reproduction of Peter Graymoor's formal portrait; the one painted at the Graymoor Estate in England—complete with riding crop and hound. I had it painted years ago as kind of a Christmas present to myself."

Amy made a face. "You must have been on Santa's stink list if you call that a Christmas present."

"Well, I like it. The original was painted right before Peter came to America. Wish the UK Graymoors would let go of it. We could hang it in Graystone."

Amy stared at it critically. "Ugh. It's pretty blah. He's not even smiling."

"It's very much of the period."

"Well, I *don't* like it." Amy looked from the portrait above the fireplace to the opposite wall. "And why'd you have to hang it opposite that big mirror? Now you have to see the same 'blah' guy no matter where you look!"

"So?" Cliff felt like she just called his baby "ugly."

"So, it feels like he's watching me; gives me the willies!"

Cliff plopped into one of the wingback chairs. It was a lot less comfortable than it looked—and it didn't look very comfortable. "Whatever."

"I'm just saying—"

The sound of a spoon banging on a pot interrupted Cliff and Amy's sparring. Kate was in the kitchen, and obviously hungry. "Well, if it won't bother your arguing too much, I'm gonna fix us some supper!"

Amy popped up from the couch, probably the most comfortable seat in the house. "Oh, no you don't. Uh-uh! You've been working like a—like a crazy woman all day; so you just put that pot down right now. We're ordering pizza for dinner!"

"You kids don't need to buy a—"

"No argument! We're buying you a big, sloppy pizza—aren't you Cliff?"

Cliff suddenly twigged in. "Huh? I am?" Amy gave him a pointed look. "Oh, uh, yeah. Sure, I'm—I'm buying a pizza."

Amy was already in the corner, on her cellphone, placing the order.

Cliff walked over to Kate. "Thanks, Aunt Kate. You know I couldn't have done it without you."

"Sure you could have. It just would have taken you twice as long." Cliff grinned. *Gotta love Aunt Kate.* Kate grinned back. "Besides, you're the only nephew I got."

Cliff placed his hand under Kate's elbow and gently guided her toward the kitchen. "Aunt Kate, I have to ask you a question…"

"Oh, here it comes—the *big* question."

"Huh?"

"The answer is 'yes,' Cliff, I'm leaving all my riches to you."

"Aunt Kate, I'm serious!"

"So am I!"

"Kate, I need to know something about the family."

"The Bane family?"

"No, the Graymoors. Do you know anything about a—a family secret?"

Silence—the *you-could-hear-a-pin-drop* kind. This was getting to be a thing with Kate, whose face was as stony and unreadable as a sphinx.

"Pizza should be here in about 30 minutes, and—" Amy stopped, looked from face to face. "Uh-oh. What's wrong?"

"Uh, nothing." Cliff glanced uncertainly at Kate's unchanged expression. "I was just asking Kate about the—the family."

"Ohh." Amy nodded knowingly.

Kate grimaced. "So, you're in on this, too. Fine. I'll tell you." Kate motioned them closer. "There's no family secret."

"Are you sure about that, Aunt Kate?" Cliff, in his whole life, had never known Kate to lie.

"Of course I'm sure. Why wouldn't I be?"

Amy planted her diminutive frame in front of the taller woman. "Because your ears are turning red, and when your ears turn red that means you're—"

"It means I'm tired of all these foolish questions." Kate turned to Cliff. Her face softened. "Clifford, digging up dead men's bones never did anyone any good. If there are any secrets buried out there—and I'm not saying there are—just let 'em lie, son. Just let 'em lie."

"I can't, Aunt Kate!" Clifford began to pace the stone floor of the cottage. "I just—I don't know why but I—I need to know."

Kate gave a heavy sigh. "Well, I can't help you. You're on your own."

"One more thing, Aunt Kate."

"Oh for heaven's sake, boy, you're worse than a reporter! I told you, I don't know—"

Clifford waved away her protest. "Don't worry, it's not a secret." He hesitated, "At least I don't think it is."

Kate sighed again, and with resignation, pulled out a kitchen chair and sat. She suddenly felt very tired and old. "Go ahead. May as well get it out of your system."

Cliff pulled up a chair beside her. "When Peter Graymoor crossed the Atlantic to come to America, did he bring his brother Simon with him?"

Silence again. All that could be heard was the ticking of the grandfather clock. Quietly, Kate simply responded, "Yes."

Cliff pressed in. "There is no record of Simon coming with his brother. None. It's not in any of the official history. But something I—I found says otherwise." Cliff sent a glance toward Amy. "So, you're saying…"

"Yes. I said, 'yes.'"

"Aunt Kate, can you prove it?"

Transatlantic to America, the RMS Charles

—March 1905

Ashen clouds rolled and twisted across the sky, their dullness reflected in the endless ocean beneath them. Waves crashed across the bow of *the Charles*, sending a spray of cold water over the figure of a man, collapsed on a coil of rope. A half-full bottle was held loosely in his hand; an empty one lay at his side. A figure in a long coat emerged from the deck below.

"Oi! Simon! Where are...?" Peter Graymoor spied the prostrate figure of his brother lying senseless and soaked on the damp coils. His heart was heavy, as if carrying a weight of stone. A heart so unlike that of his brother's. But were they so different? Were they not the same? *Except...* Peter could not bear to finish the thought. With feet like lead, he walked over to his drenched and drunken sibling. "Simon... Simon! Wake up! You will get a fever from this foolishness! You don't want to catch your death of—"

Simon shook off his stupor as his brother spoke.

"Don't *want* to? Maybe I do. Did you think of that?" He turned his eyes toward Peter, and saw the anxious, pitying look that he so often wore these days. And love—for some reason Simon could not imagine, he saw love there, too. He turned away. "I sometimes think it would be best for you if I did catch my death." Suddenly, Simon stood, ripped off his coat, and roared like a wounded animal. "I should catch my death—or let death catch me! If I had, you wouldn't have left England—left home and family—all because I—"

"Simon, stop!"

Simon sunk back down. "No. I'm too much of a coward." He looked at his brother. "I'd likely be headed for the gallows, but for you."

Peter shook his head. "He shot first. I would testify to that."

A bitter laugh escaped Simon's lips. "And what jury would believe you, my dear brother? Don't you know? I'm the infamous prodigal, Simon Graymoor, known far and wide for his wicked ways!" Simon dashed some sea spray from his eye. Or could it have once again been a tear? "Even my own father didn't believe me." Simon picked up the bottle, uncorked it, and lifted it up to his brother, in mock celebration. "And now you, you are the sole heir of the very proud and very wealthy old English family—the Graymoors! A toast to the right, honorable Peter Graymoor, descended from the throne of King John the—"

"I said stop!" Peter snatched the bottle from his hand, then continued in a lower voice, "Please, Simon—stop." He took off his coat and laid it across Simon's shoulders. "You know none of that matters to me; none of it. I couldn't bear to see you cast out of the family; couldn't bear to think of you imprisoned and facing a hangman's noose. That's why I left, I..." Peter knelt down beside his brother, "I would die for you, brother. I would die for you."

Simon looked up at his brother. "And you know I would kill for you." He pulled the bottle from Peter's fingers. "A toast then—to America!"

CHAPTER 8

It was an overcast night of a full moon; the kind where the moon shone through the cloudy curtain, constantly drifting across its face, as if moved by an unfelt wind. It gave an unreal feel to the landscape, as if setting the stage for a mystery scripted by another hand. *Ghostly. Almost ghostly,* was the thought of one of the dark-clad figures that moved through the shadows. *Colonel Mustard in the library with a candlestick,* filled the mind of another. As the moon coyly shared, then withheld her light, they kept their eyes on the small patch of illumination coming from the flashlight ahead of them. A slight, chill breeze stirred the air. Dead leaves crunched beneath their feet. A shadowy silhouette on a barren branch above their heads suddenly spread its wings and took flight.

"Ahh! What was that?" Cliff's voice broke the stillness.

"Oh, that was just an old owl, silly. Come on, Cliff—man up! You're not gonna—" A high-pitched screech followed by a flap of wings above their head cut Amy short. "Ahh!" Now it was her turn to scream.

"What's wrong—scared of a little bat?"

"I hate bats!"

"Oh, for heaven's sake, you'd think the two of you had never been out in the woods before." Kate's voice came from behind the flashlight.

"Well, not in the middle of the night! That thing nearly

scared the jiggers out of me!" Kate could hear the pout in Amy's voice.

She shined her flashlight back on the two who followed her. Her small spotlight revealed a frightened Amy holding Cliff's arm in a death-grip. "I think you can let go of him now."

Amy and Cliff looked at each other and quickly jumped apart.

Kate gave a little chuckle. "Come on, children, it's a beautiful night for a walk; let's get this done."

Amy began to grumble as she picked her way over a fallen branch. She turned to Cliff, "Explain to me why I'm walking through some woods in the middle of the night with—with weird noises and vulture owls and everything, when I could be sitting in front of a fire eating pizza?"

"It's because you're too nosy not to come along." A thought played at the edges of Cliff's mind. *And it's because I wanted you to be here.*

"Stop it, Cliff." Amy turned her big eyes up to his.

"Huh? Stop what?" Did he say that out loud? If so, he hoped that was all he said. "Never mind, come on." The bouncing dot of Kate's flashlight was way up ahead of them now.

Kate led on through the woods, following the faint gleam of a footpath until it broke free from the wooded shadows. The land opened up to reveal a broken fence surrounding a small graveyard.

"Looks like a pauper's field," Cliff broke the silence as they gazed out on small, crudely carved tombstones, randomly scattered here and there. Only one stood out as different. He pointed. "What's that?"

Kate shone the flashlight in the direction Cliff indicated. "That is what I brought you here to see."

The moon had found a break in the clouds, and its full light filled the cemetery, casting shadows everywhere. Amy leaned over to Cliff. "This is when zombies start to come up out of their graves and—"

"Don't dally you two; come along." Kate had an agenda.

Once again, she led the way as they maneuvered through a pitted landscape booby-trapped with broken tree limbs and crumbling headstones. Kate knelt down beside a large, unbroken monument, obscured by dirt and vines. Cliff held out a set of small pruning shears. "Okay, now I see why you made me bring these... Uh, how did you know?"

"This ain't my first rodeo, boy, and it's not the first time I've come up to this place. My Nathanial used to come up here quite a lot. Never was quite sure why..." Kate was still, her thoughts circling around the memory of her late husband.

"Kate, it's late. Why are we—"

The memory of her husband dissolved. She took the shears from Cliff, handed him the flashlight. "Hold it steady."

Kate made quick work of the vines, and, pulling a rag from the pocket of her coat, made quick work of the dirt, too. She stood and faced the two impatiently waiting behind her, her heart softening as she looked at them. She realized that if she had children, these would be the two she would have wanted. She shook it off. *Can't afford to feel that right now.*

"Kate?" Cliff's voice broke the silence.

Kate took a deep breath. "You asked me a question. You asked me if Simon Graymoor had come with his brother to America. I said yes. You asked me if I could prove it—well, I can. Here it is."

Kate took the flashlight from Cliff, shining it fully on the headstone before them. Cliff began to read:

Here lies Simon Graymoor 1884–1906

A tragic life, deeply loved

"Kate! This is an incredible find! I mean, in all my research I never..." He took a step toward her. "You mean, you knew about this all along?"

"All of Absalom Bane's heirs knew about it. I found it myself when I was just pecking around the graveyard 'bout six months ago."

Six months? How could she have found it if the tombstone was that overgrown? Cliff pushed the thought from his mind. "Why didn't you tell me?"

"Didn't figure it was worth mentioning." Kate took a deep breath. "Simon was a no-good rascal who liked his rum. His death was as shameful as his life. He was thrown by a horse into the flood-waters of the river while drunk. I didn't figure any of those fancy foundation folks would care for that bit of history gettin' out." *Forgive me, Nathanial.* "Simon wanted his sins to be forgotten; *he* wanted to be forgotten. Said so on his deathbed to Absalom Bane. His family has honored that for generations."

Cliff touched the tombstone. "Well, what do you know—the family secret. Hidden in plain sight..."

Amy tugged on Cliff's sleeve, pulling him away. "Cliff," she whispered. "There's something—oh, I don't know—something kind of fishy about this. Did you see Kate's ears? Bright red. I mean, even in the moonlight I could see 'em!"

Cliff and Amy took a step farther away. "I hate to admit it, but you might be right—for once. Something's just a little off here. I can't quite put my finger—"

A soft thud and a faint sound of shattering glass reached their ears. Amy grabbed his arm again. "What was—?"

"I think someone's breaking into the church!" He turned to

Amy. "You stay here." Then Cliff began running toward the old Granville Church.

Amy called after him in a loud whisper, "When I said, 'man up' I didn't mean…" She looked around at the gravestones surrounding her. *Zombies.* "Cliff—wait up!" Amy sprinted after him.

Cliff was at the door of the church as Amy caught up with him. "I thought I told you to stay put?"

"Yeah, right." Amy was still panting.

"Okay—c'mon." Cliff felt the ground until he found a broken flower pot. From underneath it, he pulled a key. He gave a soft laugh. "I can't believe this is still here. I stuck it under the flower pot when I was just a kid. Don't ask how I got it—but let's just say Uncle Nate was kind of mad when it went missing." Cliff cautiously unlocked the door to the church. As he entered, he heard a door shut on the other side of the building. "Someone was in here—and ran out the other door."

Cliff's eyes took in the moonlit interior of the sanctuary. Broken furniture, trash on the pews, pipes missing from the organ—the place was a mess. "But it's got good bones."

"Bones? Did you see bones?" Amy stood close beside him now.

"No bones. I was just thinking out loud." *I've got to stop doing that.* "Now why in the world would someone break into the church? There's nothing here worth stealing."

"I don't know. Maybe it was just some kids. Or maybe somebody else is looking for family secrets, too."

Amy stepped even closer to Cliff. He could feel her warmth next to him.

"Can we go now? This place gives me the heebee-jeebies!"

Cliff walked toward the pulpit. His hand caressed the dark, carved wood. "It's a church, Amy. It's a safe place. There's nothing to be scared of. Besides, you've got me with…"

Amy followed, coming close to him again.

"It's not that. It's..." Suddenly, Amy tugged at his arm. "Cliff! Look out!"

Cliff saw something fall toward him through the shadows—then all went dark.

White Rock River, Graystone Estate

—1907

A man in sodden clothing knelt by a swollen riverbank, a motionless figure in his arms. "Dear God, what have I done? What have I done?" He was a Graymoor. No matter what, a name with honor; it was still a name with honor. Yet, he had watched as his brother fell into the foaming waters. Watched as he struggled. Watched as he went under. At the last moment, he pulled his brother out of the torrent, barely alive. He looked in the face that looked so much like his own...

"Speak to me, Brother—speak to me! My dear God, please speak to me..."

"Speak to me, Cliff! Wake up—come on, boy—talk to me!" Clifford's head hurt—it really hurt. He couldn't remember it ever hurting so bad.

"Open your eyes, son; talk to me!"

He wished the voice would go away. All he wanted to do was crawl into a dark place and fall asleep. His eyes fluttered.

"Cliff? Cliff!" Another voice, a younger voice, called him back.

The faint form of Kate hovered over him. He closed his eyes

again. Suddenly, he felt something cold and damp in his ear. Cliff's eyes flew open.

"See—I told you a 'wet willie' would work!"

Cliff's vision cleared. He saw the triumphant face of Amy look down at him. Th two women gently moved him to a sitting position.

"Oww... What happened?"

"That whole pulpit thingy came down on top of you. I mean— it was there—then the whole thing just kind of tipped over, like somebody pushed it or something." Amy looked earnest, and a little scared.

"Nonsense! Don't start imagining things just 'cause you both ran off and got spooked!" Somehow Amy and Cliff felt like kids being scolded. "Of all the tomfool things to do—going into a rickety old church in the middle of the night—why you could have broken your..." Kate's voice softened. "I'm sorry; I am. It's just, well, it scared me to think you might..." Kate cleared her throat. "Anyway, you're gonna be okay, son; looks like you just got a slight concussion."

Cliff rubbed his head. "Oww... How exactly did I...?"

Amy plopped on the couch beside him. "It's like I said. The pulpit thing tipped over—but I pushed you out of the way!"

"Then how...?"

"Well, you kind of hit your head on the side of a pew on your way down." Amy grinned. "I guess you could say I saved your life!"

"Or you gave me a concussion."

Amy peered into Cliff's eyes, then looked up at Kate. "Are you sure he's okay? Maybe we should call a doctor."

"I was a nurse before I married Nathanial—remember? He's gonna be okay."

Cliff tried to stand up. He made it, but had to sit back down again. He wished his thoughts would clear. There was something he was trying to remember. Something about a river and Peter holding a dying Simon—or was it the other way around? He shook his head. It would come back to him, but until then… Cliff looked up at Kate. "Well, we *do* need to call the police."

"The police? Whatever for?" Kate's voice was hard again. "It was probably just a bunch of kids—if it was anybody at all. Why stir up a mess with the police when—?"

"Because if they broke into the church, they might try to break into Graystone—and I can't afford that. Not now." Cliff stood to his feet, and this time he managed to stay there. "You got any of that pizza left?"

Amy and Kate exchanged looks. A smile played around the corners of Kate's mouth. "Told you he was gonna be alright."

CHAPTER 9

Sunlight poured into the parlor of the Gardener's Cottage, filling it with a buttery glow. It looked like a painting of days long gone—cozy, warm, and utterly charming. But its charm was lost on Cliff this morning. His head still hurt, he couldn't find socks that matched, and he was stuck on his cellphone in the middle of a contentious call.

"No, I can't call them off, I... Well, I'm sorry, but it can't be helped. I did what I had to do and... Oh, great!" There was a knock at the door. "No, no, you're not great—I mean—someone's at the door, and it might be a shipment or—hello? Hello? Sheesh. Bureaucrats!" The knocking at the door continued. "I'm coming; I'm coming!" With a shoe on one foot and a slipper on the other, Cliff made it to the door.

"Good morning!"

"Amy? What the...? What are *you* doing here?"

"I felt so bad about body-slamming you into a pew that I brought you some danishes!"

Cliff sighed. "Look, that's very nice, but I don't have time for—"

"They're homemade." With her hand, Amy wafted their scent toward Cliff. The smell of apples and cinnamon filled the air. He was going to skip breakfast, but...

"Well, maybe just one." Cliff picked one from the tray and took a bite. "Mmm. Are you kidding? They're still warm! Oh,

Amy, where'd you learn to bake like this? I never knew you could cook."

"There's a lot you don't know about me, Clifford Graymoor. Got some coffee?"

"Not made. I—"

"I'll make some."

Cliff followed her. "No, Amy, you don't have to…"

Amy popped a pod into the coffee maker. "I'm making it for me too. I had to get out of the house. Kate was all grumpy this morning."

"Kate—grumpy? Why?"

"Oh, it's all those policemen hanging around. They must have asked us the same questions a gazillion times—over and over again. She's just mad that you called them."

Cliff sighed, grabbing another danish. "Well, tell her to take a number. First thing this morning, I get a call from Lyndsie giving me the third degree about last night. Then, some foundation members called—then Lyndsie called again."

"Here." Amy placed a cup of coffee in front of him. "Sounds like you're having a lovely morning."

"I'm afraid reporters are going to show up any minute now and start in on me. I'm just glad Dexter Heathstone is on my side. He's the only one not ticked off about this."

Amy sat down at his kitchen table. "Well, I'm not! I'm glad you called the police."

Cliff sat down and looked across at her. *How can anyone look so cute this early in the morning?* "So, you're not mad, even though you got asked a gazillion questions. How come?"

Amy hesitated, making little circles on the table with her finger. "If I tell you, promise you won't laugh or think I'm nutsy or something?"

"You mean more nutsy than usual?"

"Cliff!"

"Okay, okay, I'll try."

"I just feel…" she struggled to find the words. "I feel like there's something wrong here. I don't know how to explain it, but something's wrong. Like real deep down wrong. It's all twisted up, like a—a spiritual mojo gone bad."

"Spiritual mojo?" *When did Amy get so spiritual?* He never even remembered seeing her in church.

"Yeah. It's like I can 'sense' things, you know? I know it sounds weird, but I can almost see a darkness around this place." Amy looked down at her coffee cup. "You probably think I'm a fruit loop, don't you?"

"No. Not at all. It's just… Well, I'm kind of surprised." Cliff got up, walked over to the coffee pot, and put another pod in. "I mean, this is the girl who wouldn't come to Sunday School—not even when they offered cupcakes. When did you get this, uh, mojo?"

Amy was silent. It was such an unusual posture for Amy that Cliff was afraid he'd crossed a line. "Look, if you don't want to talk about it, you don't…"

Amy smiled—a little, sad smile. "No, it's okay. I want to talk." She hesitated. "I need to talk about it."

Cliff waited.

"You know, when Jake died, I just couldn't make sense of things. I mean, I thought Jake was just perfect for me. I thought it from the moment he came to the door and picked me up for the senior prom. Remember?"

"Yeah, I remember." Cliff had asked Amy to the prom, too. But Jake had beat him to it.

"Anyway, watching Jake fight the cancer, and then…" Amy

sniffed. "I just got so mad… So mad at God. I didn't get why He took him. I yelled at God—yelled at Him a lot. I was hurt—and, oh boy, was I angry. But then…" A smile crept across her face.

"Then what?"

"Kate."

Amy took a bite of danish and leaned back. She didn't look angry now. She looked…delighted. Maybe *she* was the fruit loop.

"People like Kate started popping up all over the place. Bringing me meals, cleaning my house, even giving me money. After Jake died, they just wouldn't go away!"

Cliff smiled. The same kind of thing happened to him after Andrea left him at the altar. Kate had warned him—man, had she warned him. He could hear her say, "All that red-headed beauty is just window dressing for a rotten heart." But when Andrea dumped him, not one "I told you so," came out of his aunt's mouth. Kate—and others like her—had rallied around him, fed him, supported him…

A small hand touched his knee. Cliff shook off the memory and turned back to the present—and smiled. "I know. When Kate gets her mind set, she's a sweetheart of a bulldog. So, what did you do with these pesky, compassionate people?"

"Did my best to get rid of them. I argued, made fun of them—nothing worked! They just kept loving me. It made me so mad! It's like they were made of glue or something. I finally just gave up." She dimpled. "Sure glad I did. That's when it happened."

"What happened?"

"I got the mojo."

Cliff frowned. This was getting back into the crazy realm. Stuff like that didn't still happen, did it? He felt comfortable with historical facts, not unexplainable vibes.

Amy was watching him closely. Suddenly, she threw down her napkin. "I was right! You think I'm a nut job!" She rose to leave.

Cliff looked at the small figure across from him—sparking like a live wire. He'd known Amy most of his life. She might be ditzy or goofy sometimes, but she was never crazy. "Sit." Amy still stood at the table. "I said, sit!" Cliff was surprised at the force of his own words. *Hmmm. I guess I can 'man up.'* "You may be stubborn, goofy, and overly dramatic—" Amy started to protest, but Cliff deftly cut her off, "but I don't think you're crazy—never have. Not even when you wore that clown nose to school."

A smile twitched at Amy's lips.

Cliff looked at the girl—no, make that *woman*—across from him, grinning like a kid at Christmas. All those things about her that annoyed him as a boy, then a teen, had matured—or rather, blossomed into something purely charming. *Winsome. Winsome and adorable.* He caught himself. *Winsome? Adorable? Where'd that come from?*

Cliff shook the thought away. He simply smiled and said, "You know, Amy, you're something else."

Amy looked at him in surprise. "Why Clifford Graymoor—I do believe that's the first compliment you've ever given me!"

Cliff grinned. "Yeah, well don't get used to it." Amy playfully wadded up a napkin and threw it at him.

"Oh yeah? So that's how it's gonna be? Remember, I used to pitch!" Cliff zinged a napkin back at her.

"Hah, missed!"

Just as a napkin war was about to ensue, the door to the cottage flung open. An accent right out of a James Bond film broke in.

"Sorry to interrupt brekkers, but I thought you ought to

know. There's a big lorry out front unloading a hefty lot of boxes from the UK."

Cliff jumped up. "My shipment! They weren't supposed to unload it! They were supposed to come and get me before they—"

"Not to worry, mate. There's a lady out there telling them exactly what to do."

Cliff's teeth clenched. "Lyndsie."

Cliff rushed out the door toward the manor. Amy called after him. "Cliff! Your coat!" She looked down, saw his loafer. "And your shoe!" Amy grabbed the shoe, running after him.

The stranger at the door watched with admiration as she ran out the door. Softly, to himself, "Well, this could get very interesting, Zachary old boy—very interesting indeed."

As Cliff jogged up to the large semi, Lyndsie was already barking orders. "No, no, those boxes go back on the truck. They're going in storage."

"But I was told a Dr. Graymoor wanted us to—"

"He's not here. I am." Lyndsie's cellphone rang. She looked at it. "I've got to take this. Just get those boxes I marked back in the truck." Lyndsie walked to her car and got into it, away from the cold air.

Meanwhile, a hobbling figure came up the long drive. Out of breath, Cliff called out, "Stop!" Only a squeak came out. Taking a deep breath, he spoke again, this time louder. "*Stop!*"

The driver turned to look at him. Cliff jogged up, panting, "Unload the boxes. All of them." The movers continued to reload boxes. Cliff spotted a beefy man with a clipboard. He walked up to him. "You in charge?"

The driver turned to him. "Yeah. What about it?"

"Tell them to stop!"

The driver turned to Cliff. "Look, mister, I ain't got time for this. We were told to—"

"You were told to come get me and—"

The driver began to get impatient. "Yeah? And just who do you think you are?"

"I'm Dr. Graymoor."

The truck driver looked at the jacketless man with the mismatched shoes doubtfully. "Really?"

Cliff straightened, looking as official as he could. "Dr. Clifford Graymoor. Appointed by the Graymoor Foundation to head up the restoration of Graystone. I can call the Chairman of the Board if I have to."

The driver's attitude changed immediately. He turned, called out to his men. "Stop! Get those boxes back off the truck!" Respectfully, he turned back to Cliff. "Sorry 'bout that Dr. Graymoor. I was gonna come get you—really, I was—but when we pulled up, this lady came out and said she'd handle it. I just thought—"

"That 'lady' is not in charge!" Cliff knew exactly who he meant.

A familiar, authoritative voice rang out behind him. "I told you to load those boxes back on the truck!"

Cliff turned, seething. "Lyndsie."

Lyndsie Bainbridge halted in her tracks. "Cliff? I—I was just—"

"Undermining my authority?"

"No. Trying to help. Look, I heard about the incident last night."

"Incident? I wouldn't exactly call it an 'incident'—and anyway, what's that got to do with unloading the—"

"Walk with me, Cliff." Lyndsie began walking toward the far end of the drive where her car was parked.

"Lyndsie… Lyndsie stop!" Did she think he was a dog on a leash she could just drag around wherever she wanted? "I'm not taking another step till you tell me what this is all about."

Lyndsie turned to him. Gone was the feminine and charming Lyndsie. Corporate Lyndsie was back.

"You want to know what this is about? It's about liability."

"Liability?"

"These structures are a lot less sound than we originally thought. Your little escapade last night proved that. I don't believe a full restoration is in order."

"What?"

"I'm going to recommend to the board that we only restore the few rooms that would be of most interest to the public—and for that, we don't need all the Graymoor artifacts."

Cliff was usually pretty easygoing. Conflict wasn't his style—and neither was power. But this was different. This was Graystone. His "man up" mode shifted into high gear. "You don't get it. I don't care if you are the big shot Director of the Graymoor Foundation—you just don't get it. This isn't about making some *tourist attraction*; it's about restoring the Graymoor history, making it come alive!"

"Not at the risk of public safety. These structures are too—"

"These structures were made of stone and heartwood timber—and Peter Graymoor brought over the finest craftsmen from Germany, Italy, and England to put it all together. A hurricane couldn't take this place down."

Lyndsie smugly folded her arms. "I see. And these same 'craftsmen' built the church?"

"Yes, but—"

"The same church whose crumbling structure toppled a pulpit on top of you?"

"Yeah, but it didn't—"

"Do you know how much the foundation could be sued for if that happened while a classroom of fifth graders were walking through? An accident like that could cost us millions!"

"I'm not so sure it was an accident."

Lyndsie gave Cliff a look he couldn't quite decipher. *Fear? Anger? Maybe something else; something darker, deeper.* Cliff's train of thought was interrupted by a small form briskly walking toward him. It was Amy.

"You forgot your shoe."

Cliff looked down at his feet. He saw his loafer on one foot, and his cherry red bedroom slipper on the other. He looked up and saw Lyndsie suppressing a laugh.

Amy continued, "I would have brought it sooner, but that guy started jabbering and I couldn't get away." She handed Cliff the slipper.

"Uh, thanks." He tossed out introductions. "Amy—Lyndsie; Lyndsie—Amy." The two women sized each other up. In about a nanosecond, they knew that they would not be friends.

Hopping on one foot, Cliff made the shoe exchange, handing the bedroom slipper back to Amy.

"Could you—"

Before he could finish, Amy replied, "Sure. I'll just toss it back in your closet. I've got to go back to your place to get my stuff anyway—and clean up the dishes."

Lyndsie lifted an eyebrow, "I see. You two are…"

Cliff and Amy both flushed red and started talking at once. "No! It's not like that! We didn't… We wouldn't…"

"I just brought some breakfast and—"

Their confused explanations were interrupted by a genuine guffaw from Lyndsie. "Okay, okay! Whatever you say!" That one laugh dispelled the cloud of anger.

Lyndsie smiled, softer this time. "I'm sorry, Cliff—really I am. I guess I'm just used to being in charge. I'm worried that if something else happens, the publicity could—"

"Make this the most famous place in America." The voice was very British—and very charming. Zach strolled up and took control of the conversation. He was the kind of man who could do that. He was tall, with dark hair and unbelievably blue eyes that accented his boyish good looks. He wasn't "model" handsome; he was better than that. He looked a little bit roguish, a bit playfully unpredictable, with a grin that could warm up a block of ice. The women went silent. He had their attention.

"The story of the 'haunted church' has already been picked up by the Associated Press, and may even hit the telly. Trust me—you can't *buy* publicity like this!"

Cliff suddenly felt invisible, a little resentful, and for some reason, grateful for the interruption. "I hadn't thought of that," Cliff nodded. "Anything to arouse the public's imagination might be good."

"Think about it, chappie—I can help make this place famous."

"A reporter!" Lyndsie went cold, almost hissing the words. "Now see what you've done? The last thing this project needs is—is publicity!"

Cliff saw his opening. "Really, Lyndsie? It's the Centennial Plus celebration! A little publicity could really help."

"Fine. You're the boss; do what you like. Call if you happen to need me. In the meantime, I'm going to talk to the board."

The reporter, Amy, and Cliff all watched Lyndsie walk to her car and squeal out of the drive.

Zach broke the silence. "Bit of a spitfire, isn't she?"

Cliff nodded. "Yeah, you could say that."

Amy frowned. "I don't like her. She's sneaky."

The reporter grinned again. "That's what I like, a woman who speaks her mind. Especially if she has green eyes. What's your name, love?"

"I'm Amy."

"Amy. How do you like that—me mum's name was Amy. A real looker she was, too. Must be something in the name."

He was interrupted by slight cough behind him. "I'm Dr. Clifford Graymoor, uh, Cliff." *I better put a stopper in the boyish charm oozing out of this guy, before someone—like Amy—steps in it.* "Now that you know who we are, it'd be nice to know—"

"Zach. Zachary Malone. It's a pleasure to meet you, Dr. Graymoor; a pleasure to meet *both* of you." Zach looked back at Amy.

Amy looked back, narrowing her eyes as if trying to see something inside him. "So that's why you were asking all those questions; you're a reporter!"

"The *London Star*. I'm here to do a series on the restoration of Graystone. Big UK connection with the Graymoor family and all that. Just thought I'd—"

Cliff pulled out all the charm he could muster. "Look, I really appreciate what you did, you know letting us know about the—the 'lorry'—but I just don't think we're ready for the press to—"

"Dexter said it would be okay. I got the go-ahead from him."

"Dexter Heathstone? Chairman of the Board, Dexter Heathstone?

"Call him if you like. His number is—"

"I've got his number." He patted his side for his cellphone.

Rats! He left it at home. He didn't want to run back and leave Mr. Charming alone with Amy. He felt a tug on his sleeve. Amy held out his cellphone.

"Looking for this?"

Cliff grinned. "Amy, you're a gem."

Amy nodded. "Yes. Yes I am."

Cliff quickly dialed Dexter's number.

Ring. Ring. Riiing!

Finally a familiar voice answered. "Dex? Good, I've got you…"

The phone call was brief and to the point. Cliff closed it out with a word of warning to Dexter. "And watch out; Lyndsie's on the warpath."

Amy and Zach looked at Cliff expectantly. "Um, Dex says hello, Zach."

"So, I'm in?"

"You're in."

"Great!" Zach grinned that grin again. He turned to Amy. "Amy, love, would you like to show a bloke where to get a bit of brekkers?"

Amy giggled. "Brekkers?"

No! For some reason, Cliff couldn't let "brekkers" happen.

"Amy, don't you think you ought to go and check on Aunt Kate? I mean, with the way she's been…"

Amy nodded. "You're probably right. I should go check."

Zach winked at her, "Later then, love," and walked away.

Yeah. Much later. He heard a beefy voice call out behind him.

"Hey, Dr. Graymoor, we ain't got all day. Where do you want these boxes?"

Gravesite, Granville Church

—October 1907

"Ashes to ashes…" A handful of dirt was tossed. "Dust to dust…" A second handful of dirt was tossed. Soon it would be his turn. The dirt felt cold and heavy in his hand. He would remember this day: the climb up the hill; the silent walk through the overgrown woods; the digging of the grave on this hidden patch of land within earshot of Granville Church. He would remember the dark clouds scudding across the sky; the mournful wail of a solitary bagpipe; the weeping of the women. Yes, he, the last living son of Thaddeus Graymoor, would remember this day. How well, he did not yet know.

The voice of Absalom Bane began to drone again. "With our tears and our sorrow, we commit to the earth the body of… Simon Jeremiah Graymoor. We commit this body to the ground in the sure and certain hope of resurrection, when all mankind shall stand before the judgment seat of their Creator. May God have mercy on his soul…" Absalom's voice lifted to Heaven. "For, hear me, we shall all stand before that seat to face our eternal destiny—for some the joys of heaven, and for some…" Absalom turned his dark eyes toward Simon, "…the everlasting torment and flames of Hell!"

The flames of Hell? Was that his fate for this mockery of death? Absalom caught his eye, then nodded toward the burial site. The other Graymoor brother stepped up to the open grave and looked down at the pine box that held his brother's lifeless body. He cast his eyes upward to the name graven in granite above it…

"No! I cannot do this!"

A shocked silence filled the still air. Even the weeping of the women stopped.

"He is simply stricken with grief! A moment—I must have a moment to speak to him and bring comfort to his soul!" Absalom took his arm, pulling him to the side. "Get a hold of yourself, man!"

"How can I? When I looked at the tombstone—saw the name carved into it—I knew I couldn't…"

"Enough! I said I would guide you through this, and I will, but you must trust me; you must!" He whispered in his ear, "You do trust me…"

"Yes. I have no choice."

"Good. Then go now; do what must be done. Obedience is the one hope for your soul now." Absalom's hand tightened around his arm. "And do not forget, it is the only hope for the soul of *Simon* Graymoor, as well."

He looked at the dirt in his hand, then straightened, a cold resolve hardening his features. He spoke softly to himself, "I am the elder brother, the master of Graystone—and Simon Graymoor, prodigal and profligate, is dead." He turned to face Absalom.

"The only one I ever truly loved is in his grave. May God have mercy on his soul—and mine."

The master of Graystone, the sole heir to the Graymoor fortune stepped to the grave site and slowly emptied the dirt from his hand. "Ashes to ashes. Dust to dust. Goodbye my brother," he intoned, then added a whispered, "I'm sorry."

CHAPTER 10

"Kate... Kate! Are you here?" Amy entered the small house that used to be the Gatekeeper's Cottage of Graystone. It and the Gardener's Cottage were the only two outbuildings of the estate that were still livable. "Kate?" No answer. Amy didn't know where Kate could be, but she heard a small rustle coming from the kitchen. Cautiously, she peered in. There, curled in the window seat looking out of the window, was a familiar figure.

Amy walked over. "There you are! Didn't you hear me calling?"

Kate looked up. "Oh. Morning, Amy."

"Morning? It's past noon!"

Kate glanced over at the kitchen clock. "So it is," she sighed. "So it is." Kate's form slowly uncurled itself, walked over to the coffee pot, and poured herself an over-cooked cup. This wasn't like Kate; it wasn't like her at all.

"Kate, are you alright? You're acting kind of woogie."

"Woogie?"

"You know, not yourself; kinda off. Is everything okay?"

Kate sat down at the kitchen table and took a sip of stale coffee. "I'm fine. I just couldn't get to sleep last night. Too much excitement I guess."

Amy poured herself the last of the inky liquid in the coffee-pot. "I know what you mean. All that weirdness at the church and everything. Everybody's talking about the 'vandals' who pushed the pulpit down on top of Cliff and—"

"Vandals? Don't be silly—nobody said anything about vandals. It was an accident."

Amy carefully cradled her cup of coffee and sat beside her. "The police don't think so. They found fresh scooch marks on the floor where somebody pushed it. And somebody had been knocking away at the floor underneath it. One touch and it was set to go down." Amy took a sip of inky brew. "Bleh! This is awful!" She set the cup down. "You know, Cliff could have really been hurt."

"Yes. He could have." Kate stared into the black pool of coffee in her cup.

"The whole place is buzzing like crazy this morning. One good thing, Cliff thinks the publicity will be great for the foundation—and the town!"

"Well, heaven knows, anything that's good for the foundation is going to help the town. It employs about half the people who live here. Good people—all of 'em." Kate rose, dumped the coffee in the sink, and headed out of the kitchen toward the front door.

Amy followed her. "Where are you going?"

Kate grabbed a jacket from the rack. "Out. I need to think."

Amy came up to Kate and placed a hand on her arm. They'd been through a lot together. They'd laughed together, worked together, grieved together. Amy knew her friend—and she had a vibe that something, somewhere was very wrong. "Kate, are you sure you're alright?"

Kate turned to her. "What if you stared smack in the face of something you didn't want to do—something you prayed you'd never, ever have to do—and realized," she swallowed the lump in her throat, "you realized you just had to do it anyway?"

"You mean, like going to the doctor?"

"Kind of. Only, with a doctor, you end up feeling better." Kate slipped on her jacket. "Sorry 'bout the dishes. And don't wait supper for me. I don't know when I'll be back." With that, Kate opened the door and was gone.

Amy opened the door, calling after the receding figure, "Kate!" But Kate turned a corner and disappeared from sight. Amy sighed and walked back into the kitchen. "Woogie. Just woogie…" She looked around. "Boy, you were right, Kate. This is a mess." With a sigh, Amy pushed up her sleeves. "Well, somebody's got to do it…" Amy was used to talking to herself aloud when nobody was around. It made her feel like she wasn't alone. She heard a soft thud behind her. It sounded like it came from the window seat. She looked, but nothing was there. Then she noticed something—an unusual gap underneath the top of the window seat. She put her fingers into the gap and lifted. "Well, what do ya know? I didn't even know this was here!"

Underneath the window seat was a space for storage. She saw table cloths and all sorts of kitchen linens pushed to one side, then she saw the source of the 'thud.' A book had tumbled to the floor of the storage space. Amy picked it up. "Who'd stick a book in with a bunch of tablecloths?" She opened the book and leafed through it. As she did, a look of amazement crept over her face like a sunrise. "Holy moly! I better show this to Cliff."

Grand Hall at Graystone Manor

—September 1910

S oft sunlight streamed through the tall window, illuminating a canvas. Before it stood a small man with a huge moustache, wielding a paintbrush. "Oh, but you would love Paris, Monsieur! The cafés, the wine, the Moulin Rouge! Yes—the Moulin Rouge. What a man of your wealth could do in Paris! Stand still please, Monsieur Graymoor."

It was the official portrait of the honorable Peter Graymoor, the new—and proud—master of the Graymoor wealth. But its model was growing impatient. "How much longer is this infernal painting going to take?"

"It would not take so long, except that you insist that it is so exactly like the other. Pah! You have been painted once in such a pose—even now it hangs in your halls in England!"

"Then you should know how to paint this very quickly. Or do you not like the fact that I'm paying you more than the first painter ever dreamed of making?"

"Very well, very well; I paint. But it is so...so very English! If you would but let me paint you as I wish, it would—"

"No! This painting is my..." Simon stopped himself. "This painting is to be just as I say."

The painter sighed heavily. "As you wish, Monsieur." Surrounding the posed figure was a setting worthy of an English lord; heavily carved woodwork, rich fabrics for the curtains, and walls full of books—a scene as still as the morning, with no sound but the chirping of birds outside the window. However, this peaceful silence was soon broken by heavy footsteps approaching the closed door and the voice of the parlor maid filtering through.

"But sir, you can't! The Master isn't receiving company this afternoon and doesn't wish to be—"

The library door pushed open. The Master broke his pose and turned, annoyed. "Nelly, I told you I was not to be—"

"I'm sorry sir—I'm very sorry—but the reverend insisted that..."

Absalom emerged from the shadowy hall and stepped into the library, bringing a kind of darkness with him. With a look, he silenced the girl, then, turning his dark eyes on the posed figure he ordered, "Tell her to leave us."

The painter threw down his brush. "I cannot work with these interruptions! I must—"

Absalom's voice cut through. "Tell *him* to leave, too."

A crimson flush crept up the painter's neck. Several colorful words in his native tongue spewed out until he managed to sputter.

"You cannot tell Jacque Latrell what to do! I am the painter of kings! I will not be—"

Graymoor silenced him with a wave of his hand. "Go, both of you."

"But Monsieur, you must—"

"Go. Now."

The quiet force in his words quelled the painter. The little man threw a cloth over his paints and walked out of the library, muttering all the way. "I am Jacque Latrell; I will not be treated this…" His voice faded away as Nelly shut the library door behind them.

The painter's model and the preacher were alone.

All the masterful arrogance fell away from the new heir to the Graymoor fortune. His shoulders sagged and his face took on the wary look of a hunted animal. He took a moment to regain control of himself, and with a nonchalance he did not feel said, "What do you want now, Absalom?"

Absalom walked over to the unfinished picture. "I see you have brought in a heathen artist to paint your portrait. That is an expensive proposition."

"And what if it is?"

"Why—why do this? There is another picture just like it at your father's estate in England."

The young master laughed. "Then I shall have another one."

Absalom countered. "You are playing a very risky game."

"Perhaps—but it pleases me to do so."

"It does not please me. Your father is only six months in his grave, and it's only six months since you've received your inheritance. Look at this!" Absalom gestured toward the painting. "Already you've become a—"

"Become a prodigal?" He laughed.

"Become less concerned about the welfare of the needy."

"Don't you really mean the 'Church,' Absalom? *Your* church?" The young man began to pace. "Haven't I given you everything you've asked for—and more? Now I want to live!" He took in a deep breath. "My father is finally dead, and now I'm free. Free, Absalom! How long I have dreamed of this—how long? I have waited and waited, and now my life is mine. I can have what I want, what I—"

"Deserve? Shall we really talk of what you deserve?" Though Absalom's voice was quiet, it froze the retort on the young man's lips. "And need I remind you of who you are?"

The weight of Absalom's words settled on him. He sat and hung his head. "What do you want now?"

"An orphanage."

Incredulous, he looked up at the preacher. "An orphanage? I have already built you a fine church and a school…"

"And now you must build an orphanage for those in heathen lands, so that they might repent and perhaps be saved from a fiery doom." Absalom's voice softened, but its menace grew. "Unlike the kind your own son would have gone to had you not married my daughter."

The handsome, boyish face turned pale. He rose and walked to the window, turning away from the cleric. He could not let this man who was his advisor, his father-in-law, see his pain. He could not. Absalom came up behind him, his words like a knife in his back. "Did you think I didn't know? That I couldn't see the stain of guilt in her eyes?"

"It's not as you think! I… I love her."

"You tarnished her!"

The young man broke. He turned. "I made her my wife, didn't I?" Anguish filled his eyes. "It was just after my brother died. She was so very comforting, so very…" He began to pace. "I have repented of that! Before God, I have repented!" He lifted his eyes to Absalom once again. "I am not the man now that I was then!"

"How well I know that—Master Peter Graymoor—how very well I know." Absalom placed a hand on his shoulder. "And you will build an orphanage to prove it. There, children shall learn a trade; learn to work and service the Church…" Absalom leaned down and whispered, "Just as you will service *this* church…"

Cliff stood in a high-ceilinged room, with soft afternoon light filtering in through a tall, dirty window. Some people might see a ruin around them. Cliff saw the richness of what once was the library at Graystone. He was in his glory. He busied himself with a few of the small boxes, meticulously cataloging the contents. He carefully opened the next box, talking to himself as he went. "Let's see what we have here…?" He lifted out a gilt frame, took off the wrappings, placed it on a chair, and stepped back.

"Whoa! This is incredible! They actually sent it. The portrait of Peter Graymoor!" Cliff stared at it. Something wasn't right. Cliff leaned in for a closer look. "Jacque Latrell? That can't be right." Cliff flipped the portrait to read the notation on the back. "Huh. This was painted after he came to America. Wonder why?" Cliff went to another covered gilt frame on the opposite side of the room. He uncovered it. "Wait, this is—" he leaned to look at the signature, "Whitmore. Yep, this is the original."

He looked back at the Jacque Latrell. "Huh. That's funny. He had two paintings done exactly alike. Of course, when you had the Graymoor fortune at your disposal..." Cliff grabbed the painting by Jacque Latrell. "Better take this one home. We don't want to get this mixed up with the original." *Score!* No more second-hand reproduction. A genuine Jacque Latrell was going on his wall.

Cliff went to the next box. "Look at this! Silver sets, tapestries, miniatures—this stuff is pristine! Peter Graymoor, you were one lucky guy. I don't know why it took us so long to get this stuff."

"Legalities."

The voice behind Cliff made him jump. It was clear, feminine, and getting to be very familiar.

"Lyndsie! You about scared the crap out of me!" Realizing she'd overheard his solo conversation he added, "I was just... You see I..."

"I talk to myself too." She smiled. "See Cliff—we do have something in common."

Cliff cleared his throat—and his head. "So, what's this about legalities?"

"Well, for years, the other side of the Graymoor family—your side—claimed these artifacts belonged to the Bournemouth Estate, not Peter Graymoor's. They say he abandoned his claim on them when he came to America."

"And…"

"And the foundation took them to court, and won."

Cliff chuckled. "Oh well. My loss, your gain."

Lyndsie looked at him appraisingly. "More than you know, Cliff. You do know that you are the only male left to bear the Graymoor name on that side of the family."

"Well, a lot of good that's going to do me."

Lyndsie plopped herself on a crate. "Oh, I don't know about that. You know, you're going to gain quite a reputation from this project. And," she gave him a coy smile, "you never know what else might come out of this…"

Cliff suddenly felt too warm. "Uh, so what's the real reason you're here Lyndsie? I know it's not to hear me talk to myself."

"I brought you this." She held out a paper bag. "Chicken tenders, honey mustard sauce, onion rings, and a cherry Coke."

"What? Huh? How did you know I liked…"

She laughed. "Oh, I have my ways of finding out what I want to know."

"Uh, that's a little scary, Lyndsie." Cliff gave her a sharp look. "So, why are you doing this?"

"A peace offering. I know I was a bit of a bear this morning."

"A bit?" Cliff mentally kicked himself. "Sorry. I have a tendency to—"

"To blurt. I know."

"Look, uh, maybe I've been a little insensitive. I know it's been hard for you to let go of this project and—"

"It's not that…" Lyndsie's face softened. "It's just that, when I heard about the accident and thought about what could happen to you working all alone in this house, I… I just…" Lyndsie shyly smiled. "I guess I overreacted."

Cliff was puzzled. "Overreacted? Why?"

Lyndsie laughed and put the paper bag in his hand. "Eat. Your nuggets are getting cold."

Amy Newgate was jogging up the long drive to Graystone as fast as her legs could carry her. If her legs weren't so busy, she'd be kicking herself for not taking the car. At least the cold air was clearing her head, and the jog from Kate's house to Graystone Manor was giving her extra time to mull things over. Things were getting pretty weird, and she could sure use some of that mojo Kate kept talking about. A horn beeped behind her, sending a shock through her system. She stumbled—and dropped the mystery book she'd been clutching to her chest.

"Are you alright?" She turned to see Zach Malone, his head poking out of a Mini Cooper. *Figures.*

He pulled to the side and got out, a concerned look on his face.

Amy dusted herself off. "Yeah, I guess; except you just about scared the padooky out of me, that's all."

He grinned. "Well, I didn't mean to scare you, ducks, but you were so off in another world that you didn't even see my car."

"Yeah, well, that's what I get for trying to walk and talk at the same time."

Zach looked around. "Talk? Who were you talking to," he grinned, "the moon?"

Amy caught his quizzical look. She shrugged and said, "It's complicated."

Zach reached down and picked up the book. "This yours?"

Amy's eyes widened in panic—she quickly snatched it out of his hands. "Yes! I mean, no. I mean, it is right now. You see, it's—"

Zach grinned. "It's complicated. Got it." Amy's eyes narrowed as she looked at him. "What are you doing here?"

"My job. I'm a reporter, remember? The real question is, what are *you* doing here, love?"

"I'm—I'm on my way to see Cliff."

"What about?"

Amy held the book tighter. "You sure are nosy."

"Like I said, I'm a reporter..."

"Yeah, yeah it's your job; I got it." Amy looked anxiously toward the manor. *When is this guy going to leave?*

Zach caught the look. "Lucky man."

"Huh, who?"

"Clifford Graymoor. He's one lucky man to have a girl like you on his trail. So, tell me about him. What's he like?" He flashed a grin.

He is pretty cute. Can his eyes really be that blue? She shook the thought away. "Oh, I don't know. Cliff's really smart, decent, hardworking... Kinda nosy."

"Nosy? Now that's interesting."

Amy panicked. Was she saying too much? "No—it's not! I mean, he just likes to know things; you know, figure them out. Oh—and he's stubborn. Really stubborn. He's like a bulldog when he..." She stopped herself. "He's just stubborn, that's all." She had to be careful around this reporter. He made her want to talk.

"Sounds like you know him pretty well."

"Well, we grew up together."

Zach stepped in closer to her. "So, is there anything going on between you two? Romance and all that?"

"Huh?" Amy flushed. "No, no—we're not... I mean, to him I've always just been the bratty little girl next door. We've never... I mean, he's never..."

Zach grinned. "Personally, I've always found bratty little girls incredibly attractive."

Amy gave him an appraising look. "You're really full of it, you know."

A loud genuine laugh burst out of Zach. "Thank you. I work hard at it. What's say I show you a few more of my lines over a late dinner tonight?"

"I don't think so."

"How about this? No lines; I keep it purely professional. I want to do a profile piece on Dr. Graymoor—and I need to pump that charming brain of yours for information."

As Amy looked at him thoughtfully, the words formed in her mind. *Go ahead. ...Really?* Then, with a sigh, she plunged in. "Well, okay."

Zach looked surprised. "Okay. Really? I rather didn't expect…"

"You know, you're not so full of it as you want people to think. There is more to you than meets the eye, mister. Now, I have got to find Cliff!"

"Eight o'clock then! Where do I pick you up?"

"The Gatekeeper's Cottage." Amy began to walk toward Graystone once again.

"Where's the Gatekeeper's—?"

"Figure it out," she tossed over her shoulder as she walked away.

Zach was satisfied. Very satisfied. He smiled to himself, "Brilliant, Zach old boy—brilliant. This one may prove very useful…"

The sun was just beginning to touch the horizon, shooting its dying beams through the windows of Graystone. From inside came the sound of laughter. Lyndsie's voice lilted through the library door.

"…And then Professor Malachi sat down again! He never did figure out where that noise was coming from!"

Cliff's deeper laugh followed. "I'm glad I never had a student like you! It's a wonder you ever passed his class."

"It's a wonder I ever graduated!" Lyndsie giggled. "I can't believe the things I got away with in college!" She giggled again.

Cliff took the last sip of his cherry Coke. "Who knew the foundation's director could be so giggly?"

Lyndsie looked coyly at him. "Well, I am still a girl, you know. I mean, in case you didn't notice?" Cliff noticed. Her soft, red hair fell across her face as she leaned toward him. He began to feel a little warm. He loosened his collar.

"Uh, yeah—I noticed. Well, uh, thanks, Lyndsie. You know you really didn't have to—"

"I wanted to." The scent of her perfume drifted into his senses, making him think of velvet and musk. Was it getting even warmer? Cliff looked around at the boxes, feeling totally out of his depth.

"Well, I, uh, better get back to work if I'm ever going to…"

"Cliff…" Lyndsie leaned closer, placed her hand on his. "I want you to know something. I think you're—"

A crash shattered the moment, and a scream pierced the air, followed by the high, frightened cry, "*Help*!"

Lyndsie and Cliff both looked at each other. Lyndsie frowned. "What was that?"

Cliff's heart began to pound; he knew that voice. "It's Amy!"

CHAPTER II

The Thirsty Hart Inn, Granville

—April 1911

Raucous. That was the kind of laughter that filtered through the door of the *Thirsty Hart*. Coarse and raucous. A voice shouted above the laughter, "Another round for us all, Bert—another round!"

The innkeeper's voice rose above the din, "I'm thinking you've had enough now, Willy…" But his entreaties were only met with more laughter.

So loud was the laughter, that the sound of heavy boots approaching the inn was never heard. The steps stopped, as did the laughter. Absalom Bane stood in the doorway.

Whispers floated among the patrons.

"It's the preacher…"

"What's he doing here…?"

"I hope he doesn't go telling the wife…"

A heavy-set man stood unsteadily. "I better be going, Bert…"

The innkeeper nodded, but fixed his eyes on Absalom. "This way, Parson. I put him in the back room…"

Absalom's cold stare scanned the room, confronting the faces that were so boisterous just moments ago. Eyes dropped and chairs scraped the floor as the crowd began to exit the inn, making their way home.

"Sir...?" Bert opened the door and motioned to Absalom. "I kept him back here, away from the crowd, if you'll be knowing what I mean."

Absalom turned his cold stare on the innkeeper. "At least you have some sense of decency, man."

"You may not think much of my business, Reverend Bane—or me, for that matter—but I do know a place like this is not for the likes of him."

Bert led him into a small room at the back of the *Thirsty Hart*. A fire flickered in the corner and a gas lamp shed a pale light. Absalom entered, and the innkeeper left, shutting the door behind him.

A slouched figure at a small table raised his head. "Well, if it isn't the good Reverend Absalom Bane! I see the ghost of my conscience follows me wherever I go."

"Then your conscience I will be. This is no place for a man of your position. What are you doing here?"

Simon Graymoor turned back to the table before him. "I am contemplating a bottle of rum. The drink of Simon Graymoor."

"Simon Graymoor is dead." Absalom's voice was soft.

"Is he? Do you know what I see when I look in the mirror, Absalom? I don't see myself; I see my brother! I see—"

"Then break your mirrors and let the dead be dead!" Absalom's voice was firm.

"How can I? Shall I break all the windows, too? Empty all the fountains? Drain the lakes and the ocean so no reflection can touch me? I can't..." He stopped, uncorked the bottle of rum, and poured a glassful. As he lifted it, Absalom stopped his hand.

"You can because you must. Too many now depend on the Graymoor name. Orphans, widows, and the poor and needy all draw from your benevolence."

The slouched figure laughed bitterly. "Especially you, Absalom."

Absalom lean down. "Yes, especially me. But, before God, you know that I too, have sacrificed, and that not one penny has entered my pocket. You know that, because of you, my church has grown deep and wide; and salvation, yes, salvation has come into this wretched land."

Simon shook his head. "Well, not by my hand…"

"Yes, by your hand! Don't be a fool. I have made you a tool in the hands of the Almighty. And this…" Absalom picked up the bottle of rum and poured it out. "This is not worthy of the Master of Graystone—and the poor comfort you find in it will not bring what you need."

"You don't know what I need. No one does."

"Not even God? Do not dare tempt the Holy God with your rebellious thoughts. He may yet deem that your charity will outweigh your sins; and in the end, Peter Graymoor will be redeemed."

"Will he?" Simon looked up into the immovable face of Absalom Bane. "And what of Simon Graymoor? Who in heaven or Earth will redeem him now?"

The crumpled figure of Amy Newgate sat on the floor, rubbing her ankle. Cliff rushed up and knelt beside her. "Amy—are you alright?"

Amy stood. "I think so—ow!"

Lyndsie Bainbridge came up behind Cliff and placed a hand on his shoulder. "What happened, Cliff?"

The two women looked at one another, first in surprise, then with irritation.

Amy turned to Cliff. "What's *she* doing here?"

Cliff brushed Amy's question away. "She just brought me some food. Now, what are *you* doing here?"

"Looking for you. I had just gone up the back stairs trying to find you, and I was coming down the main stairs when all of a sudden, a step cracked and I—I—"

"She fell. Right into my arms." Zach Malone emerged from the shadows.

Now it was Cliff's turn to be irritated. "What? He's here, too?"

"Yep," Amy replied. "Mr. Nosy here caught me."

"Good thing, I was hanging about, too. You could have snapped your ankle, dearie." Zach placed an arm across Amy's shoulder. "Now, aren't you glad I followed you in?"

Amy gave him a look, but Zach simply grinned. "What can I say? I have a nose for trouble."

"This is exactly what I was talking about!" A single, manicured finger pointed toward Amy. Corporate Lyndsie was back. "We should have stuck with my plan. This place is not safe!" She turned to Cliff, her tone softening, "When I think that... Well, that it could have been you that fell, I just..."

"Hello? What am I, chopped liver?" It was a diss—and Amy knew it.

"More like caviar, love." Zach whispered to Amy.

Ignoring him, Lyndsie continued, "Look, Miss Newberg—"

"That's Newgate!"

"Whatever. This isn't about you. It's about the—"

"What do you mean, it's not about me? I'm the one who fell!"

"Well if you hadn't been such a snoopy little—"

"Excuse me? And why exactly are *you* here? I may be kind of snoopy, but at least I'm not sneaky!"

The two women squared off. Cliff looked panicked. Zach looked like he was enjoying the show.

Lyndsie flushed a deep red. "You little... Do you have any idea who you're talking to?"

Amy crossed her arms. "Yep. I know *exactly* who you are! And I know exactly *why* you're here!"

Lyndsie stepped toward her, ice forming on each word. "Well, I'm afraid you're missing the point, Miss Newgate, which is, why are *you* here? *You* are not part of this project. *You* have no business poking around, bothering Cliff when he's—"

"Oh, and you do?"

"*Stop!*" Cliff's voice cut through. "Everyone, just—just count to ten or something. I need to think." There was silence for a moment.

Lyndsie took a deep breath. She was in control again. "I'm sorry, Cliff, but don't you see how dangerous a full renovation would be? Especially for you."

"Look, Lyndsie, I'm flattered—I think... But one accident doesn't mean that—"

Lyndsie hardened again. "Fine. I can see what my opinion's worth. She turned, grabbed her handbag off the floor, and headed for the door.

Cliff called out, "Lyndsie...!"

Lyndsie Bainbridge made her way down the drive of Graystone. A curious expression played across her face: an odd cross between anger and triumph. Just as this curious mix of thoughts played through her mind, a voice behind her interrupted them.

"Miss Bainbridge! Half a moment, please!"

Lyndsie stopped and turned, irritated. "What?"

Zach Malone ran up to meet her. "I just wanted to say, you handle yourself well. I'd hate to be on the wrong side of a fight with you."

"Yes. You would. Now if you'll—"

"And I wanted to say thank you."

"For what?" Lyndsie eyed him cautiously.

"For very kindly retrieving Miss Newgate's book." Lyndsie stiffened.

"What book?"

"The one in your handbag," Zach stepped closer. "The one I saw you pick up from the bottom of the stairs."

Lyndsie remained cool. "I'm sure you're mistaken."

"I'm sure I'm not. You see, the reason I know it's her book is that I saw her carry it in. Got a dandy look at it. I'm sure she's wondering where it is. Shall I go and get her—*and* Dr. Graymoor—so she can…"

Lyndsie opened her bag and thrust the book at Zach. "Here. My mistake."

Smiling, Zach pulled the book from her fingers. "Cheers, love." As she began to turn, he stopped her. "By the way, Miss Bainbridge—you wouldn't want to get on the wrong side of a fight with me, either."

Without a word, Lyndsie got in her car and pulled away.

Zach looked down at the book in his hands. "Now let's see what Miss Bainbridge was so anxious to have a look at…" He opened the book and thumbed through the pages. He gave a little laugh. "I say, this will stir the pot a bit, no doubt about it. And that will suit your plan perfectly, Zachary my man; no doubt about that, either."

Zach turned and headed back to Graystone. As he entered, Cliff was attempting to check a protesting Amy for injuries.

"If you'll just settle down so I—"

"I'm fine! Now, let me get up so I can…" Amy squirmed as Cliff pushed her back down.

"Stop squirming! You're not leaving till I check your ankle."

"And a lovely ankle it is." Zach had slipped in quietly. He had a knack for that.

Cliff was not amused. "What are you still doing here?"

"Returning Amy's book."

"My book!" Amy struggled to her feet and hopped over to Zach. "Where'd you find it?"

"In a certain Director's handbag."

Amy began to fume. "Lyndsie. See, that woman *is* sneaky!"

"That she is." Zach handed her the book.

Amy quickly thumbed through it, then let out a sigh of relief. "I mean, if Lyndsie had gotten hold of this…" Amy hugged the book to her chest. "Thank you; thank you; thank you! I could just kiss you!" Both men looked at her—Zach grinning, Cliff frowning. "I didn't mean *kiss* you, kiss you! I just meant—"

Cliff interrupted, "What's this about a book?"

"Well, it's a…" Amy hesitated, looking at Zach. "Zach, do you mind if we…"

"Of course not, lovely. I'll just go have a look at the scene of the 'accident,' if you don't mind." Zach moved back to the broken stairs as Cliff helped Amy hobble to the library.

Cliff shot a look back at Zach, then turned to Amy. "Why's this guy hanging around you, anyway?"

"It's a long story." Amy glanced around to make sure they were alone. "Anyway, this morning at the cottage, Kate was acting kind of, I don't know, kind of weird. Like she had the weight of the whole world on her shoulders or something. She wouldn't talk about it, so she went out for a walk—a long walk—to clear her head."

Cliff interrupted. "So, what's that got to do with—"

"I'll tell you what—she was hiding this book inside the

window seat in the kitchen." Amy handed the book to Cliff.

Cliff read the cover, "*The Strange Case of Dr. Jekyll and Mr. Hyde.*" He turned it over in his hands. "Wow. This looks like a first edition."

"It is. Read the inscription."

Cliff began to read. "'To Anna Graymoor, for your kindness in my distress. May fate prove kinder to you and your sons than this tale forebodes. God help you!' It's signed, *Robert Louis Stevenson*!"

"Pretty weird, huh?"

"Well, not exactly weird. I mean, Anna Graymoor and her sons spent three or four years in Bournemouth while Stevenson was there for his health. I guess they must have become acquainted."

Amy pointed at the inscription. "Yeah, but what about what this says?"

"I guess that *is* rather odd."

"Yeah? Well you ain't seen nothing yet. This was stuck between the pages." Amy carefully pulled out a yellowed page of ragged paper.

Cliff fingered the paper carefully. "Looks like a page torn out of a diary."

"Read it," Amy commanded.

Cliff nodded.

Though I am still weak, I take joy in the sons God has given me—though there is fear mixed with my joy. So alike they are, yet so different. If I were to face the two, one would form the mirror of the other. Where one reaches with his right, the other reaches with his left. And the dimpled cheek of one is on the opposite cheek of the other.

Cliff looked up at Amy, excitement in his eyes. "It's from Anna Graymoor's diary! And she's writing about Peter and Simon! They weren't just twins; they were mirror image twins!"

Amy motioned to him, "Keep reading!"

Cliff continued.

> *As opposite they were in body, so they were in temperament. Where Peter would laugh and play, Simon would cry and squirm. And whilst Peter would sleep as peacefully as a dove, Simon would fret Nanny through the night. Then, one night, as I gathered Simon into my arms to comfort him, I held my head to his chest. Lo—there was no heart there!*

Amy couldn't contain herself. "See? Now that's totally weird."

"Shush. Let me finish."

> *I could not move or cry—so terrified I became. Then I found it. His heart was not where it should be. It was on the other side. I cried in relief as the child slept fitfully in my arms. Yet, the fear of that night still lives in my own heart. A fear of what this child will become...*

Cliff gave a low whistle. "You're right. That *is* weird."

Amy pulled another small piece of paper from the back of the book. "Now read this."

"It's just a scrap of paper..."

"I know—just read it!"

Cliff looked at the scrap. It had a single phrase written in faded ink. "*The Hyde Papers*. What are *The Hyde Papers*?"

"I don't know, but I think we should find out."

The voice of Zach interrupted their speculations. "There's something else you need to find out." Once again, he'd entered silently.

Cliff muttered, "I hate when he does that."

Zach motioned for them to follow, then knelt when he reached the stairs. "You need to find out who did this." He held up a board. It was the board pulled from the broken staircase. "This was no accident, my friend."

No accident? Cliff's brain began to whirl, filled with the events of the past few days. First, he was catapulted into a position he'd never dreamed he could hold—head of the restoration of Graystone. But it seemed that dream came with a jumbled mix of emotions and events: pulpits being pushed on top of him; a mysterious warning in an antique book; secrets being kept by his favorite aunt. Oh, and then there was Lyndsie Bainbridge. Beautiful, infuriating Lyndsie. The word "dangerous" flashed into his mind. *Could Lyndsie be dangerous?*

"Dr. Graymoor?" Zach's voice interrupted his thoughts. "You really should take a look at this." Cliff took the heavy board Zach held out to him. "See how the board is sawn halfway through? Somebody wanted the board to break in half as soon as it was stepped on."

Cliff frowned. *Why would anyone do that?* He countered, "Maybe it was unintentional. Maybe somebody just made a shoddy repair somewhere along the way and—"

Zach interrupted. "What's say we try a little experiment, eh?" He motioned Cliff toward the stairway. "Now take your place, mate, here at the bottom, and make your way up to where we have the broken step."

Cliff balked. Who was this Brit to be theorizing about what

happened—especially when Cliff didn't think of it first? "Look, I don't know about this…"

"You do want to find out if this lovely lady was the victim of a malicious act, don't you?"

Cliff snapped. "Of course I do! Now, what's this 'big experiment' of yours?"

"Just start at the bottom step and do a little bouncing on each step as you make your way up to the broken one. The ones above seem to be good enough; Amy already came down them. Of course, if you don't want to risk—"

"Hey, I got this!" Cliff took a tentative step onto the first tread and bounced. "This one's good." He stepped onto the next one and bounced. "Good…"

Amy's face began to grow anxious. "Ooh, Cliff, I don't think you should—"

Cliff smiled back at her. "Relax. It's going to be fine." He was just two treads away from the broken step. Cliff planted his feet on the next one and bounced. "This one seems to be good—whoa!" The step gave way beneath him; he grasped the rail to keep from hitting the floor.

Zach called up, "Try the next one!"

Cliff stepped, more carefully this time, and bounced. The step cracked in half. Grasping the rail for support, Cliff managed to finesse his way to the bottom of the stairs.

Zach was already climbing up, pulling boards loose.

Amy hurried up to Cliff, looking anxiously in his face. "Cliff, are you…?"

Cliff smiled, "I'm fine."

Amy smacked his arm.

"Ow! What was that for?"

"For scaring me!"

Zach scrambled down the broken stairway, boards in hand. "I'm afraid you've a saboteur on your hands. These boards are sawn through, also."

"What?" Cliff and Amy spoke in unison.

"Take a look for yourself, old boy." Zach placed the boards in Cliff's hands. The cut marks were crystal clear, even in the dying light.

"Great, that's just great." Cliff's heart sank. He hoped it wouldn't sink the project, too. "I guess I better call the police."

Zach raised an eyebrow and gave a slight but clear cough.

Cliff's skin began to prickle. *Man, this guy is irritating.* "What now?"

"I wouldn't do that if I were you, mate."

"And why not?"

"Publicity."

"Publicity? I thought you said 'publicity' was good for the project."

"The right kind of publicity. A spooky happenstance in an old church rather tickles the public's fancy—but this, a flesh and blood vandal, why, it could shut down the whole project."

Cliff's eyes narrowed. "Why are you being so helpful all of a sudden?"

Zach grinned. Cliff was beginning to really dislike that grin. "If you call in the police, they'll bar my access to this place. Crime scene and all that. Not a good thing for a reporter."

A thought struck Cliff. "Yeah? How do I know…?"

"Don't worry, I won't leak any of this; that would bring a hoard of other reporters onto the scene. I want the exclusive, mate."

Zach turned to go, then turned back to Cliff. "By the way, I wouldn't share this with anyone, especially Miss

Bainbridge—unless, of course, you'd like to prove that she's right." He turned to Amy. "Oh, and Amy, love—let's make it 7:30 p.m., shall we? And bring your dancing shoes, just in case your ankle's feeling better. Ciao, bella..." With a wink, Zach turned and left.

Amy sighed. "Well, I guess I better go get ready." She gathered up her book and headed for the door. Cliff rubbed his head; had he heard right? He ran after her.

"Amy—wait!" She turned. "What's he talking about?"

"Dinner. Zach is taking me out."

Cliff began to sputter. He never sputtered. "What? Seriously? He's taking you...? Are you crazy? You don't even know this guy."

Amy placed a hand on her hip. "Oh, take a chill pill. He just wants to interview me, Cliff—about you."

"Really. He just wants to talk about me. And it just happens to be over dinner—and dancing?"

"Okay, so he's a reporter...who...who dances."

"Yeah, right. He knows how to dance, and he knows how to talk his way into anything. Don't let that cute little British accent fool you! The guy's a—a snake." His arms began to flail. He never flailed. "Don't be such a...such a girl, Amy! You can't go out with him."

Amy's green eyes began to flash. "Excuse me? Who do you think you are, Clifford Graymoor? I can go out with whomever I want to! I'm not the little girl next door anymore; the one that you can just boss around. I'm a woman now, in case you hadn't noticed."

"I noticed!" The words came out louder than Cliff intended. He continued more softly, "I—I noticed."

For a moment, they just looked at one another—really looked. Amy saw her girlhood crush, now a man. Tall—well, tallish—with an awkward kind of charm. Dark blond hair falling into his eyes. Lips, full—well, fullish—and a grin that dimpled only one cheek. And warmth. When Cliff grinned, it was like an early summer sun on a lazy afternoon. She could wrap herself in that sunlight forever. Amy swallowed hard and shoved the image away.

Cliff saw the girl next door—rather, the pest next door— now a woman. Petite, but in a way that didn't hide her curves. Green eyes that flashed or twinkled, depending on her mood. Plump lips that were quick to smile, quicker to laugh. *Lips that would be easy to kiss...* Where did that thought come from? Cliff immediately pushed it away.

Without a word, they both began walking toward the Gardener's Cottage. The silence was speaking volumes to them both. It was as if they were venturing into unexplored territory—territory they weren't sure they knew how to navigate. As they reached the door of the cottage, Cliff broke the silence.

"Uh, look, Amy, come in—just for a minute, I—" Cliff opened the door, flipped on the light. "What in the…!"

CHAPTER 12

Granville Church

—June 1920

The sun played through the new stained-glass windows of Granville Church, painting pastels on a small form hunched in a pew. The boyish face was troubled, conflicting emotions playing across it. Suddenly, a shadow fell across him, blocking out the light.

"Tis too beautiful a day for a lad such as yourself to be hidden away in the church. Are you so pious, young master?"

Startled, and a little bit frightened, young Charles Graymoor looked up at the looming figure of Absalom Bane. "No, Grandfather—I fear I'm not nearly pious enough. If I were…"

Absalom sat by the boy, placing a kindly arm across his shoulder. "If you were, you would…what?"

"I would know what to do."

"Have you trespassed against God's laws, boy? Speak."

Charles shrank from the voice that so often spoke of Hell's fires from the pulpit. "I'm sure I must have; though I don't know which one."

A ghost of a smile broke the sternness of Absalom's stony features. His voice softened. "Then speak to me, lad; perhaps I can help."

Charles hesitated, then was able to bear it no longer. "It's Father!"

A coldness stole into Absalom's voice. "What about your father?"

"He has a secret—and it frightens me."

"What kind of secret?"

The boy hesitated.

"Tell me!" Absalom's voice echoed through the church. Charles could almost smell the brimstone as it did.

"I—I don't know! I only know it makes him disappear; sometimes for days!" Tears began to fill the boy's eyes.

Absalom leaned in closer, his voice soft now. "Just tell me, my child. Place this burden on my shoulders. Yours are too small to carry such a load."

Charles leaned over and poured his confession into Absalom's ear. Absalom's expression was a curious mix of concern and cunning. He turned the boy to face him.

"You must listen to me, boy—listen and heed what I say." The young face looked into Absalom's. "Are you willing, Charles Graymoor, to do whatever I say in order to save your family—and your father's soul?"

Amy and Cliff looked around the cottage in shock at what they saw. Drawers were opened, cushions were tossed, furniture turned over, and papers were scattered everywhere. Amy spoke first.

"Oh Cliff! Who... I mean, why would...? Good grief! Somebody sure ramshackled this place!"

"Ransacked."

"Well, it looks pretty ramshackle to me!"

"Ramshackle—ransacked—whatever! The question is: why?"

Amy and Cliff picked their way through the chaos, righting

furniture and scavenging papers as they went. Cliff looked at the papers in his hand. "Huh. Weird."

"What's weird?"

"None of my papers were taken; I mean, the folders aren't even touched, but the place is torn apart like somebody was looking for something. I can't figure out why—"

"Ugh, gross!" Amy's voice interrupted. "Look." Amy pointed to the mirror above the sofa. "Is… is that blood?"

Cliff touched the red.

"Ooh, Cliff, don't!"

"It's just paint, Amy."

Cliff stood back, looked at the mirror again. Someone had written on it in red lettering. Cliff read aloud, "'Let dead men's bones sleep in the grave—or yours will join them.'"

"Well that's pretty creepy—and hokey," Amy said.

"Looks like someone is trying to scare me off for some reason. Well, it's not going to work!" Cliff picked up a handful of papers. "I put too many years of work into…" Cliff took a look at the papers in his hand. "Wait a sec. These aren't my papers."

Cliff placed the cushions on the couch and the lamp on the table beside it. He turned it on, looking closely at the papers he held. Amy sat down beside him, peering over his shoulder.

"You sure they're not your papers? You've got an awful lot of papers."

"Of course I'm sure. These papers are really old; see how yellow they are? I think whoever trashed this place dropped these. Close the door Amy, and lock…" Cliff stopped himself. "Wait. I forgot you had a dinner date."

"Well, not anymore, I don't!"

"But there might be dancing…"

"Oh, no you don't, Clifford Graymoor; you're not getting rid of me now." Amy rose and locked the door. "We're gonna see what these mysterious old papers have to say!"

A car pulled in quietly through the gates of the Graystone Manor, headlights off. The engine turned off, letting the car coast for the last few hundred feet. The door opened and shut quietly, and barely perceptible footsteps took a path through the grass toward the Gatekeeper's Cottage. Zach Malone allowed a soft whisper to himself: "Well, well, what have we here?"

From behind the cottage came the steady sound of digging.

As Zach slipped around the corner, he heard a shovel strike something hard. Katherine Bane was standing before a hole, tool in hand. She let the shovel fall, knelt down, and brushed the remaining dirt away. Then, carefully, she lifted something out of the shallow grave.

She looked thoughtfully at the object in her hands, and shook her head. "I never thought the future of so many folks could fit into such a small, wooden box."

As Kate looked up, Zach pulled further back into the shadows.

Her eyes drifted up to the evening sky.

"Nathanial—I know you're up there with the angels, having a high old time in Heaven—but if you happen to be listening…" Kate swallowed, "I buried it. I buried it for you." She wiped a tear from her face with a dirty hand. "Forgive me, Nate. Never wanted to do this. I never wanted to hurt the family—or mess up all those years of servin' God…"

Zach watched as Kate gulped back a sob. It was at times like this he almost regretted his agenda. He steeled his emotions as Kate composed hers.

"Too late for all that now, Nate. It's got to be done."

Setting down the box, Kate rose, grabbed the shovel again, and refilled the hole she'd just made. She picked up the box, and turned just in time to…

A scream caught in her throat. Standing in front of her was Zach.

"Hello, Kate. I think it's time we had a little talk."

He placed a hand on her shoulder, but Kate shook him off. "Get out of here, or I'll call…"

"The police? I don't think so."

Kate heard, rather than saw, the muted click of a gun being cocked. Zach leaned in close to her face; so close, she could feel his breath. "I don't have time for games, Katherine Bane. Tell me what you know, and no one will get hurt…"

"Hey, shut the drapes while you're at it." Cliff's eyes were fixed on the mysterious, yellowed pages in his hand. If he'd lifted his head, he would have seen an irritated Amy, hands on her hips.

"Ahem. Magic word…?"

Cliff looked at Amy and sighed. "Shut the drapes, *please*. Now, let's—"

Amy's cellphone ringtone interrupted. Strains of a Disney classic filled the room.

Cliff looked at her. "'It's a Small World'…? Really?"

Amy looked at her phone. "It's a text—from Zach. What? He's canceling our date? Well, he's got a lot of nerve."

Cliff laughed. "Amy, you were going to cancel with him!"

"It's not the same thing!" Amy shut the drapes, and walked back to the couch. She placed herself close to Cliff's side, peering over his shoulder. "Now, what's in these papers?"

Cliff tried to ignore the touch of her arm and the faint smell of jasmine that drifted from her hair. He cleared his voice. "It's hard to tell exactly what this is; the lettering is kind of faded. But it's definitely Peter Graymoor's handwriting." He pulled the lamp closer. "'The Hyde Papers.'"

Amy squirmed with excitement. "Ooh, ooh—like—oh, whatchamacallit—like 'Jekyll and Hyde'!"

"Yep. This is starting to get interesting."

"Starting? You mean falling pulpits, boobytrapped steps, and Kate hiding things isn't interesting enough? Oh—and don't forget a ramshackled house!"

"Yeah, well, this Jekyll and Hyde stuff makes it more than just some vandals trashing things. This story is tied in with the Graymoors—and that makes it *very* interesting."

Amy was uncharacteristically silent.

So silent that Cliff looked at her. "What's wrong?"

Amy lowered her eyes. "It's this Jekyll and Hyde stuff. I, uh, I sorta forgot what it's about."

Cliff looked at her, incredulously. "I can't believe you don't know the story of Dr. Jekyll and Mr. Hyde! I mean, we studied it in high school."

She hesitated. "Yeah, I know, but I kinda didn't pay attention. A lot. Could you tell me the story?"

Cliff bit his tongue. He knew if he chided Amy too much, she might just walk out. And for some reason, he really didn't want her to do that. He searched his memory to pull out as much of the story as he could.

"Well, Jekyll was a doctor who had kind of a thing about the good and evil inside human nature. So, he mixed up some sort of transforming potion that would unleash what's buried deep inside a person."

Amy shivered. "Creepy. What did he find?"

"He found a monster. A monster that was locked inside him. You see, he drank the potion himself; and when he did, he became Mr. Hyde—a part of himself that was pure evil."

Amy shivered again. "Garden of Eden type stuff."

Cliff looked at her. "Garden of Eden?"

"Oh, you know, Adam decided he was smarter than God, and wanted to call all the shots on good and evil. All it took was one itsy-bitsy bite of that forbidden fruit, and zap—everybody's got a Mr. Hyde inside."

"Huh. Never thought of it that way."

"Whaddaya know? I actually had a thought that Dr. Clifford Graymoor had never thunk!"

He could see the mischievous glint in her eye. He smiled. "Okay, brainiac, help me figure this out."

Amy scooted even closer to him. "Well, I gotta be close enough to see what you're looking at, don't I?"

"Uh, yeah, right. The closer the better." Cliff heard a little giggle. "I mean… I mean, I didn't mean… Oh, let's just read the thing." Cliff began to read aloud.

I don't know how much longer I can continue this battle—he haunts me day and night. I can't even bear a…

Simon's Secret Room, Graystone Manor

—October 1920

In a secret attic garret, hidden in a remote part of Graystone Manor, a disheveled figure was writing furiously: "…he haunts

me day and night. I can't even bear a mirror in the house, for
when I look at it, it's his face I see."

The man stopped writing and whispered to himself, "His face,
I see nothing but his face." His shoulders began to shake. Was
it the chill of the attic, or a sob lodged in his heart? He began
to write again. "I am Hyde, yet the face of Jekyll stares back at
me. Though I fear it, I know what I must—"

There was a knock. His body stiffened. He heard a familiar
voice entreating him from beyond the hidden door.

"Peter! Peter—it's Mary! For God's sake, let me in!"

Simon Graymoor whispered to himself, "Mary?"

Her voice was full of pain. "Peter, please listen! I've followed
you like a sneak thief for days just to find this secret place. Must
I now beg to be let in? Please, my darling—please!"

The secret panel creaked open, and Simon quickly pulled
his wife in. "Quick now—come in! He mustn't find me…
He mustn't…" He froze. The familiar tread of heavy boots
approached them. Mary clung to her husband, who whispered
but one word: "Absalom."

Bony fingers came through the crack in the secret door, pushing it open. Mary broke the silence.

"Father! How did you…?"

"You are not the only one who has spies in this household. Leave
us, Mary." Mary looked at the haggard face of her husband, then
back at the stony face of Absalom Bane. "No, Father! I will not."

"Do as I say, daughter!"

Mary turned her face up to her husband. He tenderly brushed
the hair from her face. "Go, my love. It seems your father and
I must talk alone." Without a word—or look to her father—
Mary kissed her husband's hand, and walked out. When her
footsteps had died away, Absalom spoke.

"So, this is where you come when you go missing for days."

"And now you have found me. What do you want, Absalom?"

Absalom studied the small room, furnished with only a cot, a desk, a lamp, and a small lavatory. His eyes fixed on the unfinished manuscript on the desk.

Simon repeated his question. "What do you want of me, Absalom?"

Absalom turned to face him. "I want you to stop hiding! You have a wife, a fine son, and a reputation to preserve. I want you to live up to your name!"

"You mean the noble name of Peter Graymoor?" He laughed.

"Yes—the name of Peter Graymoor!" Absalom stepped toward the desk—and the manuscript—but its author stopped him, blocking his way.

"You dare defy me? We shall see…" Absalom's voice was soft, menacing. "What has happened to you? What is this room…? What sins do you hide in here?"

"Sins?" His laugh approached hysteria. "This is not my sin; it is my penance! And this," he grabbed the pages he had been writing, "this is my confession!"

Absalom's voice grew low—reasonable. "You are overwrought; I see that. And I will help, if you will but let me." Absalom placed a hand on his arm. "Don't be a fool, man. I've told you that you can redeem yourself by doing—"

The Master of Graystone shook off the preacher's hand, his laughter reaching full hysteria. "It is not enough! It is never enough! Orphanages, schools, hospitals—do you think they can atone for what I am inside?" His laughter turned into a deep, swallowed sob. He sunk down in his chair.

Absalom watched with a cold eye as despair descended on his charge, settling on him like a shroud. The Reverend Bane offered no comfort; he simply waited for the sobbing to stop.

Finally, the broken man regained control enough to speak. "Do you know why I had that portrait painted? It wasn't pride; it was to remind me of who I am not—and who I really am. I am... Hyde."

"No, you're a fool. I can't believe you give credence to that heathen writer. What does he know that—?"

"What does he *know*?" The living brother's fist slammed down on his desk. "He knew my mother!" Recovering his self-control, he continued in a more civil tone. "He knew my Mother. From my youngest years, he saw what I was. I cannot escape that fact."

"You must try. Even if the devil did have a hand in shaping you, you must try!" Absalom's grip was no longer fatherly; it was like iron. "You must free yourself from this—"

"Free myself?" Preacher and penitent faced one another, the latter's expression painted with sorrow. "There is only one way I can be free, Absalom. God help me, there is only one way..."

CHAPTER 13

The night had fallen darker and colder than expected. A warm blaze now crackled in the fireplace of the Gardener's Cottage, casting cheery shadows into the room. But the man pacing in front of it was far from cheery. Cliff was frustrated.

"I know, I know, but I just can't figure it out! I mean, why did Peter Graymoor think he was a 'Hyde'—and what was his way 'out?' And why the heck was he afraid to look in the mirror?"

"Don't forget the secret room!" Amy's voice reminded him of one more twist to the puzzle.

Cliff stopped, went to his bookshelf, and pulled out a large book. He knelt at his coffee table, opened the book, and unfolded a double page in the middle of it. Amy peered over his shoulder.

"What's that?"

"The original floor plan of Graystone. See? There is no hint of a secret room! Peter Graymoor must have added it later. The question is: why?"

Amy shook her head. "Too creepy." Suddenly she jumped up from the couch. "That reminds me." Amy headed into the kitchen. Cliff turned.

"Reminds you of what?" He called out, "Amy! What are you doing?"

"Getting a washcloth."

"Don't worry about the dishes now, just…"

Amy reappeared into the room. "It's not for the dishes—it's for that stupid mirror."

"The mirror? What; you mean *now*?"

"All those icky words bug me. I can't think as long as they're up there."

Cliff smirked. "So that's why you can't think—icky words." Amy took a swipe at him with the washcloth, but missed. She stood up on the couch and began to wipe.

"Oh, great." Her arm fell to her side.

"What now?"

"Oh, it's just that Peter Perfect's over there waving that riding crop in his left hand like he's going to hit me." Amy switched the wet rag to her left hand and swatted the mirror, mimicking his pose. She shivered. "Ick—creepy."

"Oh, here, let me." Cliff kicked off his shoes, climbed up on the sofa, and, taking the washcloth, began wiping the paint off the mirror. "You know, you are the strangest woman, Amy Newgate. You're not afraid to run right in and take on a saboteur, but you won't look into a mirror because…"

Cliff stopped mid-swipe. His brain was whirling with a collection of words, artifacts, bits and pieces of history, all being caught up in a storm of thought. It was as if he was inside a snow globe that was being shaken—only everything was settling down far differently than it had been before. It was the same information, but the shape it was taking was…

Cliff looked at the mirror, then back at the painting. "Wait. That can't…"

Amy tugged at his pant leg, "Cliff—what is it?"

Something was stirring in the back of his mind, something that was still in the shadows. A flash of illumination lit up his understanding, then vanished. Whatever it was sank back into his subconscious. Cliff dropped the rag and sat, staring at the floor. He'd never felt so much responsibility resting on his shoulders. He whispered the words to himself, "Something… There's something here… I just can't quite…"

Amy could not make out his words, but watched the wrestling of emotions on Cliff's face. "Cliff?"

Suddenly, the wrestling stopped. He looked up. He knew what he had to do. "We're not letting go, Amy; we're going to get to the truth."

Lyndsie Bainbridge was tired. She never got tired, but then she'd never had more at stake. All she had accomplished—in fact, all that she *was*—felt threatened. Her eldest brother— make that half-brother—was a surgeon. Her other half-brother was a powerhouse on Wall Street. She was bookended by success, the only girl in a high profile, highly volatile family. They weren't rich, but they were very well-to-do; well-to-do enough to supplement her scholarship to Sarah Lawrence and foot the cost of an MBA at Yale.

The family had all the ear-markings of success, but like many who seem so picture perfect, fatal flaws began to crack the mask. Her father was given to philandering and misplaced philanthropy, and her mother was given to depression and drink. Throw in a few marriages, and you have an impeccably dysfunctional family. True to form, her two half-brothers were given to the same weaknesses as the parents. The surgeon had been suspended for substance abuse, and scandal followed the "Wall Street Wonder" who just couldn't seem to keep away from other men's wives.

Someone had to redeem the Bainbridge legacy, and Lyndsie

was the chosen one. She felt like the family name—and the family fortune—rested on her shoulders.

Those shoulders began to sag as she pondered the danger the restoration of Graystone presented. She already knew the secrets it held. She had known since she discovered a certain set of diaries gathering dust in the attic of the Bournemouth branch of the family. She had wheedled an invitation to visit the old estate, and even managed to plant herself there for a weekend. Early one morning, she found the stairs to the attic and began to explore. It was in a small hatbox that she found them. She slipped the volumes into her jacket, then into her suitcase. She thanked the family for their time—and headed straight for Heathrow.

Lyndsie thought she was safe. Graystone was just a fossil, and she alone possessed all the diaries of Mary Bane Graymoor. Nothing could touch her—or the foundation. At least, that's what she thought. Now, a frightening thought pushed itself into her mind. *If the truth is discovered, what would you do to protect the foundation?* The answer came to her immediately. *Whatever it takes.* Then, an even more chilling question took shape: *And if someone stands in your way…?*

At that moment, a plan began to form in her mind; one that both frightened her—and thrilled her. She pushed it away. "No. Impossible. I couldn't…"

What was she going to do?

Katherine Bane held the teacup in her hand, staring into it. She took a sip. Cold. Zach Malone sat in front of her, watching her. Waiting. The gun was still in his hand. Katherine took a deep breath.

"It's pretty late. People are going to see your car outside and start to wonder."

Zach laughed. "Worried about your reputation, Kate? It's a little late for that, don't you think?"

"You going to be here all night?"

"No. And neither are you. Grab the diaries—and your toothbrush, love. I'm taking you someplace far from any prying eyes—or ears. We're going off on a little adventure together." He gave a laugh. "Oh, and write a note for the lovely Amy, telling her not to worry about dear old Aunt Kate."

Kate tried not to show her fear. "What are you going to do with me?"

What, indeed? Zach mulled it over. It was tricky, but he knew what had to happen—and what he needed to do to make it happen. Failure was not an option.

Charles Graymoor's Bedroom, Graystone Manor
—October 1920

The fair-haired, slight frame of young Charles Graymoor sat motionless on the window seat in his room. He had locked the door and taken all the keys. He wanted to be alone. Tears streaked his face, and a lead weight sat in the pit of his stomach. At least Nanny had stopped pounding at the door, and his mother's crying had stopped too. He was the one. He was the Judas that had betrayed his own father. He had told Absalom Bane about his father's secret room.

The door creaked open. Charles jumped in surprise. There, only a few feet away from him, stood Absalom himself. Charles wondered if he was dreaming—or if some strange magic had somehow opened the door. "How did you…?"

Absalom held up a large ring of keys. "There is no part of Graystone I cannot enter. I care for this family. For me, there must be no locked doors—ever." Charles hung his head.

"It doesn't matter. I am a wicked, wicked boy; I've betrayed my father."

Absalom placed himself beside the boy. "No, my son, you've saved him. He would throw away all the spiritual fruit he has earned… Throw it away and leave his family—and his church—in poverty. And his soul…" Absalom stood. "His soul must be saved. It is only under my guidance that he can find his way!" A slight smile broke the iciness of Absalom's face. "My child, you may have just saved your father's soul."

Absalom pulled out a handkerchief and dabbed the remaining tears from the boy's face. "Now, let us dry these doubting tears! Go, leave this room, and play in the sun, my Charlie. You have done a great good!"

The trusting face of the young boy looked up into the deep eyes of Absalom. Somehow, inside, Charles knew that if he obeyed, if he took a step out of his room, he would belong to Absalom forever. Charles nodded, got up from his window seat, and left to play in the sun.

Absalom watched as he left. He knew the heart of his grandson had been secured. Now—what to do about the heart of his father? If it would not yield, Absalom knew what he had to do. Whatever the price, he must not fail.

Cliff stretched. The morning sun was peeking through the blinds. He looked over at the clock. *Nine o'clock?* He never slept that late—not even on weekends—but he felt like he could still use another couple of hours. His head felt foggy—and desperately in need of coffee. He threw his robe over his pajamas, and made his way to the kitchen. He entered the living room, the sight of which hit him like a bucket of ice water. There were the remnants of the disorder from last night scattered about his living room. It was all starting to come back. Then, he got a second shock. There on the couch was a motionless figure. A tiny snore came from it. He smiled. Amy was dead asleep with an afghan pulled halfway over her.

He took a moment to really look at her. Rumpled, dark hair. Small hands. A tiny smile on perfectly formed, pink lips. She was the same old Amy—but she wasn't. She was still pesky, but somehow different. She was…charming. Cute. Even cuddly. The little, snaggle-toothed Amy that pestered him as a kid was now a totally adorable, lovable woman. She was different than high-school-Amy, the pretty, flirty little cheerleader who thought she could wrap any boy around her finger. He knew he had been dangerously close to being wrapped himself. But that Amy was gone; replaced by something completely different.

Maybe it was the sorrow of losing her husband—or maybe it was something else. Something spiritual? He just knew that this pure and sparkly woman shined with something more. *Now, what are you going to do with this, Cliff?* Too early to try to figure that one out.

He shook his head and headed to the kitchen. He put a pod of coffee on to brew, and opened the refrigerator to see if it had anything resembling breakfast in it. He picked up the milk and sniffed. *Good enough for cereal.*

"Cliff?"

Startled, he jumped, then turned to see a sleepy-eyed Amy standing before him.

"Don't do that! I almost dropped the milk!"

"Did I… Did I spend the night here?"

Cliff smiled. "You fell asleep mid-sentence last night after helping me go through all those 'Hyde Papers.' I couldn't wake you up, so I just threw a cover over you and let you sleep."

Amy's eyes widened. "Oh no! I mean, what will people say when… I mean, they're going to think…"

He could feel Amy ramping up to a full-blown panic. "Relax! Nobody lives between this place and Kate's cottage. You could be spending every night here for all they know…" It had slipped out. Now it was Cliff's turn to panic. "I didn't mean you should! I mean, you could but…" It was getting worse. "I know you wouldn't, but, if you did, it would be…"

This was not going like he intended; nothing was coming out right. He looked at Amy, who was leaning against the door frame, suppressing a smile. "You're enjoying this, aren't you?"

"You betcha."

"You know what I meant, don't you?"

"Mmm… Don't know about that. It all sounded kind of twizzly to me. Next thing you know, you'll be offering to make an honest woman out of…" It was Amy's turn to panic.

They looked at each other, and, reaching for an exit to the topic, started speaking at the same time.

"I better go find Kate…"

"You better check in with Kate…"

Amy quickly retrieved her jacket and headed for the front door. As she opened it, she tossed over her shoulder, "I'll be back for coffee!" Then she was gone.

Cliff shook his head, confused. What just happened? Sure,

he was attracted to her, but did he have feelings for Amy? Did she have feelings for him? He groaned. He hated, and loved, the jumble of emotions that the opposite sex brought into his life. The warm, embraceable image of Amy danced through his imagination, but it was abruptly followed by an overpowering vision of the alluring, alabaster-skinned Lyndsie. Cliff groaned again, "I'd rather face a bloody mirror and a horde of vandals than…than mess with these *women!*" He grabbed his cup of coffee and went back to work on the remnants of ransacked disorder.

It was a beautiful, fall morning as seen from the expanse of windows that formed an entire wall of Dexter Heathstone's office. Dexter didn't take note of the riot of colors painting the trees, because he was not at his polished, African Blackwood desk. In fact, he was not *in* his office. Not really. He was enclosed in a room hidden behind a large, ornate bookcase. It was a small room, but comfortable. But it was more than that. It was totally secure. He had the room built for his dealings with certain government agencies, both foreign and domestic, and that made preserving client confidentiality a must. Now, he was glad for another reason. He didn't know who he could trust. He opened his cellphone and listened to the voice message again. This was bad. Very bad.

Dexter deleted the message, as instructed. So much was at stake, but there was nothing he could do. Or was there? He sat motionless as the minutes passed. He stirred; he had decided. Dexter rose from his chair and exited the secret room. For the first time that day, he looked out the window. Perched on the ledge, right in front of him, was a peregrine falcon with a pigeon in its claws. The bird stared at him with an unblinking eye, then flew off with its prey. A chill went through Dexter.

He had to watch out. He had no intention of playing the pigeon in this game.

He buzzed his secretary. "Bring in the file on Graystone and file 13001 on the Graymoor Foundation."

A voice came through the intercom: "Yes, Mr. Heathstone. And by the way, sir, your lunch is here."

Lunch? Was it that late? He checked his watch—11:45 a.m. *That's odd—they're early today.* It didn't matter; he wasn't really in the mood for food. Not with this, this dilemma hanging over him. He looked up just as his secretary entered.

"I have the file, sir."

He smiled. Jennifer Marley, the more than competent executive assistant who had been with him for the last fifteen years. If he could trust anyone, surely it was her.

She set a paper bag down, "And here is your lunch."

"They're kind of early today, aren't they?"

"It was a new guy making the delivery; actually, I think it was just a boy. He dropped off the bag and didn't even wait for a tip."

"We'll catch the kid next time. Now, the files?" The secretary laid the thick folder in front of him.

"Here you are, sir. Can I get you anything else?"

"Not now. Thank you, Jenn."

Dexter picked up the file on the foundation. This was going to take a while—especially in light of what he'd just learned. Maybe he should eat. He buzzed his secretary again. "Bring me a bottle of that sweet tea, please."

"Yes, sir."

He opened the bag and pulled out the Styrofoam box. He unhooked the tab and pulled out the sandwich. Pastrami—his favorite. As he took a bite, a fine dust and a familiar odor rose up. Dexter began to feel his throat swell and close off. His heart began to pound. He buzzed his secretary but he couldn't speak. He reached inside his drawer for a small cylinder. He found it, but it dropped from his hand. Why did his chest hurt so much? It was his lungs—they couldn't get any air. He faintly heard the voice of his secretary calling his name. Then, darkness.

Amy slipped down the back way through untended gardens as she made her way to Kate's cottage. She hoped Kate was still asleep so she wouldn't have to answer a lot of embarrassing questions—and not just about why she was gone all night. There was the book hidden in the window seat that Amy had taken. Somehow, she had to explain that. But the really big questions didn't have to do with Cliff or the book—they were for Kate; questions she didn't want to ask. Like, what did Kate know? What was that big secret that was eating away at her? Amy sighed. She sure hoped Kate was asleep.

Amy unlocked the back door of the cottage and entered the kitchen. No Kate. She peeked into the living room. No Kate. She carefully cracked open the door to Kate's bedroom. No sign that the bed had been slept in. Her heart began to race. Where was Kate? She must have never come back from her walk. Amy walked back into the living room and spied the cup and tea bag on the table. Kate *had* been here, but where was she now?

"I've got to go get Cliff." She said it aloud to fill the emptiness of the room. She opened the front door—and that was when she saw it. Kate had left a note. Amy pulled it off the door and walked back inside.

I'm going off for a couple of days, but I don't want you to worry. I'm fine. Just need to clear my head. I'll be back in soon, and I'll tell you all about it then. Sorry I didn't clean up my mess. Just had to have a cup of that fine Earl Gray tea you like so much. Kate.

Amy's radar went off. Even without it, she would've guessed something was woogie. Kate never visited people, and she never left town. But Amy's radar was pinging in a different direction this time. She looked at the tea bag, gingerly picked it up, and sniffed. Sassafras. Then what was that bit about "fine Earl Gray tea you like so much?" Amy's eyes narrowed as a hint of a suspicion formed. She had some investigating to do—and she didn't want Cliff to try to stop her.

Cliff had taken a quick shower and was staring into his second cup of coffee. Whatever was going on with him and Amy was just a sidetrack that kept winding its way back into the bigger muddle of Graystone—and what really happened to Peter and Simon. He didn't want Amy involved—it was getting too dangerous—but there didn't seem to be any way to keep her out of it. *Maybe if Kate would...*

Amy burst in the door, breathless.

"Amy! You okay? Did Kate read you the riot act or something?"

"No. Read this." Amy handed the note to Cliff.

He read it through twice. He held the paper up to Amy. "'Going off?' Where?"

"How should I know?"

"It was rhetorical, Amy."

"Well stop being rhetorical. It gets on my nerves." She plopped down beside him. "I think she's... She's either running away from something—or that 'something' is chasing her."

"Huh?"

"Maybe she's in some kind of trouble. Or—maybe somebody took her."

Cliff shook his head. This was too much like a spy novel. "That's crazy talk. Why would anybody take Aunt Kate?"

Amy held up the Jekyll and Hyde book she'd found hidden away. "Because of stuff like this. Who knows what else she's got squirreled away? I think we need to go back to the attic and—"

"Break into the trunk. You know, that may actually be a good idea."

A half hour later, armed with a hammer and chisel, Cliff and Amy were in Kate's attic, looking down at the trunk Kate had called "personal." Cliff knelt down beside it. "Okay, here goes." He placed the chisel on the lock, lifted the hammer, and struck. The padlock fell apart easily. They lifted the lid. Inside were bits and pieces of Kate and Nathanial's past: scrapbooks, photographs, and clothing. They emptied them all on the floor and went through them. Nothing. Cliff looked at Amy, puzzled.

"Why was Kate so protective of this stuff? There's nothing here but the typical stuff you'd find in an attic." He sighed. "Another dead end."

"Kate was hiding something—I know it!" Amy responded. "I can feel my radar going off all over the place. I just don't know what it... Hey, what are you doing?"

Cliff had tipped the trunk over and was tapping on the bottom.

He set it back down and studied the inside floor of the trunk. "Look at this—the depth of the trunk on the inside doesn't match the depth on the outside. You know what that means…"

"A false bottom! Kate has a false bottom!"

Cliff chuckled. "Well, at least her trunk does." He studied the inside again and spotted a small notch. "There it is!"

He dug his fingernail under the notch and lifted. Hidden beneath the false floor of the trunk was a small chamber. In it were three books. A prayer book and two black volumes. Cliff opened one of the black books and began to read.

CHAPTER 14

St. Peter's Church, Bournemouth

—May 1898

A fair-faced, fair-haired boy sat crouched in the balcony of the church, far above all the reverent flock. The solemn tones of the preacher rose up like smoke, until they curled around the boy, filling his brain with doubt. He had heard many a "sinners doomed by an angry God" sermon, and this seemed to be no exception. The boy sighed. He was afraid *he* was no exception. Though just a youth, he was filled with enough guilt to last a lifetime. The boy's brow twisted as he listened. This sermon was a little different. The black-cloaked man at the pulpit was a guest—and now his words left the beaten path and took a new direction.

He began to speak of "grace." Was there enough grace in the world cover a hopeless soul born wrong on the inside? Silently, another figure sat down beside him. Without looking up, Simon spoke.

"So, you found me, Peter."

"As always, Simon. Come down with me. We need not sit with the family if you don't wish to. I will sit with you in the back and—"

"No. I will not go down. They stare at me so. I hear the whispers. 'Is that him—is that the wicked twin?'"

"No! Surely they don't—"

"They do! I've heard them." They were both silent as the words of the preacher floated up to them. Simon heard the words "cross" and "death." Then he heard the words, the beautiful words, that spoke of love, forgiveness, and of becoming a new creation in Christ. Simon turned to his brother.

"Do you think that is true—that we can become new creatures?"

"I do, brother; I do."

"I wish I could believe it. Oh, Peter, how I wish I could believe it."

"You can, if you only will. Just ask God to—"

Too loudly, Simon responded, "I do! I do every day!" He pulled out a small, black book from his jacket. "See, this is the journal Mum gave us each for our birthday! It's all in here—can't God read?"

"Quiet, Simon!" Heads from below began to look up in their direction. "He not only reads your words, He reads your thoughts."

A tear rolled down Simon's face. "Then I am doomed."

"Come down with me, Simon."

"No."

With a compassion that far outweighed his years, Peter looked at his mirror image in his brother. "Then I will stay with you. I will always stay with you."

Without looking up, Simon said, "Then you are doomed, too."

Cliff laid down the book. "Poor kid."

"Who?" Amy felt she had been patient enough as Cliff sat and read; now she wanted the story—all of it.

"Simon Graymoor."

Amy was puzzled. "Wasn't he the bad twin?" Cliff laid down the book.

"You see, that's the problem. His mom somehow got this whole Jekyll and Hyde thing from Robert Louis Stevenson, so the kid was raised with this fear that he was just born 'wrong,' you know? A kid will always live up to—or down to—what's expected of him."

"Wow! That's pretty—oh, whatchacallit—profound. I didn't know you had profundity, Cliff."

He saw Amy's eyes shining with a new look of respect. He kind of liked it.

Amy continued, "But why would Kate hide this?"

Cliff shook his head. "I haven't a clue." Amy held out her hand for the book. She opened it, turned to the last page, and began to read. It was written in a bolder hand.

> *With sorrow, I lay the past and the boyish musings of this book aside. With new pen and new words I must wrestle now before my Maker. Wrestle with the darkness—with what I've done and who I now am. Am I a wolf clothed in lambskin... Or a lamb swallowed by a wolf? No matter. I am Hyde.*

Amy shivered.

> *Simon is dead. Hyde controls me now—or is it Peter? God help me, I have to know!*

That was the end of the diary, but for one thing. On the inside back cover, three words were scrawled. Amy showed it to Cliff. Cliff traced the words with his finger.

"'The Hyde Papers.' Could it be…? It has to be…" His voice was soft, yet grew louder, more intense. "That's it—it's 'The Hyde Papers!'"

"What are you talking about?"

Cliff grabbed Amy's hand without thinking. "Don't you see? This was hidden because it referred to 'The Hyde Papers!' There's something in them that Kate doesn't want anyone to find out." Cliff paused. A dark thought crept into his mind. "And maybe she's not the only one."

Cliff and Amy looked at each other. The pulpit. The booby-trapped stairs. The ransacked house. They both knew Kate would never hurt anyone, and that only meant one thing. Someone else was in the game; a game that just might take an ugly turn.

Cliff stood up. "We need to find Kate…"

Amy finished his thought, "…before somebody else does."

Cliff and Amy put the trunk back together, but hung on to the diary. When they reached the bottom of the stairs, Cliff's cellphone buzzed: a missed call. "Stupid phone."

"Don't blame it; blame the attic."

Cliff's cellphone buzzed again. "Voicemail. I better give it a listen. It might be Kate or something."

"Well, put it on speaker then."

"No, nosy!"

"Why? Afraid it might be Lyndsieee?" There was a challenge in Amy's eyes and—was that a glint of jealousy?

Cliff sighed. He wasn't up for a fight. "Fine. Whatever." He pushed the voicemail icon, then set it to speaker.

"Dr. Graymoor—please call Dexter Heathstone's office as soon as possible. There's been an attempt…" The voice hesitated. "An accident. Please call as soon as you can. Thank you."

Again, Amy and Cliff exchanged glances. For the first time, the looks were tinged with real fear. Silence filled the cottage. Cliff was the first to break it. "Uh, did she start to say what I think she did?"

Amy swallowed. "Yeah. It wasn't really an accident. It was an 'attempt.'"

"That's what I thought." Cliff dialed Dexter's office. "Hello? This is Dr. Graymoor... Can you please tell me—?"

"One moment, Dr. Graymoor. I'll transfer you."

Cliff looked at Amy. "They put me on hold! Gimme a break; they called me! Of all the stupid—"

"Excuse me?" A cool, male voice came through on the other end of the line.

"Oh! Uh, I'm sorry! Uh, this is Dr. Clifford Graymoor. I understand there's been an," Cliff fumbled for the right word, "incident. Is Dexter okay? And who is this anyway?"

"I'm Dexter's physician, Dr. Matthews. He's okay. He'll probably be in the hospital for a couple of days at the very least, just to make sure."

"Make sure of what? What happened?"

"Dr. Graymoor, are you aware of Dexter's peanut allergy?"

"Man, am I ever! He had only, like, a handful of restaurants he'd ever go to because he felt he could trust 'em." Then it hit Cliff. "You mean somebody put peanuts in his—"

The cool voice cut him off. "Please, Dr. Graymoor. What about the places he orders his lunch from?"

Cliff thought. "Uh, there's only one place: Georgio's. He's been using them for years. Wait—you can't think they would..." Cliff's brain made a leap. "Unless you're thinking that somebody who knew he always got lunch from there somehow got to his order, and put—"

"Please!" The cool voice began to sound human. "I can't... I mean, I know what you're thinking, and that's what I..." The doctor's voice trailed off. "But, I'm not here to offer my opinion. Dexter should be fine—but he will be out of commission for a couple of days. We're keeping him sedated because he gets very agitated. He's not the, uh, most cooperative patient."

In spite of it all, Cliff smiled to himself. "No—Dex wouldn't be a good patient." He took a deep breath. "Thanks, Dr. Matthews, for talking to me. I'm just relieved Dex is going to be alright." A new concern hit him. "I mean, he is going to be alright, isn't he?"

"They have a policeman outside his door. No one visits him. No one."

Policeman? Cliff sighed, fear mixed with relief. "Well, thanks again, Doc, and—"

The Doctor's voice lowered. "One more thing, Dr. Graymoor. He kept asking me to tell you something—but his throat was closed off. He did manage to write two letters on a piece of paper before we got him sedated."

"What were they?"

"The letters were a 'Z' and an 'A'..."

Zach looked down at the sleeping woman on his couch. Her strong features still showed through the softness of sleep. Salt and pepper hair, an almost unwrinkled face, kindness hidden behind the strength. He could imagine her puttering around a garden or baking bread. In a way, she made him think of his mum. He pushed aside the thought and turned away from Kate. He couldn't let personal feelings get in the way; he knew what he had to do.

What he had to do... There were times he hated the man he had become—the man he had chosen to be. Those choices always came with a price... and sometimes the price was worth it. His mind drifted back to a memory. Danielle. Coal-black hair and flashing green eyes, hinting at a recklessness that was both exciting—and frightening. He had never told her that he loved her—not even in those long hours spent together working out a plan. Not even in those moments after, when the danger was past and they were sharing a bottle of wine. He had wanted to protect her, to be the shield that deflected away the inevitable dangers of what they did. But he couldn't protect her... He couldn't control her. He could only love her. He hardened after Danielle was killed, pursuing his work with the cold precision of a machine.

He never thought another woman could begin to stir his feelings again—until he met that petite brunette with the bright green eyes. Again, he pushed aside his thoughts. Suddenly, another sensation stirred inside him. "I wouldn't try that if I were you, Kate." Zach turned to see Katherine Bane behind him, a large iron skillet in her hands. Kate's arms dropped to her sides. Her shoulders sagged.

"So, what now? You going to fill me full of lead?"

Zach suppressed a smile. "We're going to sit down, have a little chat, and—if you do exactly as I say—no one's going to get 'filled full of lead.' Are we clear, Katherine Bane?"

Kate nodded.

Zach nodded back. "Good. What say we have a bit of brekkers, then we'll begin."

"I have a right to see him!" Lyndsie Bainbridge had cajoled, entreated, reasoned, and now, as a final tactic, she bullied.

"I am the Director of the Graymoor Foundation—and Dexter Heathstone is my Chairman of the Board! Do you dare to tell me I can't visit, and consult with my old friend? Let me speak with the Chief of…"

The voice on the other end of the line was cool and firm. The protective order had come down not only from the local police, but the State Police as well.

"Well, you can tell your director, or whomever is responsible for the order, that heads will roll!" Lyndsie slammed down the phone.

A timid face peered through the door of her office. "Is everything alright, Ms. Bainbridge?"

"No, everything's *not* alright, Rachel. Cancel my appointments, and field any calls. I don't want to be disturbed under any circumstances. *Any* circumstances—understood?"

"Yes, Ms. Bainbridge." Lyndsie's assistant closed the door behind her.

Lyndsie got up and locked it. She went to the window of her office and looked out. She surveyed the village of Granville as a queen would her domain. Off to her right, in the distance she could see the peaks of Graystone. Off to the left, she could see the rooftop of Granville Medical Center where Dexter Heathstone lay. She had tried to visit him just a couple of hours before—but the "Queen" had been denied entrance. Lyndsie was not used to being denied. And she was certainly not used to being escorted out of a hospital by an armed police officer. Even badgering the doctor for information produced almost nothing. She was told, like everyone else, that Dexter was in the hospital and out of commission for a couple of days—no visitors allowed. She had an uncomfortable feeling about that. There was a tickle at the back of her brain that told her Dexter knew something. Something that she didn't know. Something that she needed to know.

Lyndsie closed the blinds, and walked over to her desk. It was an antique rolltop of beautifully carved dark wood. She loved the rich look of the mahogany—but that wasn't why she bought it. She sat, reached underneath, and pushed a raised knob of wood. As she did, a secret drawer popped out. She gave a smile of satisfaction; this one little trick is why she bought it.

She pulled out an aged roll of paper and carefully spread it out. She had looked at it time and time again, and still hadn't found what she was looking for. She shook her head. If only she had taken an architecture class in college, she might be able to figure it out.

Architecture… A new thought began to grow in Lyndsie's mind. There was only one person who knew more about Graystone than she did. A person who *did* have a knowledge of architecture in his resume. If she couldn't learn where it was, maybe he could find out. But if he did, then he would know too, and everything would be…

Before the thought could fully form, another, colder thought tightened itself around her. If exposure was threatened, she would have to do whatever was necessary to prevent it. *The greater good. I have to protect the greater good.* First, she had to figure out her next step. As she looked again at the paper before her, one feature caught her eye. She smiled. She sat down and began to sketch out her plan.

Simon's Secret Room, Graystone Manor

—February 1920

The face in the mirror was twisted with sorrow. All the wealth of the Graymoors could not erase it. His hand reached out to touch the image he saw, but he stopped and turned away. He sat and stared at the book that lay in front of him. He had its blank pages bound, and its tooled leather cover crafted by a bookbinder in England. No local, prying eyes; no questions as to its purpose would be asked. He opened it. Its clean, white pages seemed so pure, so innocent. It was his ink that would mar it, that would make it bleed with words. Innocence was stolen by action—this he knew by heart. From the first breath of a newborn, from its very first cry, the page of life was marred. Perhaps innocence could be regained. The man's shoulders drooped, defeated. Nothing he could do would restore what was lost in simply being born. And there was no way to undo what he had done, unmake the muddied pages of his life. There was only one course left to him now: confession. He would exorcise Hyde in his words, expose his darkness in the pure, blank pages of this book.

He scrawled on the top of the sheet: "The Hyde Papers." *May God have mercy on my soul…*

"No! Absolutely not! I won't let you!" Amy and Cliff stood face to face, squared off like boxers in the ring.

"You won't *let* me? Who made you the boss of me, Clifford Graymoor?" Amy's petite form was planted in front of Cliff, and it was clear she wasn't going to budge. "I can have dinner with whomever I want—for whatever reason I want!"

Cliff decided to try another tactic. "Amy, be reasonable. This is… Well, it's dangerous stuff. The doctor said Dex was only able to write two letters before they had to sedate him. The letters were—"

"'Z–A'—I know."

"As in—"

"Zach—I know!"

"So, you see, it would be stupid to—"

"Oh! So now I'm stupid!"

"That's not what I meant, and you know it!" Cliff ran his fingers through his hair. He always did that when he was frustrated, which was getting to be a more frequent experience since Amy was back in his life. The thought stopped him. *Amy…* Back in his life. Was she? His gut was saying that he very much wanted her to be. His head came back with, *Don't rush into things—remember what happened last time.*

Cliff remembered. It was the only time in his life that he totally, recklessly fell for someone. She was a guest lecturer at the University. A redhead with creamy white skin and long, dark lashes. She went after Cliff like a heat-seeking missile—and Cliff didn't even bother to put up his defenses. He'd never had such a beautiful, tempting, and intriguing woman make a play for him before…

Something twigged in his brain. An image of Lyndsie popped into his head. He nudged it away as a picture from the past took its place.

Her name was Andrea. Andrea Chamberlain. She opened him up like a clamshell, took out the meat and the pearl, and left him broken and emptied. Not only did she take him for a ride emotionally, she took all his research on a career-making project *and* the engagement ring, custom made for her slender finger. He swore off women after that. *They just aren't worth it.*

Now he was thinking a new thought—one that included Amy. Amy's voice pushed its way into his consciousness.

"Hellooo, Cliff? I said, give me one good reason why I shouldn't go out with Zach?"

He looked at Amy—a girl grown into a woman. The girl next door who knew all his quirks, who would never take advantage of him. *Don't go, Amy.* He almost said it—almost. "Fine. Go out with whoever you want. I'm just telling you, it's dangerous. I… I don't want you to get hurt."

Amy softened. She looked at the familiar face, a face trying so hard to hide its anxiety. *Whatcha know… Maybe he does care—for real.* And maybe the danger was "for real," too. She put on a brave face. "I know it's not safe, but—but Kate is missing, you've been boobytrapped, and even Dexter Heathstone was almost…" Amy stopped herself. She didn't want to think about that—then she really *would* get scared. "We don't even know why Dexter wrote 'Z–A.' Maybe he wants you to get Zach to help."

"Yeah, right."

"Well, he did come because Dexter wanted him to."

"Not buying it."

"Well, there's just one way to find out. I've got to—to charm it out of him."

"Amy, I don't trust the guy."

"Neither do I. But he doesn't know that, so I'm going to make a date! And that's that!"

A frown wrinkled his brow. He didn't like this—not at all. "Please… Please call me if you get into trouble. Promise?"

Amy smiled. *Yep—he cares.* "I promise."

CHAPTER 15

Dorchester, Dorset

—February 1904

A cold, gray mist hung over the gravesite as they laid Jeremiah Bane's body in the ground. Very few were there to mourn him; very few had reason to. Jeremiah died as he had lived: a kind-hearted drunkard. Young Absalom stood at his father's gravesite, situated close beside that of Abigail Bane. He was outraged that the profligate who bestowed on him the Bane name should rest beside his beloved mother. She was virtuous—so virtuous—but too generous and loving for her own good. His father didn't deserve that love. He broke her heart and broke her health.

It was only six months earlier that Absalom had stood in this very spot as her body was laid to rest. Yes, many people had been present that sorrowful day, mourning the loss of that good woman. But one man was missing—Jeremiah Bane. He was mourning his own way: sharing his sorrow with a bottle of whiskey.

Now Jeremiah was dead, taken by brain-fever and pneumonia when he was caught outside in a winter storm. No one but Absalom knew that Jeremiah was not "caught" outside. He was locked outside by his own son. He could still hear his father's pleas and his pounding on the door. Finally, exhausted, miserable, and cold, Jeremiah wandered off, seeking shelter—only to be found two days later, filled with pneumonia and close to death.

In two more days, Jeremiah Bane was gone. Absalom was wracked by guilt—at least at first. How could God ever forgive him for turning away his own father? But Absalom's mind worked in a curious way. Was not God the Holy and Righteous One who cannot even look at sin?

Perhaps it was His will that Jeremiah be slain, executed for a lifetime of debauchery. Yes, wasn't it another Hand that stayed Absalom's own as he reached for the door to let his father in? It was a guilt Absalom would bear so that justice would be done. God's greater good would be served.

Still, Absalom knew he must atone for his sin, however justified it was. He would dedicate his life to the work of God. He would build a monument of service, an edifice of personal holiness to prove himself worthy of the Almighty. He vowed this in his heart. He would redeem himself in the eyes of his Maker.

Whatever it took, he would do this.

Peace came at last. His father's death was a necessary step in building the Kingdom of God. Necessary and good, because it was making Absalom a better man.

When Absalom Bane was called to throw a handful of dirt into his father's grave, he didn't step forward. Instead, he simply turned and walked away—from his father, from his shame, from England itself. He would leave his past behind. He would go to America.

"Shall I top it off for you?"

"Sure, if you've got it."

The remains of breakfast littered the small table. The black, steaming liquid poured into Kate's cup. She took a sip, careful not to burn her tongue.

"Now, continue." The voice was firm and gently insistent.

Kate took a deep breath.

"Don't know what else I can say. That's what's in the box… And that's why I did what I did." Kate's head dropped into her hands. "God forgive me—it's why I did what I did."

Zach paced the floor of his small living room, his Glock still in his hand. Her story made sense. It tied up so many loose ends necessary to his plan. But he had to be sure of the facts, and he had to find out if Kate was going to be an asset—or a liability.

Kate watched him closely. Did he believe her? "You can put that thing away. I'm not going to try anything."

Zach stopped and looked at her.

A touch of irritation crept into Kate's voice. "Good grief, I'm a 65-year-old woman—not some ninja!"

Zach laughed a genuine laugh. "I don't know, ducks; you looked pretty formidable with that frying pan in your hand." Zach slipped his gun into a shoulder holster and held his hands out in front of her. "Is that better?"

"I reckon it'll do—at least for now."

Zach sat down in front of Kate, looking at her intently. "Are you sure you've told me everything?"

"Yes. I have told you everything. I don't believe in swearin', so you'll just have to take my word for it."

"And your plan—that's really what you were going to do?" Kate nodded. Zach grinned. "Well, you're a gutsy old bird, I'll give you that."

Kate swallowed. "So—what happens now?"

"What happens now? Well, Katherine Bane, you're going to work for me."

Katherine's eyes widened. She didn't expect to hear that. "Excuse me? What makes you think I'd…"

Zach leaned forward. He had to make her believe.

"Look, Kate—whether you believe me or not, we want the same thing. Understand?"

Kate gave a slight nod.

Zach continued, "That's why I'm going to follow your plan—and you're going to follow mine."

Katherine's shoulders sagged. She was too old for this. Why did she ever open this little Pandora's box? She was not cut out to clean up a mess made more than a hundred years ago. She shook her head.

"No, please—I just want to wash my hands of this…thing. Do what you like, but just let me—"

"No, Katherine Bane. It's too late for that." A hint of steel entered Zach's voice. "Now listen to me—listen as if your life depended on it. I am going to tell you what to do, and you will do exactly—I do mean exactly—as I say. Otherwise," Zach unconsciously patted his gun, "I can't promise that you won't get hurt. Understood?"

Kate nodded, hesitated, then spoke more boldly than she felt. "Who are you, and why are you doing this?"

Zach paused, chewing on whether to play it safe—or play all his cards. *This could make it or break it. I need to get it right.* It took a fraction of a second to decide. Too much was at stake to play it safe. *Here we go Katie-girl. You're in it whether you like it or not.* He pulled something out of the inside pocket of his jacket and showed it to Kate. Her eyes widened. Zach nodded.

"Yes... Finally, we begin to understand one another. Good. Now—where are the diaries?"

"Stupid, stupid, stupid!" Cliff was mentally kicking himself for letting Amy leave. *If anything ever happened to her...* He stopped at the thought. This wasn't just concern about a friend, it was... something else. *So exactly what do I feel?* How many times had he asked himself that question in the past 24 hours? Seemed like a thousand. Was he just that stupid, or just that scared? It made his brain hurt.

Cliff closed his eyes and leaned back on the Chesterfield sofa. He conjured the vision of Amy. Those mischievous leaf-green eyes. The expressive mouth always ready to laugh or scold. The delightful way she provoked him. He liked that. He hated to admit it, but he liked the way she teased him and called him out on things. She was maddening in a way—but not manipulative. She was just...Amy. She was spice, not sugar, and Cliff had not had spice in his life for a very long time.

More than that, Cliff knew he could trust Amy to the ends of the earth. There was nothing fake there; what you saw was what you got. *And what he saw, he wanted.*

What? How did *that* sneak into his thoughts? No, no—he wasn't ready for... Before Cliff could complete that thought, another one slipped in. This bright-eyed, petite, and adorably maddening girl from his past could slip through his fingers. Someone else could claim her, or... A cold thought crept in. Or he could have just let her walk into a deadly trap.

Somehow, he had to make sure she was safe.

CHAPTER 16

Parsonage, Granville Church

—December 1934

Nathan Bane entered his father's study. Absalom had never said it was forbidden to him, but he always felt a darkness descend as he approached his door. "Father...?" No response. Nathan came closer. Absalom Bane was bent over a bound journal, writing with a hand twisted by the years. How quickly those years had overtaken him. Nathan looked at the graying head, the once rigid spine now bowed by time and affliction. For some reason, he thought of his mother, his sweet, sweet mother, who had died when he was a child. His sweet Mary was gone too.

With tenderness he remembered her: Mary, the sister who was a mother to him for so long. And he remembered the diaries Mary had secretly read to him; the diaries his mother, Rebecca, had written:

> *I recall the hour, even the exact minute that I first met Absalom. It was a day that would seal my fate. I was but a lass; too young to be courted, my father thought, but the suitors came nonetheless. I was content to obey my father, for the suitors were but boys to me, and I had no wish to marry so soon. It was*

autumn. The air was crisp, and dying colors filled
the trees and blanketed the footpath from my home to
the village. I felt a chill wind clutch at my cloak, and
above, the clouds gathered for a dreary rain. I knelt
to pick up a perfect leaf of bright red when the shadow of a man fell across my path. It was then, in that
very moment, Absalom Bane entered my life. He
offered his hand to lift me up, and for some reason, I
began to tremble. He was tall and dark, with burning
eyes and a sense of destiny that hung about him like a
cloak. This is what I thought of him, though my parents did not agree. They saw him as just another poor,
parish minister; a suitor totally unfit and unsuitably
old for their daughter. Absalom did not agree with
my parents, and he began to woo me in those scarce
hours of time I could escape their watchful eyes.

He rather frightened me, but perhaps that is what
drew me to him. He burned with a flame that I
feared would consume me. I knew that if I once
gave in to his entreaties, he would own me, heart and
soul. In those stolen moments, Absalom told me of
the great things, great works, he would do for the
Almighty. He was to fulfill God's destiny for him, and
only then would he finally reach atonement… Atonement for what? Absalom would never speak of it. He
would only speak of what was to come.

Yet, what was to come? I tremble once again as I
think of it…

How well I remember it, the single twist of time
that changed my fate. We sat, Absalom and I, in
the arbor near the humble church where he served as

vicar. We were alone, for my parents had traveled to the city to consult with such businessmen as my father knew.

They had left my dear nanny to keep watch over me, but she was aged and sleepy, and I easily slipped away. At last we were free, away from all prying eyes. I don't think we had ever been so totally alone, and I felt shy in his presence. We spoke of small things for a while, then Absalom touched my face and turned it toward his own. His finger was like a fire on my skin, and his eyes were like black coals, burning into my heart. For the first time, he took my hands. I looked down and they seemed so tiny and fragile in his long, strong fingers. Then he spoke. The words we said are forever carved into my memory. I shall write them down as if they happened yesterday:

"I am leaving." His voice was firm and cold.

I started. "When? Why…?"

"God's hand has moved. I have been called to a church, but it is hundreds of miles away."

"So far, Absalom? Must you go?"

"It is destiny, Rebecca—a divine destiny. I have been called to a parish by a family of great repute, troubled by a blessing and a curse. Twin heirs, exactly alike as in a mirror, yet opposite in heart and temperament. An iron hand is needed to mold them— and the Almighty has chosen me to be His crucible of righteousness."

"Twins?" I knew of only one such noble family.

He continued, "This is a duty I cannot flee. I

am called to break the willfulness of the profligate son, and guide the other's good heart away from his one besetting weakness—his love for his brother."

"And this man that calls you so far away?"

"His name is Sir Thomas Graymoor."

I now knew why Absalom must go. I felt so very sad, yet I oddly felt as if a heavy cloud was moving away from the sun. How little I knew that one's fate could hang on so few words. I quaked as I asked my question again. "Must you go?"

"This noble family is in need of my guidance. It is far too good to be left without it—and far too rich." Absalom's eyes glistened. "Oh, the work I could do for God with such wealth!"

I understood. Destiny had snatched this frightening and fascinating man away from me. "When do you leave, Absalom?"

"Tomorrow."

"Tomorrow?"

"Yes. That is why you must marry me—tonight."

My head began to swirl. I was too young—too, too unwise in the ways of the world to know what to do.

"Absalom, I can't! How can I…?"

His voice was hard, immovable. "You must. That is your destiny."

For the first time, Absalom caught me in his arms and kissed me. My resolve shattered as I felt his passion envelop me. I knew in that moment that Absalom would possess me, heart and soul.

The sound of those words faded as Nathan's mind came back to the present. He looked down at the gray head before him and tried to think of his father caught up in the fervor of a kiss. He shook his head. Now, he stood over the elderly figure, the years hanging like weights on that once unbending body. He loved his father, though he was never certain if his father loved him back. He called again, softly…

"Father…"

Absalom's hand dropped as he turned his face toward his son. His eyes were feverish, and his face lined with pain. He closed the book and looked into Nathan's face. "There. It is finished."

"What is finished?"

"My life." Absalom saw the look of astonishment on his son's face. "My life is in this book—and the volumes that came before. I had to…" A spasm of pain swept through Absalom, making his pale face even paler. "I had to write it—confess my actions before the Almighty; but you must know, as He knows, that everything I did, I did for Him." His long, gnarled fingers grabbed Nathan's hand. "Tell Rebecca… You must tell Rebecca…"

His mother? But she was gone.

Absalom turned away and spoke into the darkness. "You must believe me, Rebecca; I did it all for Him, to prove my worthiness to Him. May God have mercy on my soul!"

Nathan leaned over his father. He had never seen him like this before—and he saw that it was not just emotion that was tormenting his father. "Father, you aren't well! You're in pain! Come lie down; I'll call the doctor and…"

Absalom stopped him. The old man slowly rose and made his way to a small couch. He sat. "I have seen the doctor—and he has numbered my days. They are very few, very few."

"No, Father! Please—you are all I have left!" Then Nathan did something he'd never done before. He knelt beside his father, and laid his head on his father's lap.

Absalom lifted his hand—and began to gently stroke Nathan's hair. He simply said, "You have her eyes. You have your mother's eyes."

Tears, Nathan's tears, began to soak Absalom's lap. For so long, he had thought the only tenderness that grew in this fierce, stony man was for his wife and his daughter. It was for them, and them alone. Now, at the end of all things, it was finally for him.

"It is true, my son. I shall leave you soon." He lifted Nathan's head, "There is one thing—one thing alone that I ask of you. I ask you to read these diaries—and then burn them."

"Burn them? But why…?"

"You'll know why, my son. You'll know why. Say that you will do as I ask."

"I will, Father. I will."

But he did not. Absalom died two days later, and Nathan could neither bear to read nor burn his diaries. Instead, he gave them to the only person he ever trusted: Charles Graymoor, who hid them deep in the heart of Granville Church. So deep that they were never found—until Katherine Bane came along.

Zach Malone had just opened the cover to the last diary of Absalom Bane when his cellphone rang. It was Amy. He was surprised. He thought she had probably written him off after he stood her up. More than likely, she was calling to chew him out. He chuckled softly. "Well, well—let's see what our girl Amy wants."

"Amy?" Katherine Bane had lost none of her hearing with age. "Why is Amy calling…?" Zach lifted his hand to silence her.

"Amy! So good to hear from you! So sorry about last night, love…"

Kate frowned. "You call her 'Love?'"

Zach put a finger to his lips. "It was business, you know—overseas and all that. I wish I could make it up to you, but I—"

"You bet you're gonna make it up to me!" Amy's voice was loud enough for even Kate to hear.

"I'm, uh, excuse me?"

"You heard me, mister. You are so going to make it up to me. Nobody stands me up—I don't care if it was the—the Queen calling! You are taking me out tonight to the most expensive place in this town. You are going to be on time. And you are going to bring me a gift—expensive chocolates or something. Flowers make me sneeze. Is that understood?"

Zach laughed out loud, not even bothering to cover the phone. "My, you are a bit of a live-wire, aren't you?"

"I'm just a woman who does not like to be stood up. Now, are you going to put on your big boy britches and take me out?"

"Yes ma'am! I am at your command! Shall we say 8:00 p.m.?"

"Nope, 7:30 p.m. I get too hungry if I wait that long."

"As you wish, m'lady, 7:30 p.m. sharp!"

"Good! Don't be late!" And with that, Amy was gone.

Zach stared at his cellphone, smiling. "Well, Zach old man, this should be quite the interesting evening." He stood, went over to the door and checked the alarm.

"I'm locking you in, old girl. Safer that way. I'll be gone for the evening, you know."

Kate approached Zach, some of the fire coming back into her eyes. "You're taking Amy out?"

"That I am, Kate. That I am."

"Why?"

"Well, I'm sure you heard, old girl—she practically insisted." Kate placed a hand on his arm. She felt the muscles tense.

"Look here young man—I don't care what you think of me or what you do to this old body, but that little girl means the world to me. If anything happens to her…"

Zach removed her hand. "Nothing will happen to her. I always protect an asset—and Amy most definitely is," he smiled, "an *asset*." More gently he added, "You're going to have to trust me on this one, Kate." He moved toward his bedroom, then turned back.

"You know what will happen if this goes down wrong. I told you the plan, Kate… I need you to stick to it. If you do that, *no one* will get hurt. If you don't…"

Kate gave a reluctant nod.

"Good girl. I'm going to get ready now. In the meantime…" He gestured toward the table scattered with diaries. "I left you plenty to read."

Kate sighed. She had only read the early ones—just enough to make her worry. She looked at the final volume of diaries; the one Zach had started reading when Amy called. She muttered, "Well, I reckon I may as well skip to the last one; see how this whole story ends." She picked it up and began to read. In fact, she was so absorbed in reading, she didn't even notice when Zach's cellphone rang again. And she didn't notice that he was leaving hours early, locking her in.

Zach entered the coffee shop, feeling extremely out of place amid the backpacks and hip college vibe. Definitely not the place he would have chosen—but then, he didn't get the chance to choose. He spotted a slim figure with long, copper-colored hair and moved toward her out-of-the-way table. He sat down.

"A little overdressed, aren't we?" Lyndsie Bainbridge sat facing him.

Zach studied her. She wore a simple cashmere sweater of royal blue and what looked to be expensive designer jeans. Lyndsie was even more overdressed than he; she just didn't look it. Interesting.

"I'm sure you didn't invite me here to discuss wardrobes, Miss Bainbridge. The question is—what *do* you wish to discuss?"

Lyndsie shifted into her soft, alluring mode. "You like getting right down to business, don't you Mr. Malone? Mmm, I find that rather refreshing."

Zach leaned forward. "Let's be clear, dearie. I know all the tactics in all the games. I know how to play them—and I know when I'm being played. So, let's put our cards on the table, shall we? Now *that* would be refreshing."

Lyndsie laughed out loud. "Well played. Fine. Card number one. You're not Zach Malone, reporter for the *London Star*, doing an exclusive on the restoration of Graystone. You see, I didn't call the number on your business card. I looked up the actual number of the paper, and guess what—they've never heard of you."

Zach leaned back, his brow darkening. "I see. Well, if I'm not Zach Malone of the *London Star*, who am I?"

"That's what you're going to tell me."

"Am I now? And why should I do that?"

"Because if you don't, I blow your little cover, get you kicked off the estate, and perhaps even…deported? I'm not sure a man such as you would like to get the police involved."

A little smile crept onto Zach's face. "And I'm not sure a woman like you wants the board of the foundation to find out about a certain diary that—"

"Stop it." Lyndsie looked around. "Keep your voice down!" She regained her composure. "Now what's this about a diary?"

"Lyndsie, please. I thought we agreed—no games." He leaned in close, so close she could feel the warmth of his breath on her ear. "'The Hyde Papers.'" He leaned back. "Did I keep my voice low enough to suit you that time?"

"How do you know about the—?"

"Tsk, tsk." Zach put a finger to his lips. "Our Master Graymoor wasn't the only one who kept a diary. Absalom Bane kept one as well."

Lyndsie turned pale. "Absalom kept a diary? So, what was in this…?"

"Everything."

Lyndsie looked hard at Zach. He certainly made an attractive package. He was a player alright. So was she. That's why she knew he could very well be bluffing. "And how do I know you're not just conning me, Mr. Malone? How do I know they even exist?"

Zach reached into his breast pocket and pulled out a paper. On it was handwriting that was unmistakably Nathan Bane's. Lyndsie read aloud, "'I am full of sorrow. A fortnight ago, I buried my father, Absalom, and today, we bury his diaries. What secrets they hold, I don't know. I could not bear to read them.'"

Zach grabbed the letter back. "Poor Nathan could not resist writing about them to his own sweetheart. Old Absalom must have trusted his boy quite a bit to have shared this confession with him."

Soft Lyndsie was gone. Survival Lyndsie took over. "What do you want, Malone?"

"I want what only a foundation can give. Money."

"You know I can't—"

"Oh, yes you can. I have a nice little shell charity set up—sick children and all that. All I need is a generous donation from the foundation each year—for the rest of my life."

Lyndsie stood. "No deal. No way. Ever."

"*Sit down!*" Zach opened his coat slightly to show the gun underneath. Lyndsie sat. "Look, we both know we're dealing with a house of cards—and a wrong move by either one of us could bring it down. Here is my final offer: partners."

"Partners? With you?"

Now it was Zach's turn to charm. "Of course, darling. Whatever you funnel in to my charity will be split into two separate accounts in the Caymans. I know how to work this—with or without you—but I think it would be a lot more fun with you."

Lyndsie leaned back. "I've built a name for myself, you know."

"And it benefits us both if you keep it—and if your good name is threatened, we will find a way to remove the threat." Zach reached into his pocket again, pulled out a small book, then handed it to her. "To prove my good faith, here's your insurance policy." Lyndsie opened the book. Inside was a passport with Lyndsie's picture, but a different name. Along with it was a driver's license, birth certificate, and $10,000 in traveler's checks.

Lyndsie looked at Zach.

"Your escape route, love. Just in case."

Lyndsie studied him carefully, smiled, and then tucked the book into her bag. "You have a deal, Mr. Malone. Just one more thing. Where are Absalom's diaries?"

"Safe and sound with Katherine Bane."

"What?" Lyndsie lowered her voice. "Are you crazy?"

"Relax. I've got the old girl locked up at my place—and as

a topper, I have her convinced that I'm one of the good guys, working for Interpol."

Lyndsie studied him for a moment to see if she could detect a lie. She couldn't. She relaxed and leaned back. "You know, Mr. Malone, I'm beginning to find you rather sexy. Would you like to kiss me?"

He smiled. "What do you think?" Zach stood. "But I'm afraid it'll have to wait, love. Right now, I'm taking Amy out for an evening of wining and dining. I figured you'd like to have her out of the picture for a bit?"

"Excellent." Lyndsie stood and leaned in close. "But I'll hold you to the kiss."

Diary of Absalom Bane

—November 15, 1934

There is no refuge for the wicked. There is no hope for those who rebel against the Almighty. Am I the wicked—or am I the hand of the Almighty's vengeance? I am no longer sure. There is blood on my hands. But all that I did, I did to earn the favor of the Most High, Most Righteous Judge. If I have pursued a path of my own folly, may He who is the Judge have mercy on my soul.

I set the events to pen and paper so my Rebecca would know the truth. I alone planned the deceit that would do good for so many. I, and I alone, set in motion those events that would insure the truth would never be learned and that the good deeds that have been done would never suffer the threat of undoing.

Katherine Bane set down the book she had begun to read just an hour before. It broke her heart to think of how it would hurt her Nathanial to know that his family name was...

Kate stood. She was wrong. Dead wrong. Her Nathanial would never want to cover up the truth just because it hurt. Her husband was just not that type. And he was never the type to take more pride in his family than he should. It was her—it was all her. She was fighting for something her husband would never have fought for. Was it her own pride? Or was it a way of...? Yep, that was it. She wasn't trying to protect Nathanial's memory; she was trying to hold on to it. As long as she felt she could do something for him, then maybe he wasn't so far away. Maybe he wasn't so...dead.

Kate felt like an old fool. But even as she felt the shame, she felt the forgiveness. He understood. She knew her Nathanial was in the company of the angels and that he forgave her. May God forgive her, too.

Kate reopened the book, this time at a different place. Her expression became intent. Her eyes widened as she read. A secret room? In Graystone? There was another secret, too, buried in this book; a secret only hinted at. She had to keep reading.

Amy looked at herself in the mirror. She had been fretting for the past hour over what she should wear. She wanted to look good, but not too good. She didn't want to send the wrong signals. Or did she? "Oh... Fribbit!" Amy had the habit of making up words when she couldn't find the right one. It was a habit that had brought smiles to everyone all her life. Well, everyone but her English teachers. Now, she just wished she could find the right outfit. She hoped she wasn't making a big mistake by insisting on a dinner date with Zach. She was usually pretty confident with men—but for some reason this one kind of rattled her. It was probably the accent. She always had a weakness for a British accent.

Amy finally settled on the emerald green with sparkles. Red was too racy—and the last thing she wanted was for this Zach to think "racy." She paused. What *did* she want Zach to think? Why was she doing this anyway? She knew there was something about him that just didn't fit. *Woogie. Is he a bad guy masquerading as a good guy? Or is he a good guy masquerading as a bad guy masquerading as a good guy? Confusing. Anyway, underneath all that charm and the cute little accent, he knows more than he's saying. Yup—that must be it.* Then Amy remembered the not-happy look on Cliff's face when she said she was going out with Zach. She smiled. *Okay, so maybe there's another reason I'm doing this.* She was startled out of her thoughts by the sound of the doorbell. She grabbed her purse and headed for the door. Her hand was reaching for the doorknob when she noticed a folded scrap of paper on the floor. She picked it up—it was Kate's handwriting. Before she could unfold it, the door swung open. It was Zach.

"Ready, love?"

Amy quickly stuffed the paper into her handbag. Right now, she had a bigger mystery on her hands—by the name of Zach Malone. With a deep breath, she took his arm and closed the door behind her.

Cliff looked out the window. He had alternated between pacing and looking out the window. He knew he should be going over the random pages of "The Hyde Papers." He knew that. He knew he should be trying to sort through the bits and pieces of Graymoor history to see if his vague suspicions would take shape. He knew that. But all he could do was pace, look out the window, and wonder where Zach was taking Amy.

Amy! From peskiness and pigtails to—to delightful adorabiliciousness. *Adorabiliciousness? Was that even a word? Amy must be rubbing off on me.* Well, she had…something. Why did he let her go out with that guy? Didn't Dex warn him about Zach? Cliff began pacing again. That didn't make any sense. Dex was the one who told Cliff to give this "Zach" access to everything. Dex never did things like that. He guarded the Graymoor Foundation more closely than his own business. So, what was the deal? Why would Dex recommend Zach, then point him out as the one who tried to kill him? Cliff looked out the window again. Maybe he got it all wrong. All Dex said was the letters "Z–A." Cliff's imagination did all the rest. But even if he was saying "Z-A-C-H," maybe it wasn't to accuse him.

Maybe it was something else. Maybe, just maybe…

Cliff sat back down and went over the events of the past couple of days: Zach's running interference that first day when Lyndsie tried to send artifacts away; his retrieval of the Hyde book from Lyndsie's possession. Was Zach trying to undermine the Graymoor Foundation—or just Lyndsie Bainbridge? What was really going on?

Zach was definitely not a reporter. Cliff was convinced of that. So, what was he?

CHAPTER 17

Zach stepped out of the limo he had rented. He was ready for this. He was always ready for anything. He had a bit of a flutter in the stomach, but he didn't know *why*. When Amy opened the door, he knew. Never had he felt such an urge to scoop someone up in his arms. Even the sultry Lyndsie didn't do this to him. Zach tried to take control of his thoughts. *Watch yourself, old boy. Too much at stake right now.*

Amy looked like "the boy next door's" dream. Soft brown hair scooped up to reveal a slender neck. A simple string of pearls hung around that neck, their soft sheen warmed by her ivory skin.

But what almost undid Zach was the dress—a flow of silk in bright emerald that made her eyes unbelievably green. Danielle had loved that verdant shade. Danielle was gone, but a living, breathing Amy stood before him—and tonight she was all his. He checked himself again.

Careful, now—you're beginning to sound like a romance novel.

"I say, lovely—you look absolutely stunning. Like a princess." Zach held out his arm, "Shall we?"

Amy took his arm, letting herself be guided by him. *He sure cleans up nice.* She was going to have to watch herself. Suddenly she stopped.

"Whoa! What's this?"

Zach chuckled. "It's a limo, my love. 'Our ride' you might say."

Amy looked at him inquisitively. "You didn't drive? Is it the whole 'left side–right side of the road' thing?"

Zach stifled an outright laugh. "No, dearie. I was simply trying to impress you. I rather failed, I must say."

"No—I am impressed. I think. No, I guess I really am." Amy hesitated. "It's just, the last time I rode in a limo was at my husband's, you know, funeral."

Zach felt a pang of sympathy. *This adorable woman, widowed so young...* He pushed the thought away, replacing it with, *Keep it together, man. Focus.* "If you'd rather not..."

"I'm fine. Really." She took a breath. "So—let's take this thing out for a spin."

The chauffeur opened the door, and Amy got in. Zach followed, sitting close beside her. *Ho boy,* she thought, *what have I gotten myself into?*

Lyndsie never made it back to the office that day. She had too much to think about. She fingered the book that held her new identity. A "just in case" identity. Zach intrigued her. Here was a healthy, handsome male—and she couldn't play him. He knew too much. That made her uncomfortable. But with his greed—his slick, cool greed—she was more than comfortable. She knew what it was like to want—and the length to which someone would go to satisfy that want. That was the key. Feed his desires so she could get her own.

Still, it was risky. Maybe too risky. He had something on her, but she had nothing on him. That had to change. Then there was Amy. Lyndsie was always, always the brightest light in the room; yet with both Cliff and Zach, Amy was attracting all the attention. Lyndsie could usually crush the competition, but it wasn't happening here. She needed to control these men. She needed them to be fixated on her. That was the only way she could make her plan work, but as long as Amy was in the mix… She needed to try another tactic.

An idea stirred. This Amy needed to be taught a lesson.

Soft music played, chandeliers sparkled, and a wine bucket sat beside them. Amy glanced over, catching her reflection—and suddenly she realized that she was laughing. She had been laughing, talking, joking, and eating just as if this were a typical evening out. How did that happen? She slipped into it as if it were the most natural thing in the world. *This was not part of the plan.* It was Zach—charming, boyish Zach—who was messing it up. Of course. From the moment Zach entered the limo, the conversation had been light and breezy, and he had been the perfect gentleman. Everything about him was set to put her at ease. Now, sitting across from him, she realized how much she'd let down her guard.

She was telling him stories about her childhood, even some of her girlhood dreams. She stopped. Abruptly.

Zach looked at her quizzically. "What's wrong, love?"

"Nothing…" *Oh, rats. May as well be honest.* "Okay, there is something wrong."

Zach leaned over, taking her hand. "Tell me, darling, and I'll try to make it better."

"Okay, here's the thing. I've been laughing and talking like a giggly little girl—"

"I like giggly little girls."

"Stop it! That's what I mean. I've told you all about me—and

I still know nothing about you. That why I went out with you. So I could find out about you."

Zach leaned back. Amy couldn't quite read the look on his face. For the first time that night, she began to feel uneasy.

Zach took his time responding. "So. You're here because you want to know more about me. You're a straightforward little thing, I'll give you that." He stood and held out his hand. "Care to find out if I can dance?"

Reluctantly, Amy rose from her chair and let herself be led into a softly lit ballroom where a live band played. With a firm hand in the small of her back, Zach expertly guided her onto the dance floor. He drew her close. Very close. Amy pushed herself back a bit. Still, Zach was close enough to whisper in her ear.

"What do you want to know about me, Amy Newgate?"

Amy couldn't see his face; she could only hear his voice, feel his breath. She pushed back even more. "I want to know who you are, Mr. Zach Malone." She amped up her courage. "All that stuff about being a reporter is a bunch of hooey. Why are you here, anyway?"

"I'm here because of you, Amy." He pulled her closer again.

She pushed away again.

"Hooey. That's not what I meant, and you know it." It was easier to be bold while she was dancing. *Hmm, I'm a daring dame when dancing…pretty cool.* "You know, I was going to try to beguile you…"

"Beguile me?"

"So I could trick you into telling me stuff. Guess I'm no good at the 'tricky.'"

Zach took her into a spin. "Well, you've done a good job of beguiling."

Amy pushed far enough away to see his face. "Stop it; just

stop it! You've been all kinds of charming to me—too charming. You talk and talk—and you've told me absolutely nothing about yourself. Nada. Zip."

They stopped in the middle of the dance floor, faced one another, and for a moment, Amy wasn't sure which way it was going to go. Zach's face was like a mask. Then the mask began to break. He took his hand, tilted her face up to his.

"There's a lot I can't tell you, Amy, for a lot of reasons. But I will tell you this—you can trust me. You can trust me with your life."

Without a word, they exited the ballroom and returned to the table. A little bit of the chattiness and warmth returned to the conversation, but there was a wariness now. The restaurant was beginning to thin out. Zach motioned for the bill, and they returned to the limo. They hadn't gone but perhaps a half mile, when Zach leaned up to the driver and murmured something. At the next light, the limo took a turn to the right—away from Amy's house, and toward the outskirts of town.

Zach continued to chat in a calm, friendly way—but Amy noticed the shift in direction. She tried not to show it, but for the first time, she began to feel fear. She looked out the window, and noticed fewer and fewer houses along the way. What Amy failed to notice were the headlights that had followed them ever since they left the restaurant.

Skerryvore Cottage, Bournemouth

—September 1885

Anna Graymoor sat by the bedside of the feverish man,

listening to nightmarish mutterings fall from his lips. He looked at her with eyes that seemed to see beyond her.

"Fanny..."

Anna placed a cold cloth on his head. "No... It is I, Anna Graymoor. Your wife is resting. She is distraught with worry for you, and the doctor has sent her to bed. The nurse will—"

"Anna? Anna Graymoor?"

"Yes. Now, you must be quiet and—"

The man grabbed her arm. "Then you know...you know that one is evil! One of them is evil!" With that, the man fell back into his feverish dream.

A chill crept over Anna as she stared down at the fitfully sleeping man. She had been back in Bournemouth for six months, sent there for her health. She had been sent by her doctor and her worried husband after giving birth to twins—twins that had drained her body, and even now were draining her soul. They had both been beautiful babes. One was sweetness itself in disposition, but the other... The other frightened her. He was the opposite of his brother in every way. She had noted that where Peter favored right, Simon favored left, and where Peter was calm and happy, Simon was fitful and difficult. But Anna's fear—her great fear—was Simon's heart. Where Peter had his heart, Simon did not. Was her infant son born twisted on the inside as well?

Newfound companions in her long, lonely recovery in Bournemouth were the Stevensons, Robert and Fanny. Robert was a writer, and his sensitive nature kept his health at a low ebb. She had shared many a long walk and talk with them both; so it was natural that she should confide in them. As she spoke of her infant sons, and the truly opposite way they were born, a glint sparked in Robert's eyes. He began to question her closely about them, fascinated by the idea of mirror image twins. Anna thought no more of it until she talked to Fanny the next day.

"Robert is writing like a man possessed." Fanny was an American, and could be very frank when among friends. "He had a dream last night. More like a nightmare—so vivid a one that he remembers every bit. In fact, this dream has taken over his imagination; he can think of nothing else."

Fanny and Anna stood looking at the sea. It was gray, its large breakers dashing themselves against rocks. Soon it would storm. Fanny looked Anna square in the face. "You did this, you know."

Anna was shocked. "I? How did I—?"

"The story of your twins. It has obsessed Robbie—so much so, that it's possessed him, and now is driving him to write. I pray that by putting pen to paper, it will leave his mind and live in print instead."

"I am so sorry to have—"

"I didn't say this to accuse you, my sweet friend. I only say this to explain his strange behavior, should you see him again." A look of worry crept into Fanny's face. "His health is not good. His temperament is far too delicate and changeable to…" Fanny stopped. "I have no one else to talk to, Anna. No one else who would understand."

The women exchanged knowing looks. Each fathomed the depths of the other's fears. Neither knew if the future held hope—or heartbreak.

In only two weeks, the book was written. Two weeks of manic intensity in which Robert Louis Stevenson scribed the book soon known as "The Strange Case of Dr. Jekyll and Mr. Hyde." Only the writer, his wife, and Anna, knew of the hidden meaning of this dreadful vision.

Now, with the fires of inspiration gone, Robert lay in a fever, spent by his efforts. He would recover, publish his book, and be done with it. What was but a creative burst for the writer was a constant shadow hanging over Anna Graymoor. It was simply a book for Robert Louis Stevenson. For Anna, it was her life. She feared the fiction of the writer would become the reality of her only sons. She feared she had given birth to Jekyll and Hyde.

Katherine Bane was restless. Here she was, locked in a room, while this Zach was out with a girl who had become like a daughter to her. She had warned Zach not to mess with Amy—not that Amy would put up with something like that. The problem was that Zach was so doggone charming. He could charm the whiskers off a cat.

Kate had always had in mind that Cliff and Amy should get together. She knew the attraction was there, but Cliff was too skittish to make a move. It made her want to give him a swift kick in the butt.

With a sigh, Kate went back to the diaries. She flipped through until she found the place where she'd left off. At the top of the page was written: "The Hyde Papers."

CHAPTER 18

Amy looked out of the window of the limousine, a waning moon the only light on the lonely road. Finally, she saw something she recognized: the sign that said, "Granville Sawmill—1 Mile." She quietly reached into her bag, pulled out her cellphone, and while pretending to look out the window, she texted.

"Amy."

Amy started. She quickly grabbed her compact instead of her cellphone. Did she send the text or not? Amy was so rattled, she wasn't sure.

"What are you doing, love?"

Amy held up the compact. "Just going to powder my nose."

"You look perfect, my dear." Zach gently, but firmly, pulled the bag away from Amy, setting it out of reach.

The limo pulled onto the dirt road that led to a collection of old, historic-looking buildings. It stopped behind the largest one and turned off its lights. The Granville Sawmill was a kind of tourist attraction, but it was closed for the season. In the moonlight, it looked ghostly. Amy's stomach twisted up. She was starting to panic.

"I thought you were taking me home. This is not my home." Why did she say that? It was a pretty silly-sounding thing to say, but Amy couldn't think of any other words.

"Tired of my company already, dearie?" The words were light, but Zach was not looking at Amy as he said them. Instead he was looking through the rear window of the limo.

"What are you—"

"Shh!"

"What do you mean, *shh*?"

Zach touched his finger to her lips. He leaned down to her ear, his voice low. "We've got a tail." Then, seeing the confusion in her eyes he explained, "We're being followed. They've been with us ever since the restaurant."

Amy removed his finger, keeping her voice to a whisper. "Why?"

"That's what we're here to find out."

"But—but can't you just take me home and…?"

Zach leaned in even closer. "Look, love, we don't know if they're following you—or if they're following me. If I left you alone at Kate's…"

Amy shivered. "Okay. I get it, but why don't we call for—"

"Hush!"

In the silence, they both heard the crack of twigs. Someone was approaching—someone they couldn't see.

"Come with me." Zach almost noiselessly opened the limo door, pulling Amy after him. He gently closed the door, gave a signal to the driver, who turned on his lights and took off.

"What are you—?"

Zach immediately put a hand over Amy's mouth. "Decoy. Let's see if they follow it."

Zach pulled her deeper into the shadows as they watched the tail lights recede. No lights followed. The decoy didn't work. Zach took Amy's hand, drawing her into the shadow of the building. He felt his way along until he found a door. He tried it. Locked!

"How do we get in?" he whispered.

This time, Amy took his hand and motioned for him to follow. She led him to a platform, then, scurrying up on top, felt her away along it until she found a trap door. She opened it, motioning to him. They slipped into the darkness, silently closing the lid on top of them. A few moments later, they heard footsteps creaking above them, then stopped, then step by step began to fade away. In a few more moments Zach spoke. "I don't like this. We're sitting ducks here. We need to find a good vantage point. Amy opened the lid again and motioned for him to follow. A few feet into the woods, they came to a thick oak tree with spreading branches. Nailed into the trunk of the tree were some crude wooden steps. Amy removed her shoes and began climbing, followed by Zach. A fierce whisper drifted down to him.

"Don't you dare look up my dress!"

All she heard in return was another "Shh." She couldn't see the grin on Zach's face.

They finally reached a platform about fifteen feet off the ground. It was a hunting blind. From up there, they could see everything. A shadow was moving back around the building. The figure was dressed in black—even the face didn't show. Zach looked over at Amy. Her face showed both fright and determination. Plucky. That was the look. He looked her over until his eyes drifted toward her feet.

"Where are your shoes?"

"I guess I kicked them off at the bottom of the tree."

"Oh, Amy—you didn't! You may as well have left a trail of breadcrumbs showing where we are. If they see them, they'll—"

Suddenly, something whizzed by Amy's ear.

"Stay down!" Zach pushed her to the platform floor, reached

into his jacket, and pulled out a gun. He shot toward where he thought the figure was. Another bullet whizzed by.

Amy lifted her head and saw Zach's gun. "Who are you?"

"Shh!"

Just as Zach was about to fire off another shot, headlights turned into the drive of the sawmill. The dark figure was seen running, and as the new car shut off its lights, the dark figure's car turned on its own, squealed out of the drive, and then was gone.

A familiar voice called out, "Amy? *Amy?*"

"Cliff, up here! Wait—I'm coming down!"

Before Zach could react, she was climbing down the ladder, heading toward the voice. He tucked his gun away and quickly followed her.

She came within a foot of Cliff before she stopped. Zach thought she was going to throw herself into Cliff's arms. He could tell that Amy thought she was going to throw herself at Cliff, too. He waited, hoping the moment would pass—that his rival would remain the clueless male who couldn't see an opportunity right in front of him. It passed. The clueless male won out. Cliff was the first to speak.

"What are you doing out here?" Before Amy could answer, he turned to Zach. "What were you thinking, bringing Amy out to a place like this?" He held up his hand before Zach could answer. "Wait—I don't want to know." He hesitated, then anger took over. "No. I do want to know. I don't know how guys act in the UK, but here, you don't kidnap a girl on a first date, just so you can…" Helplessly, Cliff turned back to Amy. "And what were *you* thinking?"

She tried to speak. "Cliff, it's not like—"

"And who was that I saw pull away?"

"We don't—"

"And did I hear gunshots? Was somebody shooting at you? Amy, what were you—"

"*Would you just listen?*" Amy's voice came out louder than she intended. "It's not what you think. None of it is what you think! Zach was just…" Amy looked around. "Where's Zach?"

"Right here." The voice came from behind Cliff, making him jump.

"Don't do that! Where were you anyway?"

"Just checking to see if our visitor left any little calling cards behind."

"Huh?"

"Clues. Left any clues. They didn't."

"Would someone like to start from the top and tell me what's going on?"

Zach looked at Amy and gave her a nod. She sighed and nodded back. For some reason, that irritated Cliff. What business did this Zach have giving understanding nods? As his thoughts drifted away, Amy called him back.

"Cliff—Cliff! I thought you wanted to know."

"I do. Let's hear it." There it was again—that knowing look between Zach and Amy.

She took a deep breath and began, "As we were leaving the restaurant, Zach noticed that a car was following us. He told the driver to—"

"Driver? What driver?"

"We were in a limo. So, the driver—"

"A limo!"

"Yes. Now pay attention. Just to make sure, he had the driver head out into the country…" That's why you did it, right?" Zach nodded, and Amy continued. "So anyway, he had the driver pull in here. We slipped out, and Zach sent the driver away, thinking this person would follow the limo. They didn't."

"You sent the limo away?"

"Yes! Now stop interrupting. Then, this person started kind of sneaking around, hunting for us—"

"Hunting?" A look from Amy stopped Cliff.

"We finally ended up in the old tree blind we used to play on—but dummy me left my shoes at the bottom of the tree. That's when they began shooting at us, and Zach shot back. Then you showed up, and whoosh—they skedaddled. That's about it, I think."

Cliff shook his head. "How in the world do you get yourself into these things, Amy? Well, at least you had the sense to text me."

It was Zach's turn to be surprised. "You texted Cliff? When?"

"When you told the driver to head to the sawmill. I was scared."

Zach laughed, and the cloud of fear melted away.

"Well, aren't you a clever girl, pulling one over on me like that? But," Zach lifted Amy's face with his finger, "you've got to learn to trust me."

Cliff felt a flush of anger creeping up his face, making him glad for the darkness. He wasn't used to this. He should be defending Amy's honor or staking his claim with her; instead, he simply said, "Come on, Amy, I'm taking you home."

With a searching look back at Zach, Amy began to follow Cliff to his car. She stopped and turned to Zach. "Do you need a ride or...?"

"Don't worry, love, I'll call the driver. We'll talk later."

With that, Amy and Cliff disappeared into the darkness. As he heard their car pull away, Zach pulled out his cellphone. "James? Five minutes."

Zach pulled a penlight out of his pocket and began to search the grounds, covering all the area around where they had walked.

He looked carefully at the tire tracks, nodding thoughtfully. He then made his way to the backside of the mill, searching as he went. No luck. He then moved toward the tree blind. That's when he spotted it: a small shiny object nestled in the leaves at the foot of the tree. He smiled. "Gotcha."

The limo pulled up and Zach trotted over to it. The driver was out, opening the door to the passenger's side. "Home, sir?"

"No, James. We have a little visit to pay. Be sure to keep your weapon handy."

"Yes, sir."

Zach took his place, and with that, the limo took off into the darkness.

Cliff and Amy rode in silence. Amy was fuming because he yelled at her instead of—snatching her up into his arms? Maybe. All she knew was that she was fuming, and she didn't want to deal with "why."

Cliff was fuming, too. He had such a confusing brew of emotions churning inside of him. He didn't even know what he was feeling. He hated the thought of Amy being in danger. He hated the thought of Amy with Zach. He hated himself for not saying so.

The silence was filled with unuttered thoughts all tumbling on top of each other. Why did he find it so hard to figure out how he felt about, well, about this woman? As soon as he asked himself the question, he knew. The face of Andrea flashed through his mind. The engagement, the ring, the stolen research... But Amy wasn't Andrea. Amy was...

Cliff and Amy began speaking at the same time.

"I'm sorry I—"

"I didn't mean to—"

They laughed. The tension was broken.

Amy spoke. "You first."

"Amy, I'm sorry I—well, that I—I mean, I was so worried I..." Cliff faltered.

"S'okay." She paused. "I was so glad to see you that I almost... I'm glad you came."

"Yeah, me too."

Silence again—each lost in their own thoughts.

Amy broke the silence once more. "I wonder who it was?"

"Huh?"

"The sneaky person. I mean why would anybody shoot at...?" Amy gave a little shiver.

Gently, Cliff ventured, "You know, you can spend the night at my house again."

Amy looked at him. Cliff began to fumble for words.

"You know—for safety, not for... I mean, I could keep you safer than... It's just that staying with me might be..." Amy began to giggle. Cliff blushed in the darkness. "Oh—just forget it."

Amy said softly, "No. I won't forget it—ever. Thank you." She took a deep breath. "But you better take me home."

Silence filled the car again as Cliff pulled up to Kate's house. "Are you sure you're going to be alright?"

"I'm sure."

"Okay. But call me if anything—I mean anything—is, you know, 'woogie.' Promise?"

"I promise."

One moment, pregnant with possibilities, hung in the

air—then Amy was out of the car and gone. Cliff put his head down on the wheel. "Stupid…"

Lyndsie Bainbridge was steadying her nerves with a stiff drink. Her coppery hair was loose and messy, fitting for her simple black turtleneck and jeans. But the world behind Lyndsie's eyes was anything but simple. The mixture of fear and daring was a heady concoction—even more heady than the scotch she held in her hand. She dashed it back and laughed to herself. Her plan, though improvised, was working beautifully. She was very happy with herself. Still, she jumped when she heard the knock on her door. Smoothing her hair, she went to the door.

She opened it.

"We need to have a little talk, love." Zach pushed his way into her living room.

This was not part of the plan—but Lyndsie would make it work. "So, Mr. Malone—how was your date?" Her voice was light, casual.

Zach turned on her with an unexpected anger. "How was my date, you say. *How was my date?*" He walked up to her, a cold fury in his eyes. "Sit down."

"How dare you—"

"I said sit down!" He grabbed her shoulders and pushed her down on the couch. Lyndsie didn't try to rise, and a not-so-ex-hilarating fear began to rise from her gut. She didn't dare to speak. "You fool! What were you thinking?"

Hesitantly, "I don't know what you're—"

"Oh, shut up—don't even try to game me. I know it was you." Zach held up a small, silver piece of jewelry.

Lyndsie's hand went to her ear.

"Look familiar, love?"

"I was just…"

"You were just…" His voice was mocking. "Don't try handing me a load of rubbish; I'm not some naive little professor lap-dog who'll swallow anything you feed him."

Lyndsie was getting her confidence back. She stood. "Don't tell me you're jealous, Zach—"

"Jealous? Of Cliff? He's a piece of tissue to you; you'll toss him when you've used him up." Lyndsie turned away. He was right. She'd try another tactic.

"I don't know why you're so angry. I was just trying to scare the little—"

"Scare her? *Scare her?* You could've killed her!"

"And why should you care? What is this dull, interfering little small-town piece of—"

Zach laughed. Loudly. "Crikey Moses! You're the one who's jealous! The Director of the Graymoor Foundation is schoolgirl jealous!"

The barb hit home. "I am not!"

"Oh, yes you are." Zach laughed again. "You're just used to being the center of attention—and now this lovely, fresh-faced slip of a girl comes along and outshines the beautiful Lyndsie Bainbridge, seemingly capturing the affections of Zach Malone—and everybody else. Oh, I'm not saying you're jealous just because I took her out—and had a lovely time of it, too…"

Lyndsie turned away from Zach. Her face was flushing hot.

Zach came up behind her.

"Or is it? Is *that* it? Is it because I took her…?"

The slap stung Zach's face. He grabbed Lyndsie by the shoulder and pushed her up against the wall, pinning her arms to her side. He then violently kissed her, pressing closely against her. She struggled, then she responded with equal violence, equal passion. Zach abruptly pushed her away. Lyndsie's eyes were glazed, her breathing heavy. Zach headed for the door. He turned and spoke.

"Just remember that the next time you want to pull another stupid stunt." Zach walked away from the building, then stopped to wipe his mouth with his sleeve.

Sometimes he hated himself—and what he had to do.

Stables, Graystone Manor

—May 1910

The lantern swung slowly in the dark as it followed the sound—the only sound breaking the stillness of a soft summer night. It was a sob—a muffled sob. Light footsteps followed a worn path to the horse barn. The musty smell of horse, hay, and oiled leather became stronger as the light approached. Inside the barn was a shadowed figure of a man, his back to a stall door. His head was down, and he was sobbing. Beside him was a bottle of rum. So intent was he on his sorrow, that he didn't notice the slight, feminine figure silhouetted in the doorframe. The figure holding the lantern approached. It spoke.

"Simon?"

His head remained down. The voice spoke again, whispering another name.

The man lifted his head, a frightened look in his eyes. "Who are you? Are you a ghost?"

"No—it is Mary… Mary Bane. Keep your voice low. Father doesn't know that I am here."

"Mary! Why are you…?" The man hesitated. "You called me by a name other than my own—why?"

Mary came to the hunched-over figure and, placing the lantern between them, sat beside him.

The young woman spoke again, gently, "I know what happened. I know."

Simon Graymoor looked up, suspicion and fear filling his eyes. "What do you mean by this? I am Peter Gray—"

"Hush!" Her voice was firmer. "No more lies. I know who sits before me."

"How…?"

"Small things at first. The strength in your opposite arm. The fall of your hair. The way Peter Graymoor's favorite horse shies away from you in fear. You have worked very hard to earn its trust."

Panic filled Simon's eyes. "Then others must know—"

"No, no, you mustn't fear that. The real reason I know is… I've stolen into my father's room and read his diaries."

The secret was out. The lies, the planning, the careful remaking of himself into his brother, Peter, was for naught.

Now, this woman he cared for, this pure heart that he knew he did not deserve, had uncovered his most wicked deed. "So. You know all." He hung his head. "You must hate me, Mary Bane."

Mary placed her hand on top of his. "I wouldn't be here if I hated you."

Simon raised his head. "Then why are…?"

Mary drew closer. "Must I say it? Very well, I will—even though I may never hear these words in return. I love you; I have loved you from the first day we met."

"How can you? I'm a wretch who let his own brother die. I am broken, Mary; I am beyond repair. Beyond love."

"No—not beyond. My father thinks that sins can only be wiped away by doing good. I know they can only be wiped away by love."

"Can your love, however sweet, do this impossible thing?" He lifted his sad eyes to hers.

"No, my darling, but I will help you find that love—if you will let me." Her voice faltered. "I cannot help but love you. My heart is yours, and no other will ever own it. If you cannot love me in return, I will under—"

He reached over, extinguished the lantern, and drew her into his arms. The only sound heard was a soft whisper. "I love you, Mary Bane."

Cliff's car pulled up to his cottage. He turned off the engine and simply sat. A jungle of unpredictable, almost outlandish events tangled up his mind, choking off his ability to think—and he was too tired to try to hack his way through. He thought back to the board meeting where Lyndsie pushed to have control of the restoration of Graystone. Maybe he should have let her have it.

"No!" The word flew out without thinking. It was almost like a voice from outside himself had pushed its way into his mind and out of his mouth. There was something at stake here—something bigger than Graystone itself, even though he didn't know what it was.

Let it go, another voice began to whisper. A reasonable voice. It reminded him of the risks he was taking—risks not just for himself but involving Kate and Amy. It whispered that he wasn't wired to be a risk taker. Let others deal with this mystery. He didn't sign up for this. Besides, it was getting in the way of what might happen with Lyndsie...

Lyndsie? Where did that thought come from? The picture of her red-gold hair, her flawless skin, and all her other "attributes" began to fill his brain, taking him down a road he rarely went down.

No! Lyndsie's face began to morph into the face of his former fiancée, Andrea, driving away with his research, laughing at him as she went... Then the vision of both faces morphed into something dark and...

"Stop it!" This time, the voice was Cliff's.

What the heck is going on? the reasonable voice began whispering again. It wasn't Lyndsie this time. It was Amy. He was putting her at risk, and if he'd just let go of it, then she would too, and...

That was where the reasonable voice made its mistake. Amy would never let go of this "mystery" until she got to the bottom of it. He said aloud, "Just stop it! Stop!"

Cliff felt like he was standing in the middle of a battle field with a war raging around him. Darkness or Light... Good or Evil... Truth or... or the easy way out. He somehow knew he was at one of those crossroads people talk about. The making of a choice from which there'd be no turning back—a choice that would determine the rest of his life. Cliff groaned and put his head on his steering wheel. Even to avoid choosing a side would be a choice. A bad one. One way would insure safety and a kind of security. The other would mean risk—maybe even danger.

Would he be a man willing to take a chance—or remain just a befuddled professor?

"I don't know what to do. I'm not good at this sort of thing! God help me... Please help me." One of the voices stopped.

Cliff opened his car door and got out. He knew what he was going to do. He was going to be a man.

Amy unlocked the door to Kate's cottage. She was shaken, but for some reason she wasn't afraid right now. Kate's cottage was a place of peace. It was where she would come after Jake died, have a cup of tea and then have a good cry. It was a place where love had lived. Kate and Nate had filled the place with laughter, common sense, and a simple but resolute faith.

If it wasn't for Kate...

Amy went to the kitchen to make herself a cup of tea. She picked one of Kate's tastier blends and waited for the water to boil. While the kettle heated, Amy mulled over the events of the evening. Zach was easy, so easy, to talk to. He seemed to have a way of prying her open. Very few people could do that. He was good looking, too, with that slight daredevil air that was almost magnetic. Amy shook off that thought. No matter how attractive he might be, no matter how easily he could get under her skin, she sensed a big "*no*" echoing through her brain. She recognized that voice—and she usually listened. And she usually got in trouble when she didn't.

The kettle was whistling away. Amy poured the water over Kate's handmade tea bag, and took her cup and the honey bear over to the kitchen table. Yup, Zach was appealing—and he was sure letting her know that he found her equally appealing. Not like Cliff, who...

Cliff. His face filled her thoughts—followed by that little flutter in her stomach. She hadn't felt that since dancing with Jake at her senior prom. All she and Cliff did was tease—and sometimes argue. But there was something about him. He was like a clear glass of water you could see right through. He was who he was—and that's all there was to it. Amy liked that. And as fun as Zach might seem on the surface, a man who had a lot of secrets set off all her alarms.

Amy looked down. She had emptied about half the honey bear into her tea. She sighed and pushed the cup away. She knew how Zach felt—but she didn't know who he was. She knew who Cliff was—but she didn't know how he felt. If this was a joke, she wasn't liking it too much. What was she supposed to do? Kate would know, or at least give her a clue. *If only Kate were…*

Amy suddenly remembered something. The piece of paper in her handbag bearing Kate's handwriting. She unfolded it. On it was only one letter—the letter "Z."

Simon's Secret Room, Graystone Manor

—July 1910

Mary is with child. My child. Shame is mixed with joy, for my love for Mary is great, but I have brought disgrace on this woman whose shoes I am unworthy to even touch. In her tenderness of heart, she yielded to me, and now…

Though I do not hope for it, may God forgive me. Mary has forgiven me. She has told me so. I want to become a man worthy of her love, though I do not hope for that, either. Absalom doesn't know. Dear God, may he never know. The weight of my brother's death already oppresses me; if this soiling of innocence should be added… I don't know if I would run—or if I would try to do more of the un-doable works for God that Absalom requires.

I will wed my Mary—if she will have me. I will give this child my name and my love. I will fight this devil inside me and play the role of a good man so that one day I may become that good man. I will kill Hyde. I must. For the sake of Mary—and the child she carries.

He closed his diary. He had built this room, high and hidden in the recesses of Graystone. This was his confessional. This was where his torment and rage could be wrestled with and overcome. He prayed he could overcome this beast within him. The room was built by foreign workmen, who could not—and would not—gossip to the locals. It was small, but it was comfortable. A high window was opposite where he sat—too high for prying eyes to see in.

A simple desk was illuminated by the window's during the day and by a gas lamp at night. A small water closet, a small bed, a chair, and a bookcase with a row of books were the only other furnishings in the room. But central to the room was the desk—and the manuscript on it: "The Hyde Papers."

He stared at what he had written. He went over to the bookcase and ran his fingers over it, a slight smile playing at the corners of his mouth. Softly, he reflected, "Even if Absalom makes his way here again—I will escape. I've made sure of that…"

His eyes went to a leather-bound book on the shelf. He touched it, his eyes softening. "Mary…" She gave it to him, to remind him of her love and hope for him. "My sweet Mary." He knew that, inside the book, was a slip of paper in her handwriting. It read, "Only love covers a multitude of sins. I hope you will find it here." He closed his eyes. He wanted to believe the words were true... He so wanted to believe! But it was not possible. Or was it? Could the same book Absalom used to condemn him bring him peace?

He very carefully lifted and removed the book from the shelf, turned to its second half, and began to read.

It was late when Zach got back to the house he'd rented. He turned off the alarm and entered, then carefully re-locked the door and re-set the alarm with a fingerprint scan. He sat down. He'd done a lot of things in the course of "his work," but nothing made him feel as dirty as what he'd just done.

And all he did was kiss her. He felt... He felt like he'd kissed mud—or maybe the devil. He went to the kitchen and grabbed a glass and a bottle of scotch. As he poured a couple of fingers of the brown liquid, he heard a voice behind him.

"Would you rather talk about it?"

Zach turned. There was Kate, leaning against the doorjamb.

Zach took a sip. "No. Why aren't you asleep?"

"Been reading some riveting stuff. Absalom's diaries."

Zach walked to the living room. This is not what he wanted. He wanted to somehow sort out what was going on inside his head. He needed to compartmentalize—that's what you had to do in this kind of job. He sat down.

Kate sat across from him. "Sure you don't want to talk about it?"

"I'm not in the mood, Kate. Go to bed."

"You expect me to just fall right to sleep when I've not only been kidnapped, but you stuck me with reading something that tears down everything my Nathanial ever thought about his family? Thought you were smarter than that."

Zach laughed. He didn't want to admit it, but Kate had struck just the right note with him.

"Well, Katie, love—I must admit that you have a point."

Kate gave him a hard look. "I take it that your date with Amy didn't go that well?"

"Oh, it was a simply smashing time if you like running around an old sawmill getting shot at."

"What?" Kate's jaw dropped. "Alright, mister—you're gonna spill whether you like it or not."

Zach put his drink down. It wouldn't hurt anything if he talked about it a little. "Well, your little Amy and I were having a simply lovely time. Limousine, dinner, dancing—like I said, simply lovely…"

"Go on…"

"Then, as we were heading home, I noticed we were being tailed. By that, I mean—"

"I know what it means. I don't watch 'NCIS' for nothing."

"Well, I noticed our tail, so rather than send Amy home and possibly have someone come after her in the night, I thought I'd lure this character out into the country, try to maybe pull a little trick on them."

"Didn't work?"

"Didn't work. Instead, this character began taking potshots at us. So, I started shooting back. Fortunately, your Cliff showed up to save the day."

Zach was enjoying the wide-eyed looks of surprise flitting across Kate's face.

"Cliff? How in the world…?"

"Amy. Clever girl. She texted 'sawmill' to him when I wasn't looking. When he pulled up, our 'tail' pulled out."

Zach held his glass up in salute to Kate. "So you'll forgive me if I need just a wee bit of fortifying, my dear," and with one gulp, he finished off his scotch.

Kate leaned in. "So, do you have any idea who it was?"

Zach hesitated only a split second. "No."

"Liar."

That hit Zach like a jolt. Was he that easy to read?

Kate gave a little chuckle herself this time. "Don't you go getting all paranoid just 'cause I can read you. I've been around awhile, and know a lie when I see one. Plus, you keep fiddlin' with something in your pocket. You found something, didn't you? A clue. I watch those 'Sherlock Holmes' mysteries, too, you know."

This time, Zach laughed and leaned back. "Sure you don't want my job, Kate? Yes, I did find something—and yes, I know who it was. But I'm not telling you, ducks—and that's that."

Zach stared down at the glass. He was feeling a bit better, and the banter with Kate was lightening his mood. Maybe with another two fingers of Glenfiddich, he could get the memory of what happened with Lyndsie out of his mind. He looked up. Kate was once again staring at him intently.

"Something else happened, didn't it?"

Zack looked at Kate suspiciously now. She couldn't know. She couldn't possibly know. "Of course it didn't. Why would you think—?"

"Liar."

Zach wasn't amused this time. It was hitting too close to emotions he was trying to put to bed. "Don't be such an old fool, woman. You don't know what—"

"Insults." Kate leaned back, studying Zach's face. "Must be pretty bad if it's making you throw insults my way." She closed her eyes for a second. "You did something that…that made you feel shame. A dirty deal, a dirty—something."

Zach stood up. He didn't show it, but he was shaking inside. He'd taken Kate for just a feisty old woman—but she was proving to be formidable. He was used to reading people, but he'd never been read like that before. Not since Danielle. He looked back at Kate.

The smiling blue eyes and rakish grin had vanished from Zach's face. The eyes Kate now saw were calculating, analytical, cold. She felt a tickle of fear, but held her ground. Each held the other's eyes, searching, looking for secrets—or deceptions.

Zach finally broke the silence. "You're quite the piece of work, Katie Bane. Are you sure you are who you say you are?"

"You know I am." Kate paused. "Now you, on the other hand…"

Zach paused, thinking of what he could say next. Would she believe him?

"I am one of the good guys, Kate. You need to believe that."

Kate closed her eyes just for a moment. "I believe it. Otherwise, you wouldn't feel so much like a dirty dog for doing what you did."

Zach nodded; a little bit of the smile came back to his eyes. "I've got to keep a little closer watch on you, my dear. You're a bit too sharp for me." Zach extended his hand. "Time for bed, love. We'll talk in the morning." Zach led Kate to her room. "You know I've got to lock you in, don't you?"

"As long as I got a bathroom," Kate picked up Absalom's diary, "and a book to read, I'm good."

Zach turned on the light to Kate's room, gently pushed her

through the door, and locked her in. For some reason, he felt a little more at peace—and he didn't think it was just the scotch. "Katie Bane, you've handed me a bit to think about, you have," he muttered under his breath. With that, Zach headed to bed.

Lyndsie Bainbridge poured herself another glass of wine. Gone was the exhilaration, the gloating. She'd felt the rush of being in control, of having someone's life in her hands. Now, she felt out of control—undone by a single kiss. It was quite a kiss, but still...

Zach was attractive—very attractive—and he was dangerous.

She knew that now. And she also knew that she could get addicted to that combination. She'd never had a man take control of her like that. She had always been the one who could control a man—either with her brain or her beauty—or both. Now she was the one losing control. Part of her wanted that. Part of her hated it. If Zach took control of her...

Lyndsie took a long drink of wine. She knew it wouldn't clear her head, but at least it would dull the pin pricks of doubt jabbing at her. She had to think. She had to strategize. She had to...

She closed her eyes and gave in to the sensations, to the memory of Zach's mouth on hers. Tomorrow. She would figure it all out tomorrow. Tonight, there was wine—and the pleasure of remembering. Tomorrow she would be the Director of the Graymoor Foundation. Tonight, she was...

Lyndsie got up and dead-bolted the door. She stared into the glass of wine, and with a sudden movement, smashed it against her hearth. The fire spat and sizzled. What was happening? In one night, she had held a gun and, without hesitation, shot it at a woman—and then, in an instant, was unraveled by a man she didn't even know. The wine had weakened her defenses, and the weight of her emotions hit her like a tsunami. She had been such an idealist, such a dreamer. And now… Death in her hands and fire in her body.

She felt like she was going to throw up. Instead, she started to cry.

Lyndsie lay down on her couch and curled into a ball, tears streaming down her face. Who was she? She didn't even know anymore. Tomorrow… She'd figure it all out tomorrow.

CHAPTER 19

Graystone Manor

—February 1921

"I do not agree. It is not wise—and it does not reflect well on your name."

Absalom Bane was pacing, something he rarely did. He had controlled, or "guided," as he preferred to call it, all the charitable works done with the Graymoor wealth since the *possessor* of that wealth had placed himself under the "good Reverend Bane's" care. But this, this was not something to bring honor to the Graymoor name—or to the legacy of Absalom Bane. A mission to women who sold their bodies? An orphanage for the children born of such women? A refuge for young girls at risk of being drawn into the same fate? True, this endeavor may be compassionate—but honorable? This could not be tolerated. Some sins should be left under the cover of darkness.

There was a certain purity in helping the sick, in helping the poor and afflicted, in helping even those in heathen lands. These acts of mercy would stir the passions of any God-fearing soul—and would draw tithes from such souls. Even the recovery of those enslaved by drink or opium would be a more praiseworthy cause. But this cause, this cause stank of sin. To bring this sin up from its murky depths, to expose its foulness to the light—this was beneath the names of Graymoor and Bane.

Absalom did not hesitate to say as much to the man he faced.

The man seated behind the desk stared at the black-dressed, rail-thin figure of a man standing before him. He'd placed the care of his soul and hope of its redemption into the iron grip of this preacher. He felt the intensity of his eyes, the pull of his influence. He broke away from the gaze of the Right Reverend Bane and looked down at a note held in his lap. It was in his dear Mary's handwriting, and it simply said, "Stand firm." More than anything in the world, he did not want to disappoint her. He looked back up at Absalom.

"I have heard all your arguments, Absalom; they are impenetrable, as always. This time, however, I must break from your counsel and follow my own. The mission will be built—and these women will be rescued."

Absalom leaned forward, his dark eyes burning. "This is not God's will. It will fail, and it will be your ruin! Do not defy me in this. Remember, you live in this fine manor by my good graces. Do not despise my guidance, or—"

"Or I will be exposed and disgraced?" Simon stood. "Remember, if you should make my dishonor public, the shame will not be only mine—it will be that of my wife and son also. Your daughter and your grandson." He had never dared to say these words before, but Mary had told him to, and had given him the courage. "Will you risk your good name as well as my own, Absalom?"

There was silence filled only by the slow ticks of the grandfather clock. Absalom had never been defied like this before. He felt his control slipping away, and with it, the dignity of his good name. His good name—was that his desire? To build a good name worthy of the praise of the Almighty? Absalom wavered. What of mercy? What of love? *If I have the tongues of men and angels, but have not love…*

Love. It was to earn that favor, that love of the Most High, that had driven him all these years. He thought of the love he locked outside the door that stormy night when he let his father die. He could not be loved until he atoned for that sin. He would atone for his sin by helping—or making—this man he faced atone for *his*. He had one more card to play.

"This—this from a man who killed his brother?" Absalom's arrow had hit the mark.

The man hung his head, his eyes resting on Mary's simple note of "Stand firm." Simon had, in turn, one last card to play as well. "Absalom, please. This mission came from your daughter's heart. She pled with me for it, and now I plead with you. My name need not be attached; no one need know that a Graymoor had any part of this, I promise. I beg you—let me do this—for Mary's sake."

There was only one entry point into the stronghold that was Absalom Bane, and that was the love he had for his wife and daughter—and even his young son. With eyes of stone and ice, he looked at Simon. "Not for you, Master Graymoor, but for Mary's sake." Absalom turned and left.

The note was still in his hand as he sank behind his desk. He knew he should feel a sense of victory, but instead, he felt only empty. It would please his sweet Mary, but this was not a prize he'd won for her. It was but a concession by Absalom, a choice not to exercise his will against him. He had not won; he'd simply been given a bone. One good thing would come of it. Those broken and used-up women could be given a new life.

A new life. He would give all his wealth, his family name, anything, if he could find such a new life. But how could he have a new life when he'd watched the very life of his mirror image slip away? His brother had begged for mercy, begged to be saved, but he had let him slip away. Would Hyde always plague him? He feared it would be so. Perhaps one day, this secret would be forever laid to rest, but for now, Hyde was very much alive.

Kate sat across the breakfast table, eyes wide, and, for once, she was totally dumbstruck. Gobsmacked, as Zach would say. First, she had awakened to a savory mix of aromas wafting into her room—the smell of a proper English breakfast being cooked. She walked into the dining room and was astounded to see a spread of eggs and bacon, sausages, grilled tomatoes, mushrooms, and fried bread laid out, ready to eat. Even more surprising was how good it was. She had told Zach that she'd always heard that the English were lousy cooks. Zach told her that his grandmother was French. If that was the secret sauce, it sure worked. The breakfast was outstanding.

Now, the dishes were loaded into the dishwasher, the counter cleaned, and the reality of her situation dulled the glow of a good meal. Zach seated himself across from Kate at the break-fast table and told her to just listen. He had decided to lay out the total plan—to tell her more than enough to answer every question she might ask. The result of Zach's words on Kate: Gobsmacked.

She finally spoke. "You're kidding."

"Not at all." Zach pulled something out of his pocket, showed it to her. "Now, will you do as I say? I mean, exactly as I say?"

Kate hesitated. "You know what this is going to do, don't you?"

"Yes, I know. Will you do as I say?"

Kate nodded. She didn't really have any other choice.

Zach scooted his chair next to hers, speaking softly. "Don't worry, Katie, I won't let anything happen to you, or to Amy—or to him. Now, here's what you're going to do…"

Amy had just finished her first cup of coffee when she heard the pounding on the door. Her first thought was, *Kate.* But that was silly; Kate had a key. She looked through the peephole—on the other side was Cliff. She opened the door.

Cliff's hair was mussed, his clothes were careless and disheveled, like he'd slept in them—and his eyes had the feverish look of someone obsessed. *He's never looked better.*

They stood staring at each other for a moment, then Cliff spoke.

"Well…?"

"Oh! Oh yeah, come in."

"Got any coffee?"

Before Amy could speak, Cliff was heading toward the kitchen.

She called after him, "Help yourself."

The memories of last night popped back into her head. Zach's charm. Gunshots in the dark. Cliff to the rescue, followed by his silence when bringing her home. More than that, what bothered her most was Kate's disappearance—and her mysterious note. All that called for another cup of coffee.

"Did you leave anything for me?"

Cliff looked down at the extra-large cup he had just filled to the brim.

"Um, not really. I'm sorry, you can have some of…"

Amy waved it away, and refilled the coffeemaker with water. "So, you're here awful early."

"Am I?" Cliff looked at his watch. "Aw, geez—sorry, Amy. I

guess I wasn't paying attention." Cliff stared down at his coffee cup; he never was any good with keeping track of time.

Amy smiled. She remembered when they were young, Cliff would keep her up at night sitting in the back yard, looking at the stars, trying to name all the constellations—or making up new ones. Before she knew it, it was after midnight, and they'd both be in trouble. Amy didn't care then, and she didn't care now.

"Okay, Cliff—what's going on?"

"Nothing. I just—"

"Don't hand me a bunch of juju malarkey. Uh-uh. A lot of stuff has happened; you better believe it! So, if you're here at my door at 6:00 a.m., I know something must be going on! C'mon, I want the full Monty!"

"Amy, do you even know the meaning of 'full Mon—' never mind." Cliff sat and ran his fingers through his uncombed hair. "Okay, here it is—it's…" He struggled for words. "It's everything!" Cliff sat, the weight of all the unknowns pressing him down. "I don't know. I just can't put the pieces together. I mean, there is something there, just underneath all this stuff about Graystone, but I can't quite…" Cliff sighed and took another big swig of coffee. "I mean, it must be important."

"I'll say! I mean, you got pulpits pushed on top of you, icky, bloody messages in the mirror…"

"Yeah. And stairs cut in half, hidden diaries…"

"Kate is missing, and I got…"

"You got shot at."

Both went silent, lost in their own thoughts. For the first time, it really hit Amy. She could have been killed. And for the first time, it hit Cliff that she could have been killed—that he could have lost her forever. The coffeepot gurgled, and Amy silently got up, poured her coffee, then brought the carafe into the living room with a cozy wrapped around it. She sat in Kate's easy chair.

"So, tell me, Mr. Professor—what would be so important that it would be worth killing for?"

A glint returned to Cliff's eyes.

Amy frowned. "Okay, what is it?"

"I'm not... I mean, it's just kind of a hint of... Oh, I don't know; I can't explain it." He got up and headed for the door.

"Cliff! You are not just gonna leave me hanging like—"

Cliff grinned. He suddenly didn't feel tired anymore. "Get ready and come over as soon as you can. And bring some snacks—we might be a while."

With that, Cliff exited. Amy should have been irritated; she didn't like being bossed around. Instead, she smiled. She headed toward the bathroom to shower and get dressed.

Dexter Heathstone was feeling lousy. His throat hurt like it had been hit with hot coals, and his brain was foggy. The fogginess was due to the pain meds—but the throat...

The doctor walked in, accompanied by a man in a black suit—and by an old friend. Dexter grabbed his friend's hand as he sat down on the bed. He started to say something, but his friend put a finger to his lips. Instead, the doctor spoke.

"Mr. Heathstone, I told you I would keep you fully informed, so I am—despite my better judgment. We've bumped up security on your room. We still have the local police keeping watch, but," he gestured toward the man in the black suit, "this is Mr. Johns with the FBI. We are now convinced that what happened was no accident." Dex's friend looked at both the FBI agent and the doctor and gave them a nod.

The doctor continued. "We found your sandwich not only laced with peanut dust, it also contained an acidic powder that has injured your vocal cords. It could have caused your throat to swell, completely choking off your breathing. Even your EpiPen couldn't have saved you. Fortunately, the paramedics were exceptional. You're a very lucky man, Mr. Heathstone."

Dexter's friend picked up the story. "Someone wanted you dead two ways, Dex. Someone made a plan—a very clever plan—and put it into motion. They needed you out of the way—even if it meant killing you."

Dexter motioned for pen and paper—he scribbled a note and handed it to his friend, who looked at it and shook his head.

"Sorry, but at this point in the game, we can't. We've set the trap, and we can't risk it being sprung too soon. We've got one shot—and one shot only." He smiled. "Don't worry—we'll take every precaution possible."

Dexter nodded. His friend patted his hand, and with a whispered word to the FBI agent, he exited. The doctor watched him exit, doubt in his eyes. He turned to his patient.

"I don't know, Mr. Heathstone; are you sure you trust this guy?"

Dexter scribbled a few words on paper. "With my life."

Lyndsie awoke on her couch. Her head throbbed. She went into the bathroom and looked at herself in the mirror; she saw the dark hollows under her eyes, the lifelessness of her face. This couldn't happen. Her looks had always gotten her places her brain couldn't. She could disarm men physically—even if she'd met her match intellectually—and that always opened a door for her words to get her what she wanted. But looking at herself now...

No. She couldn't let this happen. There was too much at stake. Too much...

She turned away from the mirror, chewing on the phrase. There really was too much at stake. A higher purpose—that was it. And she had to do whatever was necessary to protect it. Lyndsie felt a new surge of energy. She could do this; she could. The end had to justify the means—and the end was worth it. The crisis was over. She felt a cold clarity, a steel-hard resolve taking over, crushing all her doubts.

She needed to think. She needed to plan. But first...

Lyndsie headed to the shower. Today she had to look her best. She could do this.

Graveyard, Granville Church

—July 1919

The two boys were scrambling through the woods. One boy was fair-haired, dressed in comfortable, but well-made clothes; the other was dark-haired and dark-eyed, wearing well-worn, plain clothes. They were making their way to the small graveyard on the outskirts of the church property. The fair-haired boy was excited, laughing. The graveyard was off limits—which made it a magnet to a lad of his age.

"Charles—stop! We mustn't!" The dark-haired boy frowned as he realized where they were headed.

"Oh, Nathan—must you always be so gloomy?" He laughed. "Come along—it's an adventure!"

The dark-haired boy held his ground. "No! My father says it's forbidden."

"I don't care what your father says! *My* father built the church *and* the parsonage, and he owns the graveyard… And he has forbidden nothing!"

"Your father is a reprobate!" Nathan knew he shouldn't have said it, but the mention of how dependent his family was on the Graymoors angered him.

Charles stopped and looked at the son of Absalom Bane—his uncle, though the boy was only a few years older than himself.

"My father is a great man! You're just angry because your father's only—"

"A man of God?"

Charles hesitated. He and Nathan Bane had bickered before, but they had always remained friendly companions. This was something different.

"Why do you say my father is a reprobate?"

Nathan turned away. He cared for his nephew—who was more like a brother to him. Charles had come into the world just three years after he was born. Three years after his mother had died giving birth to him. His big sister, Mary, so much older than he, had cared for him as if he was her own. He and Charles were raised under her loving care—but he alone was raised under Absalom Bane's watchful eye. Absalom was the center of young Nathan's world, though it was clear that Mary was the center of Absalom's affections.

"Nathan, why won't you answer me?" The fair face of Charles was twisted with worry.

Nathan knew he shouldn't have spoken. He didn't mean to wound his friend, but it rankled him sometimes that his family lived off the scraps tossed to them by their benefactor. He had heard his father speak in low whispers to Peter Graymoor, heard his father's prayers through closed doors. He suspected much, but knew nothing for sure. Now, he had to find a way out of this door he had opened. "If you want an answer, talk to my father."

Without speaking, both boys headed home.

Cliff sat on the floor, photographs spread out before him. He had catalogued and photographed each and every artifact he'd unpacked; they were spread on the floor to his right. On his left was the photographic record of every item sent by the Graymoor Estate in Bournemouth—items belonging to Peter Graymoor before coming to America. Something, something was just a little off between the two sets of photos—but Cliff couldn't quite put his finger on it.

A knock came at the door. Amy must have hustled; it always took her forever to get ready. Cliff opened the door. "Well that was quicker than…" He stopped.

"Hello Cliff."

Lyndsie Bainbridge stepped inside the cottage. This was not what Cliff was expecting.

"Lyndsie? What are you doing—I mean, I wasn't expecting—uh, I'm kind of busy right now."

She looked down at the photos spread on the floor. "So I see." She bent down to look at the pictures. "Can I help?"

"No! I mean, I'm just trying to… You know, I need to get my, my head, uh, organized…"

Lyndsie laughed. "I get it. No." She started looking around the cottage, poking her head into different rooms. "Hmm."

"Hmm? What 'hmm?'"

"No Amy. I usually find her here in the mornings. Are you sure you two aren't...?" She trailed off.

"Huh? Are we...?" It hit Cliff. "Oh! You mean, are we in... No! I mean, we're not, you know, that way with each other. Not really."

Lyndsie gave him a radiant smile. "That's the best news I've had in days!"

"Huh? Why?" Again, it hit Cliff. "Oh. Oh! No, you see I don't... I mean I wouldn't..."

Lyndsie continued, wanting to hammer home her advantage.

"I mean, I really did wonder about your Amy. Especially since she and that Zach character really seemed to really hit it off. Even after last night..." Lyndsie knew she'd blundered as soon as the words left her lips.

"How did you know about last night?"

There was a knock on the doorframe. "Cliff? I'm ready—and I brought snacks... Oh! What is she...?"

Lyndsie turned to go, grateful, for once, for Amy's presence—and the distraction it brought. "I should go. But can we talk later—please?"

"Uh, sure."

With that, Lyndsie tossed him another smile and left.

Amy walked in and plopped the snacks on the table. "What was *that* all about?"

Cliff wearily sank down on his couch. Too many women, too many mysteries, too little sleep.

"I have no idea what it was about. She just showed up on my doorstep."

"That woman is after something, you know, *and* she's after you!"

"Yeah. I know."

Amy looked at him in surprise. Cliff usually was a dunce when it came to women. "You do?"

"Yeah. She more or less made that clear this morning. It hurts my head to think about it." Cliff dropped his head in his hands.

He's a good man. Those are hard to find. "Want me to make some more coffee for you? It might help your head…"

Cliff looked up gratefully. "Please. And then we need to get to work."

CHAPTER 20

Simon's Secret Room, Graystone Manor

—March 1922

Simon Graymoor lifted his head. He had fallen asleep at his desk again—not the hand-carved, solid walnut one that sat in the library of Graystone. This was the small one that sat in the middle of his garret hiding place. Absalom had found him out, but he still had not discovered the contents of "The Hyde Papers"—nor had he been able to discover the new secret lock to the door.

Not even Mary knew how to enter the room. She had wanted to be with him as he wrote, wanting to keep vigil, fearing that he might harm himself. That fear was over. It was done. He had found solace...and he had found mercy. He was no longer a man condemned—at least not by God. He was free now, and willing to accept whatever judgment man might make.

Only one more thing remained to be done. He took a final look at the title page, "The Hyde Papers," then, picking up the worn Holy Bible Mary had given him, he placed it on top of them. The confessional was complete. Now only one thing remained to be signed and delivered. He grabbed his pen, signed his name. It was done—and his fate was sealed.

A peal of thunder rattled the window of the garret. Simon thought of his wife and his son, sleeping untroubled through this storm. She needn't be troubled ever again; the deed would be done. With that, Simon folded up the paper he had just signed and stuffed it into a long envelope. Then, he quietly left his hiding place, shutting the door firmly behind him.

"You don't realize who you're talking to—I'm the Director of the Graymoor Foundation! You've put me off long enough. I need to speak to Dexter Heath—"

A cool voice came through on the other end of the line. "One moment, please."

Lyndsie felt a knot in the pit of her stomach as she waited, an advertisement for the hospital playing in her ears. Finally, a real human voice came through.

"Hello?"

"Thank God! Dex, I've been trying to—"

"I'm sorry. This is Mr. Heathstone's doctor, Miss Bainbridge."

"I asked to speak to Dexter, not his doctor."

"I'm afraid that's impossible, Miss Bainbridge. Mr. Heathstone cannot speak to anyone—not even you."

"I just need him for a minute or two. I promise I won't tire him."

The doctor cleared his throat. "Are you aware that an attempt was made on Mr. Heathstone's life? Not only was he intentionally exposed to peanuts—to which he is violently allergic—but acid was added to the mix in an attempt to totally close up his throat in case he was able to get to his EpiPen. He almost didn't make it."

Lyndsie felt a wave of nausea. She pushed it back. "I wasn't aware. I knew he was in the hospital, but I didn't know…" More nausea. "So how soon will he…?"

"Impossible to say, Miss Bainbridge. Right now, he is under the FBI's protective custody. The would-be murderer is still out there. I'm afraid that's all I can tell you."

"Thank you." Lyndsie hung up. She had to get a grip on herself. She pushed away the sound of the word 'murder.' She couldn't let that throw her. Higher purpose—she had to remember the higher purpose. At least Dex wouldn't be able to interfere with that purpose any time soon. In the meantime, she had to implement her plan.

For the sake of the higher purpose.

Morning had passed—then afternoon. It was approaching evening, and still Cliff hadn't figured it out.

"What exactly are we looking for, again?" Amy's voice was tired. She had gotten as little sleep the night before as Cliff had.

"An anomaly. That means—"

"Yeah, yeah, I know. Something that doesn't fit." Suddenly, Amy looked up. "Ooh!"

Cliff looked at her suspiciously. "What 'ooh?'"

"It's like one of those hidden object games, where you look at two pictures and try to find the differences between them!"

"Yeah, I know, that's what I said—an anomaly."

"Which means nothing! You were throwing around words like 'anomalous' and 'esoteric' and 'disproportionate.' If you'd just said it's like a game…"

Cliff was irritated. She was right. His head was so caught up in all the other mysterious stuff surrounding this that he was probably missing the obvious. If he just looked at it like a game… He shook his head. "Maybe we just need to go back to Graystone and…"

"Oh, poop!"

"C'mon, we'll be careful!"

"Oh, it's not that! After last night, it'd be a piece of cake. It's that!" Amy pointed up to the vandalized mirror hanging over the couch. Cliff saw that a corner of it still had red paint. He had to laugh.

"You do know it's just paint, Amy—not blood?"

"I know that! It's... it's just him!" She pointed at the reflection in the mirror, the reflection of Peter Graymoor's portrait hanging over the fireplace. "I just don't like him."

Amy jumped up on the couch, striking the same pose as the portrait in the mirror reflection. "Look at me, I'm Peter Graymoor, Esquire, and I've got a dog and a horse and a dead deer, and I'm sooo..."

Amy stopped with her teasing. Cliff was looking intently at her. She faltered. "I'm—I'm sorry, Cliff. I know he's kind of a relative and—"

"Strike that pose again—the one in the mirror."

"Huh?"

"Just do it!"

Amy obeyed, though she had no idea what Cliff was looking for. He grabbed a picture from the floor and held it up to the reflection in the mirror. Then, he held it up to the picture above the fireplace. His mouth dropped open. He sat on the couch, stunned.

"Holy moly—that's it! You were right—you were so right! I mean, I almost had it before, but I was thinking too much. When you said it was like a game..."

Now Amy was totally confused. "What's 'it?' What are you talking about?"

Cliff stood and started pacing. "This could be big. Oh

man, really, really big." He stopped, a light coming into his eyes. "I wonder. I mean, that would explain the whole... The whole everything!"

Amy stopped Cliff in his tracks and stood before him, arms folded. "Stop! Now explain it to me."

Cliff held up the photograph in his hand. "See this? It's the picture of the original portrait of Peter Graymoor—sent over from England. This," he pointed to the picture over the mantel, "this is almost the exact same picture—but it was painted over here in America, several years after he arrived." He moved Amy so that she was directly in front of the picture. "Now, do you remember when we found out that Simon and Peter were mirror image twins?"

"Yeah—but remind me."

"They were exact opposites in every way. One was right handed, one left handed. One's hair fell to the left, the other's to the right. Even their internal organs were mirror images of each other!"

"Okay, I remember! Mirror images. Like, Simon's heart was in the wrong place!"

"More than you know. Now look at this photo of the original painting—then look at the one painted in America..." Cliff waited a moment as Amy studied it.

Suddenly, the light went on for her. She sat down. "Holy moly!"

"I told you it was big."

Amy looked at him with wide eyes. "This is bigger than big. It's big, big!"

Amy and Cliff looked at each other, feeling the weight of their discovery.

Only a whisper came out of Cliff. "The Graymoor who inherited all the wealth, who started the Graymoor Foundation, wasn't Peter."

"It was Simon." Amy was breathless. "Does this mean…?"

"Yeah. It could mean the end of the Graymoor Foundation. That is, if we tell the truth."

Amy looked at Cliff with wide eyes again. He understood.

"I know. We've got to tell the truth." He paused. "You know, someone else must have figured it out. That's why…"

He didn't need to finish his sentence. All the threats, the "accidents" and booby traps, the gunshots in the dark… Someone was trying to stop them from discovering the truth. But who? Someone on the board? Someone with the foundation? A hired gun? A cold thought hit Cliff.

Could it be Kate?

Kate was so proud of her husband's heritage; so proud of the fact that Absalom Bane had helped the false Peter Graymoor begin his philanthropic foundation. Absalom must have known the truth—and covered it up. That would really stain the reputation and legacy of the Bane family.

"Cliff?" Amy's voice was soft. "You're thinking 'Kate,' aren't you?" Cliff simply nodded. Amy's voice was still soft. "Don't ask me how, but I know it's not her." Cliff placed a hand on hers, gratitude in his eyes.

Without removing her hand, Amy asked the big question. "What now?"

"We need to go to Graystone. We need to find the original painting from England; make sure it matches the photograph." A slight, reckless grin appeared on Cliff's face. "Most of all, we need to find Simon's secret room—and Simon's confessional, 'The Hyde Papers.'"

Cliff jumped up. "Meet me here in half an hour. Dress in black—and take the back way when you return. Let's do this thing…"

The old, outer gate to Graystone was unlocked, and with a push, opened with a loud creaking sound.

"Shh!"

"Why are you shushing a gate?"

Cliff was annoyed—Amy was grinning. The "shh" had come out without thinking. "I was pre-shushing you because I knew you'd want to talk, and—ow!" Amy had given him a solid smack on the arm. "What was *that* for?"

"Shh!"

Amy and Cliff walked through the opened gate and made their way along the outskirts of Graystone, heading toward the mansion. Cliff's arms were filled with a large, awkward bundle, while Amy carried a smaller one. Shadows seemed to flit and follow them, and a rustle in the bushes made them unconsciously draw closer together. Any other time, it would be a romantic, moonlit night—but their thoughts were far from romantic. In a way, Cliff hated to bring Amy along, but he knew it would have been useless to try to keep her away.

Besides, she might not be any safer at Kate's.

Cliff approached the back entrance of Graystone and handed his package over to Amy.

"Ooph—this is heavy!"

"Shh!"

Cliff approached the newly installed alarm system on the back door, but before he even reached the scanner, a Siri-sounding voice greeted him: "*Thumb print accepted. Access granted.*"

A mechanical clunk followed, and the unlocking mechanism was activated.

"Oh, great. Some security. Can I put this down yet?" Amy shifted the ungainly burden.

"No. Now let me think…" Cliff stared at the unlocked door. "Cliff!"

"Gotta be some kind of glitch in the system. Gotta be…" Cliff pushed the door open and motioned Amy through. They entered, and Cliff carefully closed the door behind them. He motioned for Amy to follow him as he felt his way along the hall.

"Can you take this thing from me? It weighs a ton!"

"Shh. In a minute."

Amy's shin encountered a chair. "Ow! Can't you turn on the light?"

"In a minute."

Cliff entered the library, where most of the artifacts were stored. He gave a signal, and Amy carefully placed the package against the wall. Together, they went to the windows and drew the heavy drapes. Cliff walked to back to the library door, turned a valve, and ignited the gas lamp on the wall.

"Let there be light!" Cliff smiled. He then lit the matching lamp on the other side of the doorway, and four more throughout the room. The soft light illuminated the chamber. It was spacious, and in its day, was probably beautiful. Now it was littered with a maze of boxes and workmen's tools. Cliff wove his way through the cardboard jungle, then stopped before a rectangular package.

"This is it! Bring the other one over here." Amy looked at Cliff. "Okay—*please* bring the other one over here?"

Amy picked up the bulky package and made her way through the litter of boxes. "Remind me again why we're doing this?"

"We need to do a side-by-side comparison for proof."

Amy placed the bundle against the wall as Cliff was lifting a large painting out of a box. He propped it up near the other, paper-wrapped frame. They stared at the English portrait of Peter Graymoor.

Amy moved closer to the picture—and to Cliff.

"Well?"

He studied the painting as Amy unconsciously linked her arm with his. They both leaned in as Cliff spoke.

"Now—this is the original painting Peter Graymoor had done *before* he came to America. He left it behind as a gift to his father." The portrait showed a fair-haired man, locks falling to the right side of his face, a riding crop in his right hand, and his right leg propped on the freshly felled body of a ten-point buck.

Cliff grabbed the bundle they had brought into Graystone and moved it closer to the English portrait. He stripped off the paper. Before them were two paintings. Identical paintings. Almost. The American portrait was exact in almost every detail, except that it was in reverse. Hair falling to the left, riding crop in the left hand, left foot on the buck.

Amy stared at the two paintings. They were mirror images of each other. "Wow."

Cliff wasn't finished. "That's not the clincher. Both painters were truly excellent in every detail. Look at this…" He pointed to a small scar on the left hand of the "Peter Graymoor" he'd brought from home. "When Simon Graymoor was a boy, he teased a neighbor's dog by taking away a rabbit it had killed. The dog didn't care for that, and gave him a vicious bite. Simon bore that scar for the rest of his life."

"Okay, so, back then, why didn't anybody notice…?"

"Absalom Bane. That has to be it. I mean, if *he* said it was Peter Graymoor, nobody was going to question it."

Amy bent over, studied both pictures, then pointed at the one painted in America.

"So, this picture really isn't Peter Graymoor…?"

"No. It's Simon."

"For reals?"

"For reals."

Both stared at the paintings. The only sound in the room was the ticking of the grandfather clock. Amy was the first to break the silence.

"So—what do we do?"

"We need to lock both these paintings in the vault—otherwise they might try to destroy them."

"They? Who's 'they?'"

"I don't know! The boobytrapping, cottage-trashing, shooting-at-you 'they!' I don't know *who* they are! They just…are!"

"Okay, okay! 'They.' Or 'them.' The 'somebody' who's trying to keep us from figuring this out. So, after we lock the paintings up, remind me—what do we do?"

"We look for Simon's secret room—and 'The Hyde Papers.'" Amy pulled a small bundle of papers out of her pocket, looked at it, then at Cliff.

"You think we can find the room? And suppose we do find it and the Hyde stuff and all that—what will this do to the foundation? I mean, all the money isn't theirs; it never was theirs. I know what you said, but are you gonna…?" The unspoken words hung in the air.

Cliff shook his head. "I don't know."

"The foundation does a lot of good…"

"I know." He drew a deep breath. "But a lie's a lie—even if it's a good lie. You can't build anything of lasting good on a lie."

Where did that come from? Cliff didn't know—but he knew he'd just said something important—something that went beyond the Graymoor Foundation. He looked at Amy. She had a light in her eyes he'd never seen before.

"You know, Clifford Graymoor—you are something else! Well, let's get these puppies in the vault!" Amy grabbed the portrait of Simon.

Cliff smiled. When all this was over, he and Amy were going to have a long talk, and perhaps more. He picked up the painting of Peter, and they went to a wall covered by an elaborate tapestry. Cliff pulled the tapestry aside. Beneath the weaving was a paneled wall with a hidden door—but this time it was not so hidden. The secret door was slightly open. A soft groan came from behind it.

Cliff slid the panel door into a pocket in the wall revealing a tall vault door with a combination lock. A moan was heard again. Cliff quickly entered the combination and opened the heavy door. The inside of the vault was almost pitch black. He pulled a flashlight from his pocket and shined it inside. He saw a pair of legs.

"Amy! Give me a hand here!" Amy quickly set Simon's portrait against the wall, and helped Cliff pull a half-conscious figure out of the dark chamber and into the light. That figure was Lyndsie Bainbridge.

"I know it's hard, but then what?" Cliff's voice was calm but firm.

Lyndsie was seated on the floor of the library, across from Cliff and Amy. "I found the note under my door this afternoon. That was shortly after I came over and found you…occupied." Her eyes locked with Amy's for a moment. There was challenge in Lyndsie's eyes. She turned them to Cliff and her eyes softened.

"The note told me to come here tonight or else something bad would happen to…" She paused and lowered her eyes, "…to you. So, I came."

Lyndsie grabbed her head and let out a slight moan.

Cliff reached over to brush her hair aside. "Here—let me take a look at—" Lyndsie's hand stopped him.

"I'm okay—it just hurts a little."

Amy's eyes narrowed, then she scooted toward Lyndsie. "I used to be an LPN, you know. You better let me—"

"No! I'm okay. Really."

Cliff gently pulled Amy back. "So, what happened next?"

"I found all the doors unlocked, and I came in. I thought maybe you…" She looked shyly at Cliff. "Anyway, I heard a sound in the library. I went in. It was dark, but a lot of moonlight was coming through the window. I heard a noise behind me, I turned around, and—and the next thing I knew I was in a pitch-black room." She smiled at Cliff. "Until you rescued me."

Amy wasn't going to let that pass. "Until *we* rescued you."

Cliff sighed. "I guess you didn't see who locked you in there."

Lyndsie's lips parted. She started to speak, then stopped herself. Cliff grabbed her arm. "Lyndsie—did you see who locked you in there?"

Her sad eyes looked up at him. "Cliff—it was your Aunt Kate."

CHAPTER 21

Katherine Bane was back in her home. After a slight detour—one she'd never forget—Zach had dropped her there.

She knew a lot was at stake, but she didn't like what she had to do. It scared her, though she'd never admit it. Taped to her chest was an apparatus—one that could mean the end of everything for some, including herself. She never wanted this to happen, but she had a role to play, and she was going play it. She whispered to herself, "God, forgive me for getting so many people into this whole mess."

"I don't believe it. Unh-uh, no way." Amy's voice was no more than a whisper, but it was adamant.

"Lyndsie said she saw her, Amy. She saw Kate."

"Poop. Kate would never do something like that. Never! You could turn her inside out, and she'd never do it!" They were speaking in low tones, even though Lyndsie couldn't hear. She had taken the flashlight and gone to the bathroom.

Cliff shook his head. He didn't know what to think anymore. He knew Amy was right—Kate would never try to kill someone, or even hurt them. But when it came to the Bane family legacy...

Cliff just didn't know. Besides, Lyndsie said...

Lyndsie had re-entered the room. "I'm okay. I've got a

goose egg, that's all. Now," she looked at Cliff, "what are you doing here? Did you get a note, too? And what did you put in the vault?"

Amy mouthed the word 'no,' but Cliff ignored her. "We didn't get a note. We—we discovered something. Something big." Amy was frowning at him. "We discovered that it wasn't Simon Graymoor who died in that accident at the bridge. It was Peter."

Lyndsie's eyes narrowed. "Peter? Then it was Simon who…?"

"Who created the Graymoor Foundation with money he had no right to inherit."

"Are you saying the whole Graymoor Foundation…?"

"Is built on a lie. I'm sorry, Lyndsie, I really am."

Lyndsie paused. "So what'd you put in the vault…?"

"Paintings. Ones that prove that Simon posed as his brother. The original from England is the exact mirror image of the one Simon commissioned for himself here."

Lyndsie scooted in closer to Cliff. "Cliff—you're a good man. Maybe the best I've ever met. Please, think this through. The Graymoor Foundation does so much good. *So* much good. Even *if* this proves to be true, do you really want to undo all that? All the good work, all the people they help… You can't just let that disappear."

Cliff was silent. She could tell he was affected by what she said. One more thing, and she might have him.

"And the scandal—think of the stink this would raise. Would you really want to stain the name of Graymoor?"

Amy held her breath. This was the moment. Cliff wasn't adept at penetrating looks, but he locked on Lyndsie.

"Protecting the Bane name was what drove Kate to lock you in a vault and leave you to die." He shook his head. "It's too slippery a slope. You can't build anything of lasting good on a lie." He looked at Amy—she was beaming. He exhaled. He had passed the test.

Lyndsie turned to ice on the inside, but on the outside, she gave a slight laugh.

"Well, I had to try, didn't I?" Her eyes narrowed. "But a couple of paintings won't be enough to prove that Simon was Peter. You do know that, don't you?"

"We've got more!" Amy could no longer keep quiet. She wanted to trump Lyndsie's persuasiveness. She wanted to really bad. "And that's all you need to know."

Lyndsie looked at Cliff. "Well, that's hardly fair. Look, my life was put at risk because of this—this 'whatever' you found out. I think I deserve full disclosure."

"She's right, Amy. She's already too deeply into this. I mean, she could have died." Cliff stood and pulled out his cellphone. "In fact, maybe we should call the police."

"No!" Both women spoke in unison; both for different reasons. Amy didn't want Kate arrested. Lyndsie didn't want anything—or anyone—to keep her from learning what Cliff had discovered.

Cliff shook his head. "This is getting pretty dangerous. Too dangerous, especially for—"

"For a girl?" Amy stood, hands on her hips. Cliff knew there was something more than "girl power" at play here. Her look said that she would follow him through a ring of fire if she had to. She had his back. Cliff nodded.

"Okay, okay—you two would badger me to death if we didn't finish this." Cliff held out his hand for the small bundle Amy carried. He unwrapped it. It was the collection of pages found in his cottage comprised of bits and pieces of "The Hyde Papers." He held them up.

"These are pages from Simon Graymoor's confessional, 'The Hyde Papers.'"

"So, it really exists?" The words escaped before Lyndsie could stop them.

"You knew about this?"

"No, no… I meant, I just didn't know that Simon kept a…"

"A confessional. At least that's what I call it. It seems to be the one place he wrestled with his deception. He would have fits of guilt and then disappear for a day or two. I think he was working on 'The Hyde Papers.'"

"You keep calling this alleged confession 'The Hyde Papers.' Why?"

"That's what he named it. He thought Peter had been Jekyll—and that he was Hyde. Anyway, I've picked up hints from these papers that somewhere, hidden in Graystone, is a secret room where Simon went to write. He evidently didn't trust anyone with this diary."

"We're going to find the room. And 'The Hyde Papers'—and then the truth will come out. About everything." Amy directed these words not at Cliff but at Lyndsie—and Lyndsie knew exactly what she meant. But Lyndsie smiled at Cliff.

"Well, what has to be, has to be. Let's find the room." Lyndsie stood up once more, and promptly collapsed on the floor.

"Lyndsie!" Cliff knelt down beside her and looked at Amy. "She fainted. Lyndsie! *Lyndsie!*" Cliff began patting her hand as Amy knelt on the other side.

"That's not how you do it." Amy took a half full water bottle, poured it onto her forehead. Lyndsie shot up, sputtering.

"What the—?" She stopped herself. "You little idiot. What do you think you're doing?"

"Reviving you."

Cliff stood. "Enough!" He helped Lyndsie up. "You—you're going home, and you're going to call the police and explain what's going on." He turned to Amy. "And you—"

"Oh no, no, no—you're not getting rid of me!"

"Fine. But you do exactly as I say, understood?" Amy nodded. Cliff turned back to Lyndsie. "Well?"

"Maybe you're right. I... I don't feel so good."

"Here—take the flashlight. Remember to call the police." Lyndsie gave a weak smile, and left.

Amy had a troubled look on her face. "That was too easy."

"Huh?"

"She left without a fight."

"She just got her head knocked in; what did you expect?"

"Whatever. I just know that the sooner we find this room, the better I'll feel."

Finding the room. It hit Cliff just how little they knew. He pulled out the papers, began to flip through them once again. "Yeah, well, it may be a while before you feel good again. It's like a jigsaw puzzle of words."

"Cool, cool, cool! I love jigsaw puzzles! So, c'mon, read it to me!"

"Well—it can't hurt, I guess." He pulled out a page. "Here's one. '*I've been up so many hours, still I cannot sleep. The moonlight streams in from above me, and...*'"

"From above? You mean, like a skylight?"

Cliff's eyes opened wide. "Exactly like a skylight! That means the room is on the top floor. And on the north side. That's the only part of the roof that has skylights."

"So, it's the third floor on the north side?"

"It's got to be!"

"Okay, okay—what else?"

Cliff hurriedly began to flip through more pages when, suddenly, everything went dark.

A heavy exterior door creaked open, then shut again. A dark-clad man entered; soft footsteps followed. The door opened again, and the man quickly hid himself.

"Hello? Is someone there?" Lyndsie felt a knot of fear. "Cliff—is that you?" Only silence. She spoke out loud, "Stop it, Lyndsie! You've got this." This was not the time to let her imagination run away with her. She left the dark of the mansion and entered the moonlit yard, closing the heavy door behind her.

The man emerged from the shadows. "Close one, Zach, my boy, close one." He moved to a small window and carefully peered out. "We'll just wait for Miss Director to come back—and lead us right to where we want to go." With that, Zach slipped back into the shadows. He loved it when a plan came together.

"Shh."

"Where are we going?" The voice was just a whisper.

"To the pantry. There's a lantern there if we can find it."

"*If* we can find it?" Amy was annoyed. She was walking blind and had knocked her shin once again. "Great time for the power to go out. I mean, even the gas lights…"

Cliff stopped. "Amy, this may not be an accident."

"What do you…?"

"Shh."

Softer, "What do you mean?"

"The easiest way to disable the alarm is to cut the power. And the best way to put us in the dark is to cut the gas. I could think one of them was an accident—but both?"

Cliff felt along the wall until he found a door knob. They had reached the pantry. His fingers felt through the items on the second shelf until they found the glass globe of a lantern.

"Hold this…" He grabbed the lantern and placed it in Amy's hand. He fumbled along the rest of the shelf until he found a small box. "Aha—gotcha!"

"Shh." It was Amy's turn to be cautious.

Cliff struck a match. Amy noted his face looked eerie in the light of the flame. He quickly checked the lantern to make sure it had enough oil and wick, and with another match, he lit it. They both sighed with relief.

Amy held the lamp up and looked around. "Now what?"

"Now let's see if we can find any other clues."

Cliff pulled out the packet of pages once again. He stopped on one sheet. "You know, Simon was really metaphorical sometimes." He turned to Amy. "That means he used a lot of images to—"

"I know what it means, Clifford. I didn't totally sleep through English. But how do you know it's metaphorical?"

"Well, listen to this: '…*though they may search for me, none will find me. I am protected by a wall of words.*' I guess he thought his writing was a kind of defense against—"

"Is there a bookcase on the third floor?"

The question stunned him. Wall of words. Bookcase. Of course!

"Yeah, there is—and I know exactly where to find it! Amy, you are a flippin' genius! I could just kiss you!"

Amy was looking at him in the lantern glow, hoping he didn't notice the red creeping into her face. She paused just long enough to calm her voice. "Well, what are you waiting for? Let's go find that room!"

Old houses have a way of speaking in the dark. Creaks and cracks, leaves scraping against a window, unidentifiable moans from the shadows… All this gave Amy the feeling that she and Cliff were not alone. Maybe it was just the sounds of the old house. Maybe it was more. She just knew that as they got closer to their goal, the knot in her stomach grew tighter.

"I've got a bad feeling about this." She could hear Cliff breathing, nothing more. "I said, I've got a bad—"

"I heard you." He paused for a heartbeat, then added, "I'm not crazy about it either. Here's the last set of stairs."

Amy hesitated. Her sense of 'wrongness' grew stronger. "Maybe we *should* call the police. Tell them about…"

"Mirror image paintings and an old diary?"

"There's the accidents and—and the thingy with the vault." Amy hesitated to mention the vault.

"Don't worry. Lyndsie's supposed to call the police—remember?"

"Yeah, right. I remember."

Cliff stopped, turned back to Amy. "You really don't like her, do you?"

"No, I don't. She's a snake and maybe… Oh, I don't know. I don't trust her. You shouldn't trust her either."

Cliff turned back, smiling to himself. Yep. She was jealous. "C'mon. I'll feel better once we find that room."

They climbed the stairs until they found themselves in a narrow hallway. Cliff led Amy a few feet down the hallway, then stopped. "Here it is. The wall of words."

They were facing a bookcase filled with a variety of volumes. Cliff handed Amy the lantern and began to feel around the edges, trying to find a latch or lever. He stepped back in frustration.

"I think this whole bookcase is a door. Look—you can see a faint light coming from right there, underneath. I just can't figure out how it…" Cliff suddenly stopped. He lowered his voice to a whisper. "Did you hear that?" There was a tap-creak, tap-creak sound getting closer. Footsteps. Someone was coming up the stairs.

"We've got to find a way in—fast!" Cliff started frantically pulling at the edges of the bookcase, until Amy grabbed his arm.

"Wait." She reached up and pulled out a book, then pushed it back in place. The bookcase silently unlatched. Quickly they stepped inside, pulling it back in after them. They held their breath, listening as each footstep brought an unknown someone closer.

The footsteps stopped, moved away again, then disappeared.

Cliff felt his stomach unknot a little. "I think we're okay." He turned to Amy. "Okay—so, how did you get the door to open?"

"I grabbed a book and pulled it forward."

"Which book?"

"'The Strange Case of Dr. Jekyll and—'"

"'Mr. Hyde.' You know, sometimes, you are brilliant. Just brilliant." Cliff looked at her with a new appreciation.

Amy flushed with pleasure. She gestured toward the small room they were in. "Uh, don't you think we ought to, you know…?"

"Yeah, you're probably right."

Cliff held the lamp out to survey the space they were in.

He spotted several candles plus a small oil lamp on a desk. "Hey, this still has oil in it!" He turned up the wick and lifted the glass. "I wonder if…?" He struck a match and put it to the wick. Light poured out of the lamp.

Amy tugged at his sleeve. "Look over here—there's a lamp here by the bed, too!"

"There's a bed?"

Cliff lifted his lantern and walked over to an antique bed-stead where he found a second lamp on a small nightstand. By the time all the lamps and candles were lit, the room was flooded with a golden light.

Amy's eyes grew big. "Wow."

"Yeah—wow!"

Cliff and Amy felt like they'd stepped into another century, another life. They surveyed a room that hadn't been seen in almost one hundred years. It was covered with dust, but other than that, it was well-preserved. A small bookcase sat in the corner, filled with volumes by authors of the day. The small but comfortable-looking bed sat against the opposite wall, covered by a handmade quilt.

A modest but expertly crafted desk filled the other wall, and on it was placed a book—but not *just* a book. It was a journal. Cliff stared at it. *Could it be...?* "Amy..." Cliff's voice was soft.

Amy came up, stood beside him, and caught her breath. "Is it...?"

Cliff opened the book. At the top of it was written: "The Hyde Papers."

Cliff grabbed Amy in his arms and swung her around. "We did it! We found Simon Graymoor's confessional!" Just as suddenly, he put her down. Their secret door was opening.

"Enjoy your little victory, Professor Graymoor. I'm afraid it won't last very long."

In front of them stood Lyndsie Bainbridge—and she was holding a gun.

Chapter 22

The thunder rolled as a dark-clad figure made its way from Graystone, moving from shadow to shadow. It slipped its way into the barn, moving quickly to one of the stalls.

"Steady boy, steady. Soon this will be all over."

"Simon…" A soft voice greeted him—and a familiar form emerged from the shadows.

"Mary! What are you…? Go back to bed. You are soaked to the bone."

"And so are you. Where are you going—and why now, at this time of night?" She moved toward him, opening the dark lantern she held. "You are not thinking of… of…"

"Hush, my darling. You have no need to fear anymore. I'm at peace. I am finally at peace. And at last," he held up a small packet, "I know what I must do." He drew her near in an embrace and whispered, "And you know what you must do. Protect 'The Hyde Papers.'"

Mary lifted a frightened face to him. "Father will never stand for this! Your, your benevolence has—"

"Has made a name for Absalom Bane." He stroked her hair. "I'm sorry, my darling, but it's true. You know that it is. That's why I must end this."

221

Mary buried her head in Simon's chest, clinging to him until he gently pulled away. "It's time, Mary."

"Come back to me, Simon. Promise that you will come back to me."

Simon lifted her face and gently kissed her on the forehead. "I love you, Mary Graymoor—do not fear." He grabbed a saddle and threw it on the back of a horse.

"You're taking Brightmoor? She's never liked you."

"I began with her; I shall end with her. Besides, I can't take the motor car—not in this rain. The road's too rutted. She will have to endure me one last time." Simon mounted the horse, which stirred restlessly. "Don't worry, my sweet Mary. All will finally be well."

With that, Simon Graymoor spurred the horse forward and disappeared into the darkness.

Mary's face was in her hands as she heard the hoof beats get swallowed by the sound of thunder. She whispered, "God be with you…"

Suddenly behind her, there were footsteps and the creak of a stall door. Grabbing her lantern, she turned to see a tall, familiar figure mounting a dark horse.

"Father!"

Absalom and the horse entered the light. "When did I lose your heart, Mary? When did I lose my daughter's heart?"

"What are you doing here?"

"You won't answer me? It's just as well. Perhaps in the days to come, you will learn wisdom instead of the foolish passion you feel for this filthy reprobate…"

"Stop! He is my husband—and he is a good man!"

"He is the devil and wants to destroy the works of God I have built!"

Mary looked steadily at the unbending form of Absalom. "*You* have built, Father?"

Absalom felt the weight of her words, but he stiffened his resolve. "You dare school your own father? Enough! I will not let your 'good man' do this!"

With that, Absalom spurred his horse away into the night.

Mary, panicked, not knowing what to do. Then, with a strength she didn't know she had, her own resolve steeled her will.

Quickly, too quickly, she saddled her own horse and mounted it. "I will not let you stop him, Absalom Bane; I will not!" Mary rode off into the wind and the rain.

The thunder grew louder as Mary tried to spur her horse on, but it was a timid creature, unlike the one her husband rode, and at best, Mary was only a fair rider. A lightning strike near the road proved to be too much for her poor beast, and it took off at a gallop, leaving the road and heading into the woods. It wasn't far into the tangle of trees that Mary was struck by a branch and knocked to the ground. The horse continued on, leaving its mistress behind. Mary's head was bleeding and her leg was broken. Something had pierced her side, and every breath hurt. Still, she couldn't let her father... Do what? The fear she felt covered her in a wave of nausea. She had to reach Simon.

Inch by inch, Mary tried to drag herself back to the road. Inch by inch.

She didn't know how long she had crawled. Minutes? Hours? But now, the road was but a few yards away. Silly thoughts were entering her head. Simon had her in his arms, and they were dancing at a feast dressed as harlequins. She was just a few feet away, now. The music must stop so she could warn him... She must warn her beloved. She must stop the music. A voice was now blending with the sounds, singing, "When did I lose your heart, my girl; when did I lose your heart?"

Mary Bane Graymoor was just two feet away from the road when she slipped into unconsciousness.

Simon was galloping through the dark, but he needed no lantern to show him the way. The path was imprinted on his memory from fifteen years before when he had met his brother—his mirror image—on this same road. For so long, that night had haunted him. The vision of his brother, crying out for help, and he, frozen, watching him suffer—watching him drown. He remembered the guilt that swallowed him after those minutes of hesitation, crucial minutes that would claim Peter's life. Now, Simon pulled up. There was the bridge where it happened, where his drunken struggle sent them both into the icy waters. His tears flowed freely—more freely than the rain. He called out, "Forgive me, brother—as God has."

A voice answered. "He will never forgive you!"

Lyndsie stood in the doorway of Simon Graymoor's secret room. Her hand was steady as she held the gun pointed right at Cliff's heart.

"Lyndsie? What are you doing?"

"What do you think? I'm saving the Graymoor Foundation."

"What?"

Amy drew closer to Cliff. "I knew we shouldn't have trusted her!"

"What are you talking about? Why do you have that—that gun?"

Lyndsie laughed. "You really are a piece of work, Cliff. Are you actually that naive? I was on to this "secret diary" long before you were. I just didn't know where to find it. You have been such a helpful boy, showing me exactly where it is."

Cliff gave a helpless gesture. "But if you knew about it, why didn't you…?"

"Really, Cliff? I mean, really? If word of this ever got out, the foundation would lose everything! Simon Graymoor was disinherited. And you know what that would mean…"

"That Simon had no right to the Graymoor fortune, none of this belonged to him, and the whole foundation was built on a lie."

"A lie that has changed the lives of thousands—maybe hundreds of thousands!"

"Yeah, I know, but…"

Lyndsie lowered the gun. "Just think of all the children who have been clothed and fed, all the families that have homes, all the hospitals that have been built! Cliff, do you really want to undo all that?" Lyndsie's voice softened and became warm. "I—I don't know how you feel about me, but I know how I feel about you. There is so much—so much I want to say. Oh, Cliff, darling—please! Trust me on this. So what if it had shady beginnings? Now, *now* is what matters, and now, it is doing so much good! Darling, listen to me—the truth can never be known."

There was a split second, a moment when neither Lyndsie nor Amy knew what Cliff was thinking. Then Amy broke the silence.

"That's the biggest bunch of dookie I've ever heard. Lady, you could sell ice cubes to an Eskimo!"

Lyndsie's grip tightened on her gun. "Shut up!"

"You don't care about thousands and thousands of children! You care about being the Director of a big whoop-de-doo international foundation, and all that juicy power it gives you. You won't admit it—I betcha don't even admit it to yourself—but that's the truth. You know it, too!"

"I said, shut up!" Lyndsie lifted her gun and pointed it right at Amy. Cliff stepped in front of her.

"Lyndsie, you can't…!"

"Don't be such an idiot, Cliff. I most certainly can."

The events of the past few weeks fell into place. He *was* an idiot. He got suckered by a redhead again.

"You did all the sabotaging, didn't you? The pulpit, the steps…?" Cliff hesitated. "Dexter?"

"Very good. I did everything but trashing your cottage. I suspect that was Kate."

"You could have killed Dex! What were you thinking?"

"I was thinking Dexter Heathstone was in the way. If he was out of commission, good. But if he happened to die, well, that was a solution, too. That's not what I wanted, but it's an acceptable loss for the greater good."

Cliff was still in shock. How could he have been so blind? He never suspected that anyone so beautiful could be so ruthless. So—evil.

"The whole thing. You planned the whole thing—even down to the vault. And I never even suspected…" Cliff looked straight at Lyndsie, pain printed on his face.

Lyndsie didn't want to kill. Not face-to-face. That was for Zach. She would let Zach do it. The thought of it all made her queasy, but she was in too far to back out now. "I'm giving you one last chance, Cliff; one last chance to save the foundation. All you have to do is say nothing. Just say nothing."

Amy was ticked—really ticked. She popped out from behind Cliff, who was still standing between her and Lyndsie. "He won't play along with you, Missy. Nuh-uh. And even if he did, I wouldn't! No way I won't tell the truth."

Lyndsie pointed her gun at Amy again. "Acceptable loss. What do you say Cliff? Last chance."

"No, Lyndsie. No. Please. You don't have to—"

"Enough! Enjoy Simon's room, Dr. Graymoor, while you still can!" Lyndsie backed out of the room, grabbed the edge of the door, and slammed it shut. They heard a ripping sound from outside the room.

Cliff slammed his shoulder against the door. It wouldn't budge. "It's jammed—or broken."

He turned to Amy. For the first time, he saw fear in her eyes. He wanted to protect her—to get her out of this somehow. He wanted to… He sighed. It was probably too late for that. Right now, she didn't need to hear how he felt about her. She needed to hear how he was going to keep them both alive.

"I can't believe how stupid I've… I'm sorry, Amy. Man, am I so, so sorry. I should have never gotten you involved in—"

"I'm not."

"What? Huh?"

"I'm not sorry." He saw the spark rekindling in her eyes. "I wanted to be part of this. I wanted to," she hesitated, "I just wanted to help you figure this out." That's not what Amy wanted to say—but Cliff didn't need to hear about feelings right now. They needed to work on a way to escape.

Cliff smiled. "Okay, then. Let's figure this out." He went over to Simon's desk and sat down. "Seems like some of our pages were torn—or copied—from the back of Simon's journal. Let's see if we can piece some of this story together."

Cliff carefully turned the yellowed pages until he reached the last few. "Look at this:

'I know what I must do, but I fear discovery. Should Absalom find a way of entry, I must find a way of exit, a way to preserve the truth. Should he try to remove and destroy the confessions of Hyde— he will find himself trapped. God help me, he will be trapped!'"

Cliff stopped. "So, even if Lyndsie hadn't jammed the door, we would have been trapped if we'd tried to remove the journal."

"Well, that's creepy." Amy shivered even though the room was growing warm.

"Simon wasn't thinking of future generations. He was only thinking of Absalom Bane."

"Well, this isn't helping, so keep reading."

Cliff turned up the lamp a little more and began again.

This is for you, my Mary. Should you find yourself in this room, trapped by your father, there is a way out. You must take the journal, though it may try your strength to remove it. By doing this, Absalom will be blocked from entry, but you can be set free. You must turn to the Way, the Truth, and the Life. This, and this alone, will be your way of escape.

I am finished now, my Mary. I am now at peace. I am no more a man condemned, but a man forgiven. Forgiven, my darling! Simon is now Peter—not in life, but in spirit. I will tell the truth. I will tell the world that I am Simon Graymoor, and whatever the price, I will pay it. Then we both shall be free.

This is my legacy to you, and to our son. Let these words never die.

Simon Graymoor.

Amy looked at Cliff. "Is this thing saying what I think it's saying?"

Cliff nodded. "Simon Graymoor created an escape route. We've just got to figure out what it is!"

The room was becoming warmer—almost hot—and a familiar smell was creeping in under the door.

"Cliff? That smell—is it…?"

"It's gasoline! Lyndsie's setting fire to Graystone!"

Amy's voice cracked. "And we don't know how to get out!"

The Bridge, at the Edge of the Graystone Estate
—March 1922

"He will never forgive you!"

Simon Graymoor heard a familiar voice behind him. He had been so lost in thought that he hadn't heard the second rider approach. Now, he turned to face him. "So, Absalom, you have found me."

"I have, Simon Graymoor. I see that you have returned to the scene of your crime. 'As a dog returns to his vomit…'"

"No more of that, Absalom! You have turned and twisted the Holy writ to your own ends too many times. This time, I will not listen. This time, I am truly going to follow what it says. 'The Truth will set you free!'"

"What is truth?" The thunder rolled as Absalom pulled his horse closer. A bolt of lightning struck nearby, spooking Simon's horse. It shied away, backwards, until its feet were on the bridge.

Absalom's voice rose above the torrent and the thunder. "Am I not God's voice to you? Am I not the one who has led you in the paths of righteousness for His name's sake? And now you defy me! No—you do not defy *me*; you defy God! How can you, stained with the blood of your brother, hope to know the truth? *I* am your truth, Simon Graymoor!"

Simon felt the chill and power of Absalom's words. For a moment, quicker than a flash of lightning, he almost yielded to them... Then, he remembered the words he had read. No condemnation. "I know the truth—and it is not you, Absalom. I will not be under your whip again. I am going to the authorities, and the truth will be told!"

Simon turned his horse to go when he heard a loud crack—but not of lightning. His horse reared, dancing along the edges of the narrow bridge. Simon caught a glimpse of Absalom, holding something dark and smoking in his hand. Absalom's hand rose—another crack, and Simon was thrown into the turbulent waters.

Simon's head went under, but he forced himself to fight against the current. He grabbed a rotting tree root to keep from being swept away.

"Absalom! Help me! For God's sake, help me!"

Absalom came to the edge of the waters. Gone was the smoking object—now there was something round and heavy-looking in his hand. He stood on the tree root, which began to crack under his weight.

Simon looked up into the preacher's face. It was like carved stone. Tears filled his eyes as he realized what Absalom was doing.

"Forgive. Absalom, I for—" The root broke, and Simon felt something hard come crashing down on his head. He slipped into unconsciousness and was swallowed up by the torrent.

Absalom stood in silence. Thoughts of his father, crying to be let in from the storm, pushed their way back into his mind. He had tried; he had tried so hard to please God, to make up for his sin, and now…

Absalom turned away from the riverbank and mounted his horse again. It was too late. His course was set. He may have done evil, but it was to serve the greater good. He would serve the greater good.

When Absalom returned to the stables, he saw Mary's cloak on the floor—and the empty stall that housed her horse. A wave of sickening cold fell on him. He didn't see her along the road, and he had seen no sign of her horse. Hoof beats and a whinny sounded behind him. He turned.

"Mary, child, you should not have…" He stopped. There was Mary's horse, but it was rider-less. "Mary…" No, not Mary! God had already taken his sweet Rebecca; what if his daughter was…? Absalom became a man filled with fury. He raised a fist to the sky, "This is how You repay me? I do Your work, and *this* is my reward?"

Absalom ran from the barn to the manor to rouse the house. They must help him! They must search until they find her! His cold reasoning crept in. He must tell them the master was missing, that they must search for them both. Two hours later, Mary was found, drenched and unconscious. Simon's body was not found until the next day. For a day and a half, Mary Graymoor tossed and turned in a fever, calling her husband's name. The doctors gave little hope. She had broken ribs, a broken leg, and an injury to her head. Absalom was there, by

her side. She looked so much like her mother; so much, except…
In a lucid moment, Mary turned her eyes to her father. She
whispered, "Simon…?" Absalom could not face her, could not
risk her reading the truth in his face.

He lowered his eyes. In that moment, Mary understood.

"Charles! I must see my son! Charles!" Mary lifted herself up,
trying to rise from her bed. The nurse struggled to calm her
down, but the more she was restrained, the more she called
for her son.

The nurse turned to Absalom. "For goodness sake, man—go
find her son! She'll get no peace till she sees him!"

In a few moments, Charles entered the room. Absalom had
forbidden Charles to see his mother, but now it didn't matter
what Absalom said. His mother was calling for him. No matter
the hold Absalom had on him, he couldn't touch the bond of
love between Mary and her son.

The boy came to his mother's side and took her hand. With
the tiny bit of strength she had left, Mary commanded, "Leave
us!" Absalom and the nurse didn't move.

Charles turned to them. "You heard my mother! Leave us!"

The nurse moved to leave. "I'm in the next room. You call if
she worsens."

Absalom stood firm.

Charles met his eyes, not wavering. "Leave."

Absalom turned and walked out.

Charles drew closer to his mother. "I wanted to see you,
Mum, but they wouldn't—"

"Shh. Listen…" Her voice was a whisper. "The room…you
must protect it. Let no one…" Mary closed her eyes.

"Mum?"

Mary rose up in her bed. "'The Hyde Papers.' Keep them

safe. For me, my Charlie. For your father. He loved you…"

"Mum…"

"Promise me…"

"I promise."

Mary fell back in the bed, a small smile on her lips. Charles grasped her hand tighter. "Don't leave me! Please—don't leave me!"

A last whisper, a last breath sighed from his mother, "Promise…"

Mary Graymoor was dead.

Mary and Simon Graymoor were buried side by side near Granville Church. Charles stood by his grandfather, Absalom, and his cousin, Nathan. They were his family now—his only family. As Charles cast his handful of earth on his mother's grave, her words echoed in his head. "Keep them safe… Promise."

Absalom had his arm around the shoulders of his grandson. The old man's heart weighed like lead in his chest, though his face remained unchanged. These two, his son and his grandson, were all he had left of his wife and his daughter. He must not lose them, too.

He turned to Nathan, his voice gentle. "Leave us, son. I need to speak to Charles alone." Nathan gave Charles a searching glance, then walked a distance away. Absalom led Charles to a stone bench on the edge of the church grounds.

"You have lost your mother, and I my daughter, due to the sins of your father, who—"

"He loved me."

"What?"

"In her last breath, she told me that he loved me. I believe her."

Absalom paused. This was not what he expected from the boy. "Even a sinner will love his children. But that doesn't mean the sin must not be dealt with. We must deal with the sins your father left behind; the sins he so arrogantly recorded."

Charles gave Absalom a cold look. Again, this is not what Absalom expected. He must tread lightly on Simon's memory.

"Yes, your father recorded his sins, but he would not want them visited upon his son whom he loved, surely you must see that, boy."

"They shall not be."

"Good! Don't worry, son, I will protect you. We must go to your father's hidden room, break down the door, and destroy—"

"No!"

The young man's voice was strong, powered by grief and the memory of his mother's voice. Absalom was startled. Never before had Charles defied him; the boy had always bent to Absalom's will.

"No? You reject my counsel? Child, do not make the mistakes of your father, who—"

"I promised her."

Absalom began to understand. "Promised?"

"I promised my mother I would protect Father's room. That I would keep his papers safe. As she died, she made me promise. I will not break my promise!" Charles then turned his eyes up to his grandfather. "Nothing must happen to that room, Grandfather. Not even an accident." His eyes were narrowed. He suspected what his grandfather was capable of.

Absalom lowered his head and thought. He still could work this to his purposes. He lifted his head and let a smile break through the stiffness of his face.

"You will keep your promise. No one shall touch the room. No one shall know that it exists. It will be a reminder of the wages of sin; a reminder to you to walk the straight and narrow.

We must keep it our secret, you and I. No one must ever know. You promised your mother; now promise me. No one will ever know."

Charles hesitated. His mother simply said keep "The Hyde Papers" safe. They would be safe if no one knew they were there.

"I promise, Grandfather. No one will ever know."

CHAPTER 23

Cliff was slamming his shoulder against the door again and again.

"Stop it!"

"Amy, we could burn…"

"I know what could happen; don't remind me."

"Well, what am I supposed to do? Sit back and let it happen?"

"No, I—"

Suddenly a sound came from the other side of the door. Amy and Cliff both began pounding on it.

"Hello! Help! We're trapped!"

A muffled voice came through the wall. "Amy! Cliff! Where are you?"

Cliff spoke as loudly as he could. "Behind the wall of words—I mean, bookcase! We're in a secret room!"

Amy piped in, "Lyndsie trapped us in here!"

Cliff and Amy heard coughing, then the muffled voice. "Don't worry, love. I'll get you out."

"Zach? Is that you?"

"Just stay as far away from door as you can."

Amy and Cliff heard footsteps moving quickly away—and just as quickly, they moved away from the door.

"Zach! Who'd have thunk it?" Amy turned to Cliff, trying to hide the anxiety in her face. "Think he can, you know, do it?"

Cliff put his arm around her small shoulders. "I don't know, *love*. I don't know." He moved back to the desk. "But in case he can..."

Cliff closed the journal, and, with a great effort, yanked it from the desk's surface. He heard gears grind, then stop.

"Man, Simon had this thing clamped down good." He went to Amy and sat beside her on the bed. The floor was too hot.

Cliff looked at her. Soft brown hair. Clear, green eyes. A mouth ready to smile or laugh at a moment's notice. Even when covered with fear, that face had a hold on him. How could he have been so blinded by Lyndsie that he didn't go for what was right in front of him?

"Amy, I know we could die..." Amy's eyes grew wide. Not the time for a stupid blurt. "What I meant is, if we ever make it out of here, I just... Well, I wanted to tell you..." He faltered.

Amy laid her head against his shoulder. "I know."

Smoke began to come in from under the hidden door. Amy sat up.

"Remember in 'The Hyde Papers'—that way of escape thingy? You think maybe...?"

Cliff flipped open the journal. "May as well try. Let's just see." He turned to the last pages of the journal and re-read Simon's final words.

"'*Should you find yourself in this room, trapped by your father, there is a way out...*'"

Amy cut in. "Well, that's sure us. Keep reading."

"'*You must take the journal*'—we did that—'*though it may try your strength.*' It was pretty tough..."

"Skip to the escape part!"

"I'm getting there! '...*You must turn to the Way, the Truth, and the Life. This, and this alone, will be your way of escape.*'"

Amy and Cliff were both silent. The words made no

sense—and breathing was getting harder. Amy coughed out her next question. "Is he—is he talking about death?"

Cliff struggled to get enough breath for his answer. "I can't believe that. Why put it in code if he means death?"

"Well, he's quoting the Bible…"

Cliff jumped from the bed, though the floor was almost too hot to stand on.

"The Bible—that's it!" He dragged Amy over to the bookcase in the corner, and scanned through the volumes as best he could through the smoke. "Bible… Bible—c'mon where are…?"

Cliff's hand reached for a leather-bound book and yanked it down from the shelf. Nothing. "That should have worked!"

"Push it back—like I did with the Jekyll and Hyde book!" Cliff pushed the book back in place. As he did, a slow, grinding noise began. The bookcase swung open, but stuck halfway. Too small to get through.

"Cliff!"

Air from the secret exit drafted flames into the room, the oppressive heat searing their lungs with each breath. As Amy choked, Cliff got a shoulder into the opening and pushed with all his might. The bookcase stood firm.

"Amy! *Help me!*" As the inferno began to consume the bed, Amy's fear transformed into one hundred and five pounds of pure adrenaline. She pushed against Cliff's ribcage with all she had as his shoulder continued to press into the bookcase. It began to budge an inch, then another.

"Keep pushing!" Cliff cried out. As they gave one more heave—a loud crack rang out. A rusty, hundred-year-old counterbalance spring had snapped with the force of a cannon, swinging the hidden door open with a great rush. White-hot flames were sucked into the room. The sudden giving way of the bookcase hurtled Cliff and Amy through the opening, plunging them into a freefall in the pitch darkness...

A shadow moved across the window of the Gatekeeper's Cottage at Graystone as a car coasted to a stop in front of it; both its engine and lights turned off. The car door quietly opened and closed, and a slim form clad in black soundlessly approached the cottage.

Lyndsie Bainbridge hesitated just a few feet from the door. She had to steel herself. "You can do this, Lyndsie. You've *got* to do this." She repeated the mantra: "It's the greater good—you're protecting the greater good..."

It was one thing to sprinkle peanut dust and let things happen. It was harder to actually set a fire—but she didn't have to watch anyone burn. She almost lost it at the thought of flames licking the flesh of... She shoved the image away into a remote compartment of her mind. Now, with an untraceable gun from Zach in hand, she was ready to deal with the final loose end. Why couldn't Zach have handled this one? Why did he have to call her—tell her that Katherine had Absalom Bane's diaries? Now *she* had to deal with things.

Where was Zach? It didn't matter. Nothing mattered. Maybe Zach wanted to see how strong she was—see if she could handle it. She would show him. She would show everybody.

Lyndsie came up to the door and tested the handle. It was unlocked. Little small-town idiots; they trusted everybody. She kicked open the door.

"Don't move—not if you know what's good for you." Did she really say that? She sounded like some cheesy mobster movie.

"What the...?" Katherine Bane reached for the phone.

"Don't try it! This is a loaded gun—and I *will* use it. Just do as I say, and you won't get hurt." More cheesiness.

Kate withdrew her hand from the phone and looked right at Lyndsie. "Girl, you and I both know that's not true." She sighed. "Well, that's neither here nor there now. Want some tea?"

"What? No! I don't want some tea—I want—"

"Oh, I know what you want, but why don't you go ahead and tell me?"

"I want the diaries of Absalom Bane!" Lyndsie was beginning to feel disoriented. Why wasn't this woman scared?

"Cliff won't like that, you know."

"By the time I… By the time this is over, Cliff will be… He'll be dead. Now, where are the diaries?"

"That's right—she's started a fire at Graystone! The place is going up like straw! …I don't care—two people are trapped inside, and… That's right. Hurry!"

Zach rarely got rattled. Rarely. But he was rattled now. He knew Lyndsie might try something crazy—but to set fire to Graystone? Amy was in there, and she could be… He wanted to stay; he wanted to run into the burning building and try to drag her out, but he knew that was useless. His duty was with Kate. Kate. He had to hurry. Lyndsie would be there by now.

"What do you mean Cliff will be dead?" Kate rose up, the casualness gone from her demeanor.

"I mean, I set fire to Graystone—and Cliff and that pest, Amy, were foolish enough to be inside. Now, where are the diaries, Katherine Bane?" Lyndsie's voice sounded steadier than she felt.

Kate advanced on Lyndsie. "Screw the diaries! I'm gonna take you out, girl!" Lyndsie stepped back, but cocked the gun. "Stop right now, or I'll—"

Lyndsie heard a click behind her and felt something cold and hard against her neck.

"Unh-uh—I wouldn't, if I were you." She lowered the gun and turned to see Zach Malone pointing a gun at her head.

"Zach?" As she spoke, flashing blue lights pulled into Kate's yard.

Kate took a deep breath. "It's about time you showed up!"

Minutes later, as Lyndsie was being read her rights and tucked into a police car at Kate's, Zach and Kate were already pulling into the drive at Graystone. Flashing lights and the sound of sirens greeted them.

"Why didn't you stop her?" Kate was glaring at Zach.

"Kate, I… You're right. I didn't see it coming. I didn't think she'd burn down Graystone just to get rid of the diary. I… It's all my fault, Kate. I should have…"

"No, no." Kate put a hand on his shoulder. "I'm just a scared old woman. You can't blame yourself for this." She took his arm and they walked toward the fire engine.

Zach couldn't stand it any longer. He unlocked his arm from Kate's and ran ahead. "Where are they? Did you find them?" He grabbed a fireman. "I said, did you find them?"

Cliff and Amy found themselves in the dark. Totally in the dark.

"Amy…? *Amy!*"

"Here! Over here!"

After a few moments of groping in the blackness, their hands touched.

"Are you okay, sweetie?" The term of endearment popped out of his mouth, apparently of its own accord.

"Yeah—how about you?"

"Yeah."

"Where are we?"

"From what I remember of the house plans, this must be part of the wine cellar, and—" a detail struck Cliff, "—and the cellar has a tunnel leading to the outside. This is Simon's escape route!"

"So, how do we find it?"

Cliff pulled out the matches he still had in his pocket, and struck one. Briefly, the room was illuminated. At the far end of the cellar, there seemed to be an opening.

"We just follow the wall."

It was a slow process that seemed a lot longer than it was.

They made their way along the wall, with Cliff periodically striking matches whenever they hit an obstacle. Finally, moonlight streamed in ahead of them. Quickly as they could, they moved toward the light until they found themselves facing an iron gate placed in the middle of a hill. The gate was locked, but they heard not-too-distant voices. They looked at one another, then together cried, "Help! Help! Over here!"

Zach sat on the running board of the fire truck, Kate beside him. Both were silent. Both not only feared, but believed the worst. The plan had worked—but at such a cost. Zach spoke first.

"I didn't know how very desperate she was. I thought exchanging her gun for one with blanks would be enough."

Kate placed a hand on top of his. "Evil can surprise you." She nudged him, "Especially if you're not evil yourself."

"Maybe. But I'm not positively good like you—or Amy."

"What about Amy?"

Zach jumped to his feet. Standing in front of him was a familiar petite figure, wrapped in a blanket.

"Amy?"

Kate rose. "Cliff?"

Amy smiled. "Over there, still getting the once-over."

It took only a moment for Zach to recover. He snatched Amy up in his arms, spinning her around. "Amy... Amy! I thought I'd lost you!" He planted a kiss on her mouth. Amy pushed him back in surprise.

"Hey, hey, hey—what's going on here?"

Cliff was striding across the lawn, wrapped in a blanket. "What's the idea? Let her go!" Cliff pulled Amy out of Zach's grasp. His eyes narrowed. "Okay, buddy—who are you, anyway? You're no reporter..."

"He's Inspector Zachary Malone of Scotland Yard, and he's been part of a sting."

The voice was hoarse but recognizable. It came from a gray-haired man approaching them, accompanied by a woman in white and a man in black.

"Dex? I thought you were...?"

Zach interrupted. "Heathstone! You were in protective custody..."

"And under medical care." It was the nurse who spoke. "But Mr. Heathstone insisted on coming here. He's a very stubborn man."

Dexter smiled, put an arm across her shoulder and whispered, "I was not going to miss out on the finale." He turned to Zach. "Now, what about this fire? What happened, Malone?"

Zach shook his head. "Lyndsie. She was more deranged than I—"

"Enough said. I never thought she'd try to kill me, either."

There was silence for a moment, but Amy, abhorring a sound vacuum, demanded, "Okay, so what's this about a sting?"

Dexter moved over to the running board of the fire truck and sat down. After a sip of water, he began.

"I received an anonymous tip concerning some hidden diaries—and the possibility that Peter Graymoor wasn't who he said he was. Some diary pages were sent with it, making the claim plausible. That set some wheels in motion. Around the same time, I was contacted by Scotland Yard." Dexter motioned for Zach to continue.

"We had been doing a few investigations of our own due to the discovery of some letters penned by Rebecca Graymoor and her daughter, Mary. Then, when *we also* received an anonymous tip, I reacquainted myself with Dexter Heathstone."

Cliff was next. "Reacquainted?"

Dex answered, "Inspector Malone and I worked together on some Mideast issues that affected both of our concerns. And that's all you need to know."

Amy was persistent. "Get back to the sting. Did you ever find out who sent the anonymous tip?"

Dexter and Zach both looked at Kate. In unison, Amy and Cliff said, "Kate?"

Kate gave a slight smile. "Sorry to pull such a trick on you youngsters, but... Well, there were facts to dig out, and I knew if I dropped some clues, the two of you would be on it like a dog on a bone."

Amy grimaced. "So, *you* wrote on the mirror and left all those clues, and—"

Cliff continued, "But the pulpit tipping over and the—"

"Not me! I would never put you in harm's way! Those things were all that Lyndsie woman. She has a killer's heart. She tried to kill you two and then me." Kate shivered.

"You? Why?"

"The diaries of Absalom and Mary Bane."

Granville Church

—March 1934

Charles Graymoor sat alone in the church, a worn volume in his hand. He was no longer a boy, he was a man now—a man who had just buried his grandfather. He opened the book, turned to the last page, and began to write.

> *"I complete this diary of my grandfather, who has now been laid in the ground to meet his doom. I was but a lad of 12 when my father and mother died—and Absalom became both father and mother to me. I accepted this, but it was not without a price. With his love came the burden of the lie he created, the lie of my father's identity, and now my own. I may not have chosen the right path, but I have chosen, and I will bear the consequences as my father, Simon, did, and as Absalom did. May God forgive me."*

With that, he shut the book.

"You should burn it." Charles turned to see his closest living kin, Nathan Bane, standing at the back of the church.

"Perhaps. But I will not."

"Why?"

Charles walked up to his young uncle, Absalom's only son. "You know why. Burning this would never erase the truth. We must live with that, but hopefully it will not consume us like it did your father."

Nathan bowed his head. Though he looked like his father, his heart was more like his mother's. He felt the weight of what Charles had just spoken. Without a word, he left the church.

When Charles knew he was alone, he went to a loose stone at the base of the pulpit. He wrapped the diary in oilcloth, and placed it in the opening, snugly fitting the stone back into place. There it would remain until another hand pulled the stone loose and discovered it...

And that would be the hand of Katherine Bane.

Katherine Bane was crying, as the relief of it all being over hit her. "It was I. It was I all along. I stumbled onto Absalom and Mary's diaries, and I found out it was all a sham. That great legacy of Nathanial's was all a sham. I knew it, but I just couldn't bring myself to be the one..."

She took a gulp of air, trying to regain control. "I'm just a foolish old woman. I put it on somebody else's shoulders to figure things out—and it almost got you killed."

Cliff went up and wrapped his arms around his aunt. "It's okay. We're all okay."

Dexter cleared his throat and continued. "I'd had my eye

on Lyndsie for quite some time. Her ambition was boundless, and when she began her studies of Graystone, I knew it wasn't because she loved history. She was after something. Long story short, we set a trap, baited it, and discovered the truth about Simon Graymoor."

Zach picked up. "The truth, quite right. Sorry, old boy, but you're going to have a bit of a time proving it without the diary."

Cliff held up a journal. "You mean this?"

Now it was Dexter's turn to look amazed. "You found it?"

Zach's eyes held a glint of approval. "Brilliant, old man!" He started to say more, but the insistent buzzing of his cellphone interrupted him. With a wink to Amy, Zach stepped away and took the call.

Cliff caught the wink, and shifted the focus. "Yep, we got the proof, Dex. In a way, I'm kind of sorry. I know you're Chairman of the Board of the foundation, and this thing will—"

Dexter waived it off. "You can't build anything good on a lie, Cliff."

Amy poked Cliff in his already sore ribs. "See, you were right!" She paused. "So, if Simon wasn't the heir, who was?"

Cliff shrugged. "Well, I imagine Peter and Simon's uncle— the brother of Sir Thaddeus—was next in line. That's the way the Graymoors usually did the inheritance thing back then. The eldest eligible male always got the money."

Amy persisted, "Soo, now, that would be who?"

She was interrupted by Zach's laughter. He held up his cellphone. "Just got off the mobile with the Yard. You want to know the rightful heir to the Graymoor fortune?" He walked up to Cliff and clapped him on the shoulder. "Cheers, old boy, looks like it's you!"

"Huh? Me? I mean, how…? Why…?"

"Well, Dr. Graymoor, seems you're the eldest son of the eldest son of the…"

"Okay, okay—I get it. I think." He shook his head. "I'm the heir…?"

"I'm sure there will be some legalities to straighten out, but after that… Well, laddie, you'll be a very rich man! The fate of this whole bloody mess is in your hands."

Dexter Heathstone was looking at Cliff, a slight, sad smile on his face. "I trust you to do what's right, Cliff. Always have. Even if it means shutting down the foundation."

Cliff paused. It was only for a few moments, but for all around him it seemed like an eternity.

"I'm not shutting down the foundation, Dex. I couldn't. But… But I'll probably want to make a few changes as to how things are done."

Dex smiled. "Whatever you say, Cliff. You're the boss."

Zach's phone began to buzz. "It's the Yard again. Got to take this. Don't take off, Amy, love. We need to talk."

Amy was uncharacteristically quiet, eyes down, studying her shoes.

Cliff walked up and turned her toward him. "Amy. Look at me." He gently lifted her head.

"We need to get a few things straight. No more getting shot at, or getting trapped in burning buildings. And absolutely no intimate talks—in fact, no talks at all—with charming British guys, even if they're inspectors or Dukes or…"

Amy flung her arms around him. "Oh—just shut up and kiss me!"

"What?"

"I said—"

Amy was unable to finish because her lips were duly engaged

with another pair of lips—belonging to the new heir of the Graymoor legacy.

Zach walked up and saw the two in an embrace. "I suppose I shouldn't have taken that call."

"Don't think it would have made any difference, son. Those two were bound to happen."

"Well, nothing's final until there's a ring and a ceremony. Fair game and all that..."

"Don't count on it. She's had her heart set on him since high school."

"We'll see, ducks."

Zach turned to Kate and offered his arm. "In the meantime, would you care to join an inspector with a bruised ego for a late dinner?"

Kate took his arm. "Only if you're buying."

Cliff and Amy's lips were still getting acquainted as Kate and Zach walked away.

About the Author

Sandy Brownlee is a redhead (according to the bottle from Sally's). She is a wife (according to her husband, Denny). She is an actress. She is a writer. She is a creator.

So—what has she "created?"

Seven full-length radio dramas, eight full-length stage productions, an original screenplay or two, eight original sketch comedy dinner theaters . . . and she was co-creator of *Discovery Jones*, an original children's TV program for the Christian television network, INSP.

From the days of writing and performing drama for her church, winning the Grand Prizes in drama from the Gospel Music Association, and years of using her gifts for Family Life, a regional ministry in New York and Pennsylvania, Sandy and Denny have lived the creative adventure God has penned for them.

Now they have begun another chapter in their lives, in Nashville, Tennessee, working in the areas of film, and TV, and for Sandy, writing stories.

The Mirror Lies is Sandy's first novel... but certainly not her last.

ALSO AVAILABLE FROM
WordCrafts Press